ORCHARD BOOKS
Carmelite House
50 Victoria Embankment
London EC4Y 0DZ

This edition published in 2015 by Orchard Books

ISBN 978 1 40833 738 7

Text © Val Hudson 2015

A CIP catalogue record for this book is available
from the British Library.

1 3 5 7 9 8 6 4 2

Printed and bound in Great Britain by Clays Ltd, St Ives plc

MIX
Paper from
responsible sources
FSC® C104740
FSC
www.fsc.org

The paper and board used in this book are made from wood
from responsible sources.

Orchard Books
An imprint of Hachette Children's Group
Part of The Watts Publishing Group Limited
An Hachette UK company

www.hachette.co.uk

BOYWATCHING

CHLOE BENNET

ORCHARD

For Caroline Sheldon,
best of agents and best of friends

Rules of Engagement

'Bet you don't dare sit next to him,' said Sally.

As best friends go, Sally is probably no more annoying than most, but on this occasion she really deserved the icy glare I gave her. The train was full of people we knew, and I hardly wanted them to notice how I'd been staring at an empty seat – or rather, at the person sitting next to it.

That person was Mark, who was looking at his haughty best (haughty is my new favourite word) – rather cool in a standoffish way, but tousled, curly-haired, and with what I think you might call darkly brooding good looks. He had a reputation for being scarily brilliant as well as brooding, but I was convinced that the very attractive dimple in his left cheek meant that deep down he had a great sense of humour.

I went back to staring at the empty seat, imagining

myself in it, making bright conversation and astonishing Mark with the breadth of my knowledge and the depth of my reading (or do I mean the other way round?). Just as I was getting to the bit where he was laughing fondly at my jokes and finding me utterly charming, Maggie sat in the seat.

Maggie. Arch Queen Beeeeeyatch, the one with the four-inch wedges (to disguise her height. Or lack of), and the one who could make your life a misery if she chose to, which she frequently did.

On this Friday morning she sat there – in the seat that surely destiny had meant for me – looking straight ahead, and looking like butter wouldn't melt. But Mark was gazing out of the window, earphones dangling from his perfectly formed ears. I held my breath; only one more stop. With any luck there won't be time for QB Maggie to try to work her twisted charms.

Distracted by a crinkly noise by my side I saw that Sally was offering me her last crisp. I guess it must have been that obvious that I needed cheering up. As the train drew into the station, Mark got up and off without making eye contact with the evil one. I lived to breathe another day.

There are in fact three boys in Year Eleven at St Thomas's called Mark. But this one, who'd been sitting in the seat by the window, is by far the most fascinating. His full name is Mark Anderson, but I like to call him Mark A-Star. Obviously I don't call him that to his face. In fact, I don't call him anything to his face. He and his friend Charlie are way too grand to chat with the likes of us.

St Thomas's, being the only boys' school for miles around, has been the focus of our attention for as long as I can remember – not all day and every day, of course, because quite a lot of time has to be spent listening to people try to teach us things as well as coping with our various weird families, but it's certainly right up there at the top of the List of Things We Talk About.

Because we're young and curious and female, and our school, Queen Mary's, is an all-girls school, our thoughts quite often turn to Boys. I don't think this makes us in any way vacuous (an excellent word. Just to use it means you can't possibly *be* it); on the contrary, we can only learn about the unknown by watching. And we do like to learn. Boy Watching is probably our second favourite hobby after…well, it's probably our favourite hobby actually.

I guess I should explain who 'we' are before I start elaborating on the watching, and the weird bits and the sad bits and the happy bits. (I have to do all the elaborating, plus some observing and reflecting, because my big ambition is to be a prize-winning writer, and you have to practise elaborating, observing and reflecting for that.)

So, I am Chloe, best friend of Sally, and also friend of Amy and Gemma. Chloe Bennet is not my real name. Well, the Chloe bit is, but the Bennet part is made up – to protect the innocent, and confuse the guilty. Plus it's an homage to my favourite heroine, Elizabeth Bennet, whose wit, wisdom – and boyfriend – are a constant source of inspiration.

I will start with Sally. Sally is my best friend and I try not to hear a word against her, but if there's a stick with a wrong end to get hold of, or an 'it' to put her foot in...she will. But she means well, even if she does tend to engage mouth before brain, as the old saying goes. This sometimes makes her seem rather foolish, but fortunately she very rarely notices that, so mostly she's happy. This is extra great because she has two younger twin brothers who would try the patience of a saint, plus a mother, Liv, who, as another old saying goes, is often out to lunch. Literally and metaphorically. Usually literally.

Sally has red hair (which looks great and which she

loves) and braces (which don't look great and which she hates). She adores Harry of 1D with a passion bordering on the unhealthy, and she could also get excessively attached to Justin Bieber if we let her. She is *definitely* and umbilically attached to her phone.

Amy has wavy brown hair and almost always looks lovely. She is the sweet one of us. She looks sweet, she is sweet and she just is one of those people who never have a vile word to say about anyone. (Unlike, for instance, and just as a matter of record, the above-mentioned Maggie. Maggie is not known as the Queen Beeyatch for nothing. She is incapable of having the slightest hint of a kind thought. In fact, she probably wouldn't recognise a kind thought if you slapped her in the mouth with it. I think if you climbed inside her head all you would see would be rottenness and rust. But I digress...) So, Amy. She is lovely, her parents are lovely, plus she is very good at playing the guitar (see below for more about this).

And finally we come to Gemma. Gemma is a bit of an enigma. She has the longest legs, the straightest hair (sooo envious, mine never looks like that even with the help of all the latest electrical equipment), the best clothes and the coolest manner of us all. She's done most of the things we haven't – and shouldn't. She has a rich and famously rude and boring father, who nobody – least of all Gemma – likes, and a missing mother who she hasn't seen for eight years. I like to think she's fond of all of us, but mostly she seems to dote on a Scottish boy called Jezza, who plays the guitar. And the field.

We are all in a band. It's called Overgrown Throttle and the Tempted Obscurity. OTTO. Me on vocals and keyboard, Sally on the drums (it suits her being at the back, as she can be a bit shy, probably something to do with the braces). And then there's Amy on guitar. Amy is actually incredibly good at playing the guitar, not that she'd ever tell you that, and she's the one who keeps us all together. Then there's Gemma on bass guitar. We are still not sure whether Gemma can actually play the guitar, but she's got a brilliant sense of rhythm and when she swings all that straight hair of hers all over the place she looks great.

The day I'm writing about, being a Friday, was band practice day. This was always a good end to the week, plus it was Art in the afternoon, which could be almost as amusing.

One of the Art projects for that Friday was photographing an inanimate object against a contrasting background. I thought of photographing

Sally against a beautiful painting (which I thought should be amusing enough), but I was foiled by there being no beautiful paintings in the Art room.

So in a moment of inspiration, I photographed a huge bee which had met a sticky end on the window sill. I blew it up and shot it (how *violent* photography can be) against the background of a pair of denim shorts. Rather arty, I thought.

Our Art teacher, Mr Pampledousse (he is Greek, and incredibly hairy) professed himself pleased with me. Sometimes it is a bit hard to tell what Mr Pampledousse (who of course we called Mr Pimplemouse) was professing, because his accent is so thick you could almost imagine he was speaking in the original Greek.

'This is bitter, Chloe, you are engage with shape,' he said to me. 'You are seeing with your eye more.' He nodded approvingly, and moved on to Julie Duxworth's model of her mother's head. (Julie's mother was an actress and very beautiful, but you certainly couldn't tell that from Julie's sculpture.) I wanted to ask Mr Pampledousse what else you could be expected to see with other than your eye, but the moment had passed.

Sally had made a collage of an iPhone out of bits of her mother's oven gloves. I told Sally I thought this was brilliant: a statement of how a woman's place has changed in the world – the old nurturing/caring/cooking image of a woman cut up and made into characterless technology. She looked at me like I was a little bit mad. Sometimes I think my insights are wasted on my friends.

Then the bell went, and freedom and the weekend beckoned. Sally and I set off down the studio stairs to wait for Amy and Gemma, who had to get their guitars out of the music room.

This was the bit of the week where you could do the best Boy Watching. It was when the Year Elevens from St Thomas's came to the gates to meet our Year Elevens (we're Year Nine, so we didn't really get noticed. Or not yet…). If you lurked by the side entrance to the school you could observe, assess, dismiss or generally wonder at the golden creatures waiting outside the gates.

They were 'golden' because they had a sort of dark yellow uniform. They were 'creatures' because, well, because I think the word 'creature' is just about right. It could conjure up something fabulous, like from a fable, something spellbinding and attractive: a 'magical creature'. Or it could be some enigmatic, puzzling thing: a 'mystical creature'. Or it could be something smelly and horrible: a 'creature from the deep'.

On this occasion they looked to be none of the above. In fact, I'd have said the only thing they looked like was show-offs. They all had their ties artfully twisted halfway round their necks, they all chewed gum in the same too-cool-for-my-trainers way, and they all looked at their phones like they'd never seen them before.

Mark A* wasn't there but his friend Charlie was. Charlie – tall and gangly with fluffy hair – was bouncing around in a well-meaning-looking way. He was always ready with a smile, especially for girls, a bit like a Labrador with an out-of-control labido. I think I mean libido.

We were well placed for Boy Watching, but Sally suddenly announced that we had to go because her braces had slipped and she had to take them out and she didn't dare smile. We were a martyr to Sally's braces. They never seemed to fit properly, and whenever she found them uncomfortable we all had to stop what we were doing so she could hide, take them out or rearrange them.

'Good practice for when you're old, I suppose,' I said unkindly. 'You'll be the go-to old person in the care home for Denture Management Advice.'

Amy and Gemma now came out of the door with

their guitars. Gemma was swinging her long straight hair in what I thought was a rather artificial fashion, but I could see some of the golden creatures looking her way. Amy, with her curly dark hair and sweet smile, seemed blissfully unaware of the creatures. Although one of them, Charlie, was looking at her as if he wanted to practise smiling at her. I wondered what that was about. I decided to think about it later.

We headed off to Gemma's house.

Gemma lives in an increeeeeedible modern house behind some tall and slightly sinister electric gates. Her dad is richer than any of ours because he invented a TV game show format that had sold all over the world. None of us know which one it is, and he's very secretive about it. We think that is probably because it is either very stupid or very smutty.

But it did pay for a great big garage which was perfect for band rehearsals, even though we had to squeeze the keyboard in between the Harley-Davidson bike and the Suzuki jeep thing, and the drums behind the exercise bike. (Unused, if the size of Gemma's dad is anything to go by.)

'Hence the term Garage Music,' my Ghastly Stepdad, Ralph, had said when he first heard about us. He'd looked up expectantly when he said it. If he was expecting gales of laughter he was sorely disappointed.

By this time Sally had adjusted her braces, and was putting on her best drummer expression. This is where you look vacantly into the distance because you're so brilliant you don't actually have to concentrate. The trick is not to change your expression at all if you do happen to go wrong. Sally was very good at all this, especially the going wrong bit.

I switched on the electric keyboard and played a chord. I had at least ten chords in my repertoire, but if I was singing that turned into about two. There are only so many things you can do at once, after all.

For some reason nothing seemed to sound any good that day. Sally's drums always seemed to come in in the wrong place, I forgot half the words, and Gemma pretty much forgot to play at all.

I think she was depressed. You could always tell when Gemma was depressed by the way she chewed her lower lip, and said nothing rather aggressively. (I think you can say nothing aggressively, there's something about the silence.)

Part of the problem was that she had heard the St Thomas's band, Shedz, playing the week before. Which meant she'd seen Jezza. Jezza is the tall, stick-thin Scottish boy who leads the band. He's got wristbands right up to his elbow, long, greasy, blonde hair and jeans so artfully ripped that he flaps in the wind. Despite all this ventilation, he always seems to be covered in a thin sheen of sweat – which I don't think is very attractive. But whenever he's on stage you can see all the girls (except me) gawping. Absolutely gawping. Especially Gemma. (I often think it's just as well we don't all like the same boys. How awkward would that be?) But the thing that had made her depressed was QB Maggie being in the front row. Gemma was convinced there was something serious going on between her and Jezza.

But I digress again. (I get a lot of low marks in English because of digression. Our fierce English language teacher, Miss Brewer, is quite strict about it, but personally I think digression is a sign of a lively mind.)

We decided we'd better stop our band practice before we really depressed ourselves, and we went into the house to strategise.

Going into the house takes some time as there's a series of codes and outer doors that Gemma has to negotiate before we can get in.

Eventually we found ourselves in a huge sitting room with one wall entirely devoted to a big black screen. It looks kind of threatening, but I expect that's just because we're all busy imagining the dodgy movies that Merv (that's what Gemma's dad is called. Really.) watches on it in the middle of the night.

We went through into the kitchen, where all the pizza and Coke is. There's a state-of-the-art microwave in the corner that Gemma fills with many pizzas. We sat down on the bar stools (Of course Merv has to have bar stools, I thought) and cracked open the Cokes. Fortunately Merv himself was upstairs, or somewhere else, anyway. The main thing was that he wasn't in the kitchen telling us how great he was.

We started to talk, as we always seemed to do these days, about What Happened Last Summer.

What Happened Last Summer

It all started off normally enough. Well, normally for us. It was last summer and the day of our first Snog Fest or, as the teachers prefer to call it, the St Thomas's and Queen Mary's Annual School Dance. We had got together at my place in the afternoon To Prepare. This meant taking over the bathroom for at least five hours. (Although that would be high speed for Sally, who's been known to take whole *days* getting ready to go out. I exaggerate. To make a point.)

Between us we had enough product to stock a small branch of Boots. By the time we'd built up a vitamin-cream base, dabbed on tinted moisturiser, compared mascaras, rubbed off the blusher (we can blush fine by ourselves, we decided), swapped eyeliners and put a hint of a tint of lip gloss on, we were starting to feel quite pleased with our faces.

Although then of course we had to address the burning issue of The Eyebrows. Mine needed a lot of attention with the tweezer and the gritted teeth. Eeech. After that we wore out Mum's hair straighteners and practically burnt out her styling dryer (Mum's a professional hairdresser, so she's got all the kit) but by that stage we were almost pleased with our hair.

Gemma was wearing a red wraparound dress that made her look taller and cooler than ever, Sally was wearing a cute blue skater dress, Amy her familiar green dress (we'd seen it before about seven times – I guessed Amy just liked to go with what she knew) but with a new sparkly belt, and I'd gone the skinny jeans and sparkly top route. I thought we all looked pretty presentable, and we went off to the bus stop in high spirits.

We arrived at the venue, a huge hall on the high street, which, when it wasn't doing gigs, housed everything from bingo, am. dram. Shakespeare performances, and Merv's swanky New Year parties (featuring 500 of his closest friends/AKA anyone who fancied a free drink).

It was off-the-scale noisy, which I found faintly depressing. I realised that my mordant ('mordant' is good, I think it's going to be a new favourite) wit would be drowned out, and I'd have to depend entirely on the eyeliner, the newly straightened hair and the sparkly top to attract attention. But I regretted the pumps. I *really* regretted the pumps. Even though I'm quite tall, I looked borderline short compared to everyone else, who seemed to be wearing stilts. (I took some comfort in knowing that they could barely walk in them, let alone dance.)

All around us were groups of boys, and a few groups of boys with girls in them. Everyone was dancing, or sort of dancing, drinking things and generally looking cool.

The four of us headed over to a trestle table and each took a glass of a liquid that looked either dark yellow or bright orange, depending on how it caught the strobe light. Whether you drank it at a yellow moment or an orange moment it still tasted unusually disgusting.

We took our glasses over to a corner of the hall that was a bit emptier than the other corners.

'Stability plum fest,' Sally yelled into my ear.

'What?' I yelled back.

'Plaster mass window stubble,' she shouted.

I realised I was right about the mordant wit challenge.

I think I saw Jezza at exactly the same moment Gemma did. He was gleaming with sweat as he threw QB Maggie round and round on the dance floor. And just as we were looking at them, the music went all slow and they were immediately in what can only be described as a clinch. How QBM could bear all that liquid so close to her face, I don't know. But she seemed to be loving it just as much as Gemma was hating the sight of her. I never really knew what they meant when they said someone turned 'ashen', but I got the picture as I watched Gemma looking at QBM.

'He's only dancing with her 'cos he doesn't know you're here yet,' I yelled, rather hopelessly – in every sense – into Gemma's ear.

She looked at me vacantly like she hadn't heard – which very possibly she hadn't.

Seconds later the slow music had stopped and I saw QBM's vile friends crowd round her. They had their phones in their hands and for a paranoid moment I thought they were turning them towards us.

I decided to think about that later, because right now we needed a strategy to break into the groups of boys. We'd been standing on our own for long enough.

'I'm going to say hello to that boy in blue,' said Amy during one of the rare gaps in the ear-splitting noise, 'I'm sure he's the one who gets the number 9 bus.'

I didn't think this was going to be quite a strong enough opening conversational gambit, especially if he *wasn't* the one who took the number 9 bus, but I had to admire her courage.

Still no one was coming anywhere near us, so Sally thought she'd do the same, and headed off towards a boy in a pink T-shirt, who was standing in the corner with a very tall boy dressed all in black. She said she liked the pink of the T-shirt, so decided he must be nice. I wasn't sure that the two things were necessarily connected, but before I could argue the point she'd headed off.

I looked around for Gemma, but she seemed to have melted away. I reckoned she'd probably gone in the direction of the toilets, which at least had the advantage of being the other end of the hall from Jezza and QBM's group.

So there I was; completely alone in a sea of people, all of whom were having an absolutely fantastic time. Completely short (thanks to the pumps), completely silent (thanks to the noise) and completely having a horrible time.

Then I thought I could see in the distance that things weren't going according to plan for Sally. She'd turned a T-shirt shade of pink and seemed to be trying to bat away the six-foot boy dressed in black, who was grabbing her arm and seemed to be trying to pull her off in the direction of one of the exits, presumably to try to put the Snog in Snog Fest. There was no sign of the one in pink. Sally was looking desperate. Then she must have yelled at him – I thought I could make out the words 'must' and 'toilet' – and she rushed away from him off to the back of the hall.

Then I saw Amy standing the other side of the hall, surrounded by four boys. They seemed to be taking it in turns to stay stuff to her, and every time one of them said something her lower lip seemed to – there's no other word for it – tremble. To make matters worse, I could see the cow Maggie looking on with an expression of scorn and amusement on her face.

I was just about to head over there when, to my shame, I was utterly distracted by this gorgeous, curly-haired skinny boy in a black V neck jumper (I have always loved the V neck jumper) who came over to me.

'You here on your own?' he shouted.

May every deity ever invented forgive me, but I said, 'Yes.'

He gently edged me away from the crowd to a corner where we could hear ourselves speak.

'What's your name?' he said.

'Chloe,' I said. 'You'll find it's very hard to type. Your fingers always want to type Chole. It'll be very irritating for my biographer.'

There was a pause. I could feel the beginnings of a wave of redness coming over me. Here we go, I thought. WHY should he ever want to type my name? WHY did I say that?

'Better than actually being called Chole, I'd have thought,' Handsome Boy said.

'Oh quite,' I said, starting to get excited that we were actually having A Conversation. 'But I'd always thought I was more of an Emma, as in Jane Austen's Emma. Although my real heroine is Lizzy Bennet, who's actually very wise despite her prejudice, not like Emma who makes mistakes all the time which means you like her all the more. Not that any of that stops them ending up with handsome heroes, although not as handsome as they might have been if they'd been allowed to wear V neck jumpers.' I paused.

Handsome Boy had glazed over a bit, but then started to move towards me and to my utter amazement began to lick my ear. Lick. My. Ear. Why would anyone do that? I was rigid with shock and awkwardness. Who knew that talking Jane Austen could make your ears sexy?

Then I heard a boy's voice in my other ear. 'Scored another one, Tim, have you? Come on – I think your girlfriend's waiting for you. Best get moving.'

'Tim' laughed, and without a backward glance, headed off towards a redhead who looked amazing in leather trousers and fifty-six-inch heels.

Feeling sick with humiliation and self-loathing, I turned to see Sally coming back from the toilets. Oh god, her skirt was only caught in her knickers. Everyone was looking and laughing like crazy. And the only worse thing that could distract me was the sight of Amy escaping at last from the four bullies and running towards me. At that moment Sally realised what had happened, pulled out her skirt and put on her most determined I-will-not-cry face.

Amy's face had given up the fight. She had tears pouring down it. Apparently the tall guy, Brian from Year Ten, had brought his friends over to tease a 'real-life lesbian'. Utterly random. And not true. And vile to tease her for it anyway, even if it were. But none of that was the point.

Everyone and everything had got very noisy by now.

The good news was that at last no one was looking at us, also that Gemma had appeared from somewhere. But that was all the good news there was.

We took our sorry selves off to the bus stop and had only one thought between us:

Boys. Dontcha just hate 'em?

The next day we could add another thing to the list of things to hate. QBM. As if we didn't already. Only the Queen Beeyatch could have created the Facebook page called 'Snog Fest – the Loooooooosers'.

Under it were seven – *seven* – pictures of us four looking alone, unhappy, tired, short, fat or ugly. Or all of the above. Maybe we weren't all fat and ugly. But we sure looked like losers.

Since then, I'm happy to say that time has marched on, wounds have healed, and we are now determined to look on the bright side and see the best in people. There. Four clichés in one sentence, but still true.

Sitting in Gemma's kitchen that Friday night we talked about the next Snog Fest. I told them, in my Pollyanna way (who *was* Pollyanna? And why *was* she so optimistic?) that maybe it wouldn't be so bad.

Maybe some miracle would happen and we'd all have a nice time.

'Bums,' said Sally, who has a rather unimaginative way with words. 'It's going to be just as awful as last time. No boy is going to look at us. It's all going to go wrong again. I haven't got any clothes I look good in. I'm never going to have a boyfriend. I might as well be dead.'

I told Sally to look on the bright side. She could actually be dead. Also, she might have a boyfriend she didn't like.

'Imagine. He might be horrible. He might be a humourless bully, who, when he isn't beating you up, is out with his mates getting arrested. And who keeps starving dogs in the basement that he feeds with torn-up songbirds and bits of pet cat.'

'You,' said Sally, 'are very sick and need help. And there's no sign of your miracle judging by last week, when Sunny Side Up tried it on with me in Starbucks.' (Sunny Side Up was a Year Ten St Thomas's boy so-called because he has a yellow nose and a smeary face and so looks like an underdone fried egg.) 'He seemed to think that telling me I had big ears and that he'd scored fifty-nine levels in *Angry Birds* was going to endear me to him.'

'Endear him to you,' I said pedantically.

'OK. Well. There wasn't any endearing either way round,' said Sally. 'I hate *Angry Birds*, and HIS ears were covered in spots. Can't believe he thought I'd want to go out with him.'

'Huh,' said Amy. 'That's nothing compared to Purple Anorak Boy,' (so-called because, well...you get the idea) 'on Tuesday. He asked me to go paintballing with him. He got so close to me I could see right up his nostrils. AND he smelled of blocked lavatory.'

Poor Amy. She is the cleanest person I know. I was torn between feeling sorry for her and rather admiring her use of language. Being Steve's sister, I knew exactly what a blocked lavatory smelled like. Plus, the last thing someone as gentle as Amy would want to do is fire large lumps of paint at people.

My own recent encounter with Master Wrong was last month when (Ghastly Stepdad) Ralph's nephew came to stay with us. He was called George, was sixteen and had a weird obsession with Justin Bieber and Meg, the girl in *Family Guy*. He kept trying to explain to me – with lots of touchy-feely action – the science of the sports bra. Apparently it was invented in the 1970s by a girl who sewed two jock straps together. (Incredibly, this is true. I looked it up afterwards.) If

Ralph thought we were going to get together and unite the family estate (ha) like in *Downton Abbey*, he was barking up quite the wrong family tree.

Listening to the others, and thinking – as we so often did – about how it felt to be the school Loooosers, I suddenly had A Moment. I stood up.

'Now, *look*,' I said, and I think I might even have stamped my foot. 'I've had enough of this. We are not flotsam and jetsam, drifting about in the tide, waiting for disaster to overtake us. We are not little pieces of rubbish on a river rushing headlong into catastrophe and humiliation.' In the heat of the moment my vocabulary was coming up with some real crackers. Words I hadn't even known I knew.

I went on: 'The Boy is not the enemy determined to humiliate us. Or not necessarily, anyway. If we can only understand The Boy then we can learn how to know which one is the right one to get off with at the Snog Fest.

'We do plenty of Boy Watching, but so far it's just been a hobby. We are now going to take control, and turn Boy Watching into a science, share our observations and properly work out who's the right one for each of us. And then we can all look forward to the Snog Fest, because we'll have someone to snog. And we will never, ever be featured on any beeyatch's list of losers.'

I was getting a bit out of breath by this stage, and starting to repeat myself, but I knew I was on to something. 'I can feel a spreadsheet coming on. We'll be like twitchers.' I noticed a more than usually blank stare from Sally. 'Twitchers,' I said, slowly and slightly witheringly, 'are bird-watchers. We will be to boys as twitchers are to birds.

'We will note down all the positive, nice Boy Things, and the characteristics we'd each most like in a potential boyfriend. We can award points for cuteness or a sense of humour.'

'Or not having acne, or having muscly arms,' said Sally.

'Or being able to dance and wash their hair,' said Amy.

'Or looking cute or being kind to children and animals,' I said.

'We could award them points for talking to us rather than texting, and then black marks for gross-out behaviour, or ignoring us,' said Amy, entering into the spirit.

'And then we'll multiply the square root of their cuteness by their inside leg measurement,' said Sally, introducing a rather admirable mathematical element.

'And when a boy has scored—' I said.

'Well, then it's game over,' interrupted Gemma.

'No,' I said patiently. 'When a boy has scored enough in our categories, then we'll know he's The One, and we'll go off into the sunset and the Snog Fest together.'

'You make finding The One for the Snog Fest sound like the ending of a Jane Austen novel,' said Gemma, who'd never actually read one but she'd seen all the movies.

'What's wrong with that?' I was a bit belligerent, because my love of Jane Austen was absolute – in fact, you can't be planning a career writing prize-winning novels, as I am, if you don't appreciate literature in general and her in particular. Gemma had a large spot coming on her chin, I couldn't help but notice. I mentally congratulated myself on not pointing it out.

'Absolutely nothing,' said Amy in her calm, let's-move-on sort of way. 'But where do we start?'

'We start by making the spreadsheet. We'll start tomorrow.'

I somehow knew this would work. If we pooled our observations about the 'creatures', we would come to a sort of group wisdom that we could all learn from. That way we would have our partner for the Snog Fest, and have the best night of our lives rather than the absolute horriblest.

'OK. I'll start by observing Jezza,' said Gemma. (Time had eased the pain of seeing Jezza with the Queen Beeyatch, clearly.)

I wasn't completely sure that she'd really got the point about this being a group activity, but I was sure we could all learn a lot from observing Jezza, so I let it go.

We finished the last of the stilton and apricot pizzas – Merv was between wives, and he let the local deli do his shopping for him, which meant that he had the most unnecessarily exotic store cupboard in the whole of the north of England. We decided that we would reconvene the following morning at mine to start work on our plan.

As it was quite late by then, Gemma went off to find Merv (reluctantly, I think she sort of hated having anything to do with her dad) so he could drive us home. This was a mixed experience. Being in close quarters with Merv – who wore denim from top to toe, and spilled out of every seam – was pretty alarming. He'd always make a point of having his arm round you or on your elbow in a supposedly fatherly, looking-aftery sort of way but was actually just incredibly irritating. But the up side was that the jeep was full of gadgets and still smelt of new car. Which for me, Sally and Amy was a real novelty.

Merv came downstairs. This evening he was dressed in black denim. I couldn't decide if the black made the spilling out thing worse or better, so I decided not to think about it and got into the front of the car, with Sally and Amy in the back. Front or back was always a toss-up: in the front you take the hit on being talked at, but you do have the advantage of not feeling car sick, Merv being a jerky driver as well as a jerk.

He dropped me off first, so that was good. Not so good was that the house was ablaze with light. Ablaze might be a bit of an exaggeration, but there were enough lights on to indicate that Ghastly Stepdad and (not so Ghastly, but still pretty annoying brother) Steve were still up. I unlocked the main front door as quietly as I could so as not to disturb Albert downstairs (very hard to know when Albert was going to bark, he was an unpredictable sort of terrier), and crept up the stairs to our front door. If I could just negotiate the hall there was a good chance that Ralph's TV—

'That you, Chloe?' came Mum's voice from the kitchen. I paused only a second to wonder for the five hundredth time who on earth else it could be. Then I told myself not to be pedantic (another good word that really only applies to Ralph) – it was just Mum's way of saying hello.

'Did you have a good practice?' Mum came out of the kitchen drying her hands on her 'Keep Calm and Drink Wine' tea towel.

'Better than last time, but not as good as next time.' I was quite pleased with this response. 'But now I'm going to bed, Mum. Got an early start tomorrow. Everyone's coming round at ten o'clock.'

Avoiding the eye-rolling – for someone who has to go to work at eight in the morning on a Saturday, I guess the idea of an early start at ten is more irritating than amusing – I headed to the bathroom where I'd decided I would achieve at least twenty plucks of the eyebrows. Thirty was my record, but none was my more usual score.

Tomorrow was another day.

Boy Science

The loud slam of the door interrupted a very deep sleep. I was dreaming Merv and Ralph had joined Overgrown Throttle and the Tempted Obscurity, and we were performing at the Snog Fest. Neither of them could sing a note, and all I could see from the stage was Mark A*, with QB Maggie draped round his waist, looking on, doubled up with laughter. All in all, I was pretty glad of the slam.

It must have been Mum leaving to go to Happy Hairliners. (The name of every hairdresser seems to have to be a dreadful pun. Except the one that Mum worked at, which sounded a bit like some old men being relaxed about having a receding forehead.)

Mum never liked her early starts on a Saturday, hence the door banging.

I got up slowly and realised Steve was occupying

the bathroom, as he always seemed to do whenever I needed to use it. There were some inexplicably explosive watery noises coming from behind the door, which I decided not to think about.

You'd imagine that having an older brother would be a fantastic advantage – access to his cool friends, being even more popular because your friends wanted to meet him, that sort of thing. Unfortunately, fate and my parents had given me Steve, who has long wispy hair, acne, a penchant for quoting from all three of the *Iron Man* movies, and no beautiful charismatic friends that I've ever seen. He's perfectly well-meaning, and possibly even quite bright, but on a boy-magnet scale of one to ten he was useless to the power of minus a hundred.

Plus he occupied the bathroom for *hours*.

When he finally emerged, he was dressed in skinny jeans and a T-shirt saying 'I Put the Sex in Dyslexia' which is actually quite a witty choice for such a dull boy. He was going out, he said, in his usual gnomic way, (since he looks like a tall, skinny gnome, that *has* to be an extra good description) and loped downstairs and out of the door.

Apparently, Ralph had announced that he was off to do a spot of overtime at the Jobcentre (where he was Acting Assistant Manager, as he never tired of reminding us). Always one to spot the opportunity for extra fun, he does like going into the office on a Saturday. I had no idea what he did when he got there. He always said that the staff did all the paperwork and he did all the work, so you had to wonder what he found to do on a Saturday morning with no one else about.

By then it was nearly 10.00 a.m., and the doorbell was ringing away like it knew it was safe to do so.

It was Sally. She had had a little moment with Albert downstairs and was looking rather red in the face. Even though Albert's the cuddliest, snuffliest, teddy-beariest border terrier, he's still a DOG. And therefore he barks and sniffs, and has claws and a tongue. All of which means he might as well be a bull terrier, or a Maths teacher, each in their own horrible and fearsome way the most hideous thing on the face of the earth if you're Sally.

'How can you bear it?' she said when I open the door.

I decided to pretend I had no idea what she was talking about.

'I'm fine about having the house to myself,' I said disingenuously. (SUCH a good word that. It always confuses the grown-ups, because they half think you mean ingeniously, and then they try to work out what 'ingenuous' means. Ha.)

Just as she started to explain how Albert had jumped up at her, the bell rang again and in came Amy and Gemma.

Amy was looking rather calm and sweet – actually, she pretty well always looks rather calm and sweet, except when she's having a horrible time at a Snog Fest but we don't talk about that – but Gemma was looking a little bit hyper.

'My *pig* of a father,' she said without any preamble.

Ouch, we all thought. At least, I was pretty sure we were thinking that – Merv's always seemed such a pig to us it was no wonder she was saying it out loud.

'What's he gone and done now?' Sally asked.

'He's only taken my phone away. He says it might stop me downloading rubbish from the internet and making arrangements to go out, instead of working. He knows nothing about my life. *Nothing*. I loathe him.'

We all went a bit silent. Hating people that much usually only happened in the plotlines of over-written soap operas on TV – ones where the episode ends with something bloody happening with a knife.

None of us could think of anything to say. So I decided to try to move things on a bit. Taking Mum's secret box of chocolates out of the top cupboard (there would be hell to pay, but I'd worry about that later), I told everyone to help themselves. Sometimes you've just got to throw chocolate at the problem.

I got everyone to sit round the kitchen table where I'd positioned Ralph's laptop in pride of place and began.

'Right,' I said, in a commanding sort of voice. I had decided I had to take charge. It was my idea. Plus I knew how to get Ralph's laptop to make spreadsheets. I was still sure that whatever else we did, we had to start our Boy Watching with a spreadsheet.

'Let's check out Jezza's Facebook page,' said Gemma, who, without her phone was showing all the classic signs of Hysterical Loss. She was also behaving as if she were a bit sceptical about the whole Boy Watching thing. I knew she thought that Jezza was The One, but, for her own good, I was sure she needed to be persuaded that:

a) perhaps he wasn't

b) she should get to know other boys apart from skinny-Scottish-guitar-playing-smelly-freaky-ignory boy.

'No,' I said even more sternly. 'We are going to create our Boy Watching spreadsheet.'

I began to type:

BOY WATCHING – Prat One

'Not a good start,' said Sally. 'I think we can find our own prats without typing out a list.'

'BOY WATCHING – Part One,' I typed, while gritting my teeth.

Key Observation Points/Positive Attributes:

Availability (must not be obviously tied to anyone, esp QBM)

(un)Boringness (ability to be funny and fun, and talk about things other than football)

Bums (desirability of – on the move and stationary)

Chat-up Techniques/Good (list of TBC. See also **Chat-up Techniques/Bad,** below)

Danceability (can he?)

Hair (ability to wash. Extra points for styling)

Hips (how they look in jeans from front/sideways/behind; see **Bums**)

Humour (a sense of. Defined by actual witty comments, not laughing like drain at *Modern Family*)

Intelligence (can he hold conversation, spell and/or pass some exams?)

Kind to Children and Animals (this category speaks for itself)

Spottiness (not)

Key Observation Points/Negative Attributes

Chat-Up Techniques/Bad (assumes you're interested/ suggests totally inappropriate thing to do on date/is drunk)

Farts (and finds it amusing)

Teasing (in a horrid way)

Ignoring you when he's with his mates

Compatibility Points

Says something

Looks you in the eye when he says something

Calls instead of texts

Doesn't ignore you

Suitability Points

TBC

Sustainability Points (Will it Last?)

TBC

BOY WATCHING – Part Two

Under this heading, I set up whole sections of blank columns, with room for boys' names at the top, our names down the side, with different sheets for each list of attributes. It was fiendishly complicated. But I was sure it would make more sense once we started recording our watching.

Triumphantly, I exited the spreadsheet. As a reward for her patience, I let Gemma have a brief look at Jezza's Facebook page. (Although not before noticing the drop-down menu on Google showing Ralph's previous searches. This time it was 'careers in beer tasting'. Ralph's exposure to jobseekers seems to have left him with a perpetual longing for job satisfaction. His previous searches had included 'LEGO sculptor' and 'chocolate consultant'. As if.)

After Gemma had posted 'likes' all over Jezza's pictures of him posing (and I do mean posing) with his guitar, I very kindly, and rather expertly – though I say so myself – made us all pancakes. Amy and Gemma and I had them with lemon and sugar. Sally, being a gastronomic law unto herself, had hers with chocolate ice cream and golden syrup. I do wonder whether she was actually born with any taste buds.

While we were polishing off the last of them, it started pouring with rain. Perfect weather for movie-downloading, we decided.

It was Sally's turn to choose. '*The Perks of Being a Wallflower*,' she announced firmly. 'Like an insurance policy. You know, if all this doesn't work.'

We were all a little bit silenced as the credits started rolling, then Amy asked what we thought it meant about accepting love we think we deserve. I was all set to have a deep existential conversation when Sally's phone suddenly started making a sound like a New York police siren. That's her mum's calling tone, specifically designed to make Sally jump to attention.

It worked.

Sally had to get her mum's shopping for her. Her mum, Liv, had been laid up with some hideous lurgy that meant she couldn't get out of bed. In the olden days I think they'd say she had a touch of the vapours. But these days I think you'd call it a hangover.

As a general rule, Liv is either drinking mineral water – in a sanitised glass, no ice – or a small bucket of Tesco's finest Pinot Grigio. 'Darlings, I must have another glass of Pinot Greeeeegio,' she drawls rather loudly and quite often.

Anyway, we offered to help Sally – these shopping trips always ended up being very heavy, what with the bottles of mineral water and all – and as it was still pelting with rain, we grabbed at the coats hanging by the front door. By the time we walked out of the front door, Amy looked fetching in a plastic number of Ghastly Ralph's, Sally in Mum's best winter coat (not sure what she'd say about that, but that's just another thing to worry about that later) and Gemma in Ghastly Ralph's fisherman's coat. I ended up with Steve's anorak. A kind of sickly orange colour, it had a rather suspicious-looking stain on the front. Just as well we were only off to do a good deed, and not to go on a date with Harry 1D or Orlando Bloom.

But as we turned the corner to the bus stop we drew up short. There were QB Maggie and three of her nastiest friends. They were heading in the direction of the school playing-fields, where I happened to know that St Thomas's were playing football against King Edward's School for Delinquents. (Not their real name.)

Bloddy bloddy hell. We all looked just about as uncool as it's possible to look, especially me.

'It's too late to turn round. Let's keep calm and carry on walking,' I said, sounding a bit like a tea towel.

So we walked very quickly towards them, feeling a bit sick. Well, I felt a bit sick. I expect Sally felt even sicker, what with the chocolate ice cream and the golden syrup.

'Well, look at this, my friends. London Fashion Week's early this year!' QB Maggie's voice was penetrating and shrill. And then all four of them whipped out their phones and started filming us.

It was pouring with rain, we were dressed in the most unbecoming outfits known to man or boy, there were LOADS of boys just round the corner, any one of whom could have walked out of the playing-fields at any moment, and the most poisonous cow in the school was filming us.

'Life can't get any worse than this,' I said to the others.

'And that,' said Amy in a trembly voice, 'is where you're wrong.'

She was spot on. Out of the gates on the other side of the road, and just as the sun came out and the rain stopped, came five tall, ambling boys. They were wearing their football kit. They looked muddy but unbowed. They looked fit and fun. They looked friendly

47

and funny and a bit like sporting gods.

One of them was Mark Anderson. Mark A*. Top Mark.

He was slapping Charlie on the back and laughing. The other three were laughing too. But in a nice way. They all looked like they were laughing with Charlie, not at him. For a moment, I thought: what an amazing picture of boyhood, how glorious they all look. And then a split second later I realised that I wasn't watching a film...I was in it.

The laughing stopped as they saw QB Maggie and her three witches, with us behind them. Various expressions flitted and floated over their faces. Surprise at the sight of Maggie – who of course had pulled herself up to her full three foot three inches – and her friends. And then a slight horror (although I could see they were politely trying to hide the horror bit) at the sight of us caught behind.

Our faces were red. Perhaps it was from trying to overtake QBM, but probably, and really, from a deep desire to dissolve into any available puddle.

Queen Beeyatch and her horrible cohorts stopped their filming (so every cloud etc) and turned their attention to the Golden Ones. 'Mark! Charlie!' said the QB. 'We were coming to watch you play. Don't say we've missed all the action! Bet you won, though!'

By now we were close enough to see the hairs on their upper lips. (The boys' that is, although I was pretty sure that QBM had a bit of a moustachio going on on the QT.)

There was nothing for it. We had to leave the field to QBM and the cohorts. Smiling awkwardly we marched onwards to the bus and the supermarket. Hey nonny ho. We will regroup, re-dress and be better next time.

Sunday started off rather more satisfactorily. For a start there was no one in the bathroom when I got up. This meant that not only was there no Smell of Steve, but I also had a moment to catch up on the plucking front, and scored a good fifteen plucks of the eyebrows.

Yowza!

Mum and Ralph were in the kitchen finishing off what looked like three pounds of sausages and a whole panful of bacon. Being in a sunny mood, I decided not to lecture them on the dangers of eating vast quantities of processed meat.

'Want some breakfast, love?' Mum said as she rose,

a bit stiffly, I thought, or perhaps she was just very full, from the table. I said I'd pass on the bacon butty option and go to the shops for the papers.

The Sunday papers were a ritual for the old things, and going to get them gave me an excuse to get out of the house.

When I got back, Mum was looking a bit less stiff and a bit more cheerful. 'Ralph is going to take us for lunch at The Hand and Arm,' said Mum. Clearly the thought of having another meal so soon was the best sort of Sunday news for a mum.

Now, this is another tradition for the old things: Sunday newspapers – and lunch at the pub. You'd think we lived in the middle of a Midsomer village. Where everyone walks the dog on the green, goes to church, and then sucks their teeth (how DO you do that?) over the tales of murder and mayhem that they read about in the *Sunday News of Whatever*.

'Fantastic,' I lied.

Because. Honestly. Words could not describe how much I didn't want to sit round a sticky 'faux' (not sure what that means but know it's not good) wooden table, on a swirly-whirly carpet, waiting for a sliver of rubbery steak and a plate of frites, while the jukebox is playing a hit from the late seventies (probably Status Quorelated), and watch Ghastly Ralph burp his way through three pints of Special, as Steve and I toy with glasses of Coke which we could have had much more pleasurably with our friends watching a film...

From all of which you will gather that 'going to the pub' in our world is a definition of hell.

I texted Sally. I thought it only fair she should join in my distress. I made her promise to get her mum to take her and her brothers to the pub too. Her brothers, for the avoidance of doubt, were not babe magnets in any way either. In fact, they were eight-year-old twins who always seemed to be either silently locked in mortal combat with their phones, or shouting and swearing at each other in public places. They were called Harris and Jock – because of Sally's father being a bit Scottish, which is really all we know about him. Well, except for the photograph of a very handsome man in RAF uniform that occupies pride of place in their living room.

It was all just as terrible as I foretold. Ralph had an argument with the barman, saying his pint was too short. Mum said her pie was undercooked and she couldn't eat it (though I think having had twenty-seven sausages for breakfast might have something to do with that), Steve spent the entire time playing *Angry Birds Star Wars* on his phone and Sally's mum took them all to Pizza Express instead. Lucky them.

I walked home ahead of the others, because I think you should walk fast if you want to look successful, plus I didn't want an amazingly handsome boy I'd just noticed on the other side of the street to think I was related to Ralph.

Mid-stride, my phone suddenly made the sound of the Tardis taking off. This can be rather alarming to outsiders, but those of us who knew of Sally's obsession with Dr Who were very used to it. It was a text message from her:

1ST BOYWATCHING POINT GOES TO…ROB.
10/10 FOR SWEET/KTCAA.
CALL ME SXXX

Rob was the drummer in Jezza's funky band. Except he wasn't funky, in fact he was rather quiet for a drummer.

'Rob's playing Frisbee in the park with his little sister,' said Sally when I called her. 'That's definitely a Kind to Children and Animals point.'

I had to agree. Rob had scored. Not in a Jezza sense. But definitely in a BW sense.

I looked across the road at Handsome Boy. He was looking at the trees and the sky and the birds and the bees.

'New rule, we're going to have random points for Cuteness,' I said to Sally, who was still on the phone, very pleased with her spot. 'And I am awarding one of those to the boy with blond curly hair on the other side of the road from me right now.'

Obviously we needed a record, because random points for Cuteness couldn't be awarded on any one person's say-so. So I took a very discreet photo – just for the record.

OMG. He saw, he saw... The *humiliation*. I began to walk sooo fast. I must have looked soooo successful.

I didn't look back. (Never look back, as I'm sure someone once said.) But I went to my room as soon as I got into the house, and opened up my private, secret blog. And there I wrote at least three paragraphs on the nature of embarrassment.

Tomorrow was another day. Again.

Hard Times

I don't like Mondays at the best of times. But this one had a particularly gritty feel about it right from the off. For a start, everyone at home was fighting over the bathroom at the same time. For a second start, everyone's favourite breakfast thing had run out. And for a third, it was pouring with rain, and there was a general air of deep gloom.

By 11.30 am that morning, the gloom had turned to terminal depression.

It started with one or two of the nicer girls I didn't like looking at me rather pityingly. Then one or two of the nastier girls I didn't like looking at me with expressions of evil triumph.

When I found Sally and Gemma and Amy I realised we all had the same expression of Terror of the Unknown on our faces.

'Here,' said one of the nicer girls I didn't like, holding her phone in front of me.

It was a Facebook page headed 'Ugly Chart Year 9: The Girls Least Likely To'. And it was us four, in our rainwear, courtesy of Mum, Ralph and Steve.

All sorts of thoughts rushed through my brain. Was it possible to blow up Facebook? Kill QB Maggie? Turn back time? Spontaneously combust the whole world?

We were saved by the bell. Well, not saved of course. Not saved in any way, shape or form. Our hell was merely interrupted by a bell which told us we had to go to...Maths. Our most hideously hated lesson in the history of lessons.

Does it get any better than this? I wondered.

'Does it get any better than this?' said Sally in a rather green little voice behind me. (Voices *can* be green – timid, off colour, tinged with fear.)

I turned round. She was pulling her hair off her face in a rather brutal way. If I said (and I think I have said) that her hair was of a ginger hue, and her face had a green tinge to go with the voice, then I think I'd be painting a pretty accurate picture. Behind her Gemma looked pale, and Amy, hiding behind her thick curly hair, just looked incredibly sad.

On the one hand it was rather sweet that the others looked to me for comfort, but as I didn't have any to give, that just made it all worse. We looked a sorry bunch. Because we were a sorry bunch.

Together we walked into the Maths room, in a head-down-hide-behind-our-hair-pretend-we're-not-really-here sort of way and sat down round the edges of the classroom. Somehow I thought if we weren't all together we might not make such a big target. One or two of the nicer girls I didn't like looked sympathetic, especially when QBM and her nastier cohorts marched in after us, gave us a sneer, and sat down at the back.

Happily, and just at that moment, Miss Grunbar, the Maths teacher, and without doubt the most vile teacher in the school walked in. She eyed me with a beady eye. I never would have thought I would be almost relieved to be eyed with that beady eye. Talk about referred pain.

'Chloe,' she said in a tone that indicated the anticipation of pleasure gleaned from cruelty and humiliation. 'Your last Maths project is rather unusual. I think the class would like to hear about it.'

Perfect. (Not.)

The project had been 'mathematical puzzles'. And

I'd chosen to write about Ada Byron (no, come back, stay with me!) who was Lord Byron's daughter and who virtually invented the computer before she died tragically young at thirty-six.

I had been really pleased with my project, which had been as much a human interest project as a Maths project, but…

'I think we've got a bit of a clever-clogs here, girls. When we are studying Maths, *she* is studying History! And Poetry!'

There were titters. And sniggers.

I will remember this moment, I said to myself, when I go to university to study English ('and Poetry'). I will raise a glass, full of 'poetic' irony, to the Maths teacher who put me off her subject for life.

At last it was time to go home. Sally and I had gathered up our stuff and were walking out of the gates when we spotted Sunny Side Up and two of his (also quite greasy) friends approaching.

'Boy alert at four o'clock,' I said, using what I thought was a rather clever code that fighter pilots and spies used to identify the position of the enemy.

'What? It's only half past three,' said Sally, completely missing the point. Too late, Sunny Side Up was standing in front of us.

'So you coming out with me on Saturday?' asked SSU, ignoring me and looking rather threateningly at Sally. I thought this was an interesting seduction technique, but decided not to interfere.

'I can't,' said Sally. 'I've got to go to Blackburn with my long-lost uncle from Africa whose daughter's in hospital with third-degree burns.'

SSU looked rather taken aback. One day I must remember to take Sally aside and give her some proper White Lie Training. Less is more, I shall tell her.

But on this occasion it seemed to work, and we marched purposefully off into the sunset, or what would have been the sunset if it hadn't been half past three in the afternoon.

'Now I've got to hide all Saturday,' said Sally, rather despairingly.

'Never mind,' I said reassuringly. 'We'll just go out after dark. And besides, it's an interesting entry for our BW spreadsheet. We can work out the ratio of Number of Spots on Face to Poor Chat-up Techniques.'

I'd had enough of the day, and was quite glad to get to the station for the journey home. Not least because it was by then pouring with rain – the perfect end to the perfect day.

In the crowd on the platform I spotted Jezza, king of cool, who was talking to Rob the drummer who's Kind to Children and Animals, and, in the distance at the other end of the platform, Mark A*. He was on his own, looking quite indescribably yearn-makingly handsome, even though the expression on his face was of – well, superiority might not be overegging it. Still, he had much to be superior about, not just because he was so handsome and clever but also because – unbelievable to relate – he was reading A Book.

'Will you look at that?' I said to Sally. (Somehow the shock must have given me an Irish accent.) 'He's only reading a book.'

Sally didn't seem to understand quite how significant this was. In my world, people who read books could do no wrong. And I was massively intrigued that this really (really) handsome boy was, for once, on his own and engrossed in a book.

I was determined to see what he was reading. I started to walk down the steps to the platform, straining with all my might to see what the book he was holding was. It was crowded and slippery, and suddenly I felt my right foot shoot out ahead of me. I slid down the last ten steps, landing with my head on the platform and my feet three steps above me. I'd hit my head, twisted my knee, cut my elbow, bent my arm, and there was definitely blood coming from somewhere else. The pain was excruciating but as absolutely nothing compared to the humiliation as I hazily saw Jezza, Mark A* and Rob looking down on me, with Sally – whose mouth seemed to have frozen in a perfect O – looking on from a distance.

In that moment, crippled by pain and wounded pride, I still managed to analyse every expression on the faces above me.

There was Jezza, rather amused, Rob looking concerned, and Mark, well Mark was looking a bit shocked (perhaps he could see my beige underwear, oh God) and worried. In the mixture of emotions that swirled around inside me, the one that seemed to loom largest was surprise that the book he was carrying was *The Diary of Anne Frank*.

I opened my mouth to ask him how far he'd got, but then the edges of everything went blurry, and all I could make out was a robust red face, a purple nose and the cap of authority. The station master had taken charge, and with that I passed out.

I'd never been in an ambulance before, and I've often wondered what it would be like. Would I be given oxygen, or morphine? Would I feel the bumps in the road? How loud is the siren from inside? So it's very annoying to report that I was completely unconscious, until I woke up in a hospital bed. I'd missed the whole thing.

Mum was sitting by the bed. She was looking v. worried.

'I'm fine, Mum, I'll be out in no time,' I said to reassure her. This had the effect of making her look even more worried. I guess this was because there was a large lump of cotton wool in my mouth (or that's what it felt like). So I sounded as if I was an alien who'd only just been given the power of speech and didn't really know how it worked.

The nurse came back into the room at that moment, tweaked the drip that was connected to my good arm, and I was dead to the world again.

Three days later, and though I'd recovered from the concussion, I was still bruised, with a broken arm. But I was feeling better and bored. The novelty of being at home wore off incredibly quickly, even though there were lots of compensations – like not having to face the rest of the class in the first flush of the Ugly Facebook page. Or having to go to Maths lessons. Or Biology. Plus I had lots of sympathetic messages about all my injuries, or at least most of them were sympathetic.

On Day Four, Saturday, Amy came to see me with a posh box of chocolates, and a small unidentifiable plant.

She'd come round to watch *X Factor* with me and give me the benefit of her opinion, and she'd also made some notes on some first-hand experience in Boy Watching (I realised Amy can be a tirelessly hard worker when she sets her mind to it).

No sooner had she sat on the bottom of the bed to file her report than Albert downstairs started some manic barking. For whatever reason, the very hint of a whiff of Sally sets him off. Amy let her in – Sally was ashen from her experience as usual, but bravely clutching the very shade of purple nail varnish I didn't know I wanted.

'I hope you like it, but if you don't, I'll have it,' said Sally.

I couldn't help thinking this was a tricky one for Miss Manners. On the one hand it was a positively gruesome colour that made me feel a bit queasy just to look at (perhaps I wasn't so much better after all), on the other, Sally meant well, and we shouldn't throw a gift in the horse's mouth. Or something.

To deflect the purple question, I asked Amy what she had to report from her B Watching activities. I was hoping it would be something fruity, because we didn't have Gemma (she'd been grounded by horrible Merv for some unspecified but probably non-existent crime) who could usually be relied on for fruitiness.

Amy's report was good, solid work. She and her dad had been out shopping. (Absolutely extraord., but it's true. Amy's dad was definitely the winner of the Dad Who You'd Most Like If You Didn't Like Your Own prize. He was a photographer, and always first with the jokes, but in a nice way. Plus he would take Amy out just for fun.)

They had bumped into Charlie, he of the flowing locks and the ready smile, at the bus stop.

Amy's dad knew Charlie because he teaches him Visual Arts at St Thomas's.

'Charlie, you know my daughter Amy, don't you?' said the Dad Who You'd Most Like.

'Yes, of course,' said Charlie. And he'd looked at Amy deeply and intently and intelligently, with a wide friendly smile playing on his lips. This is Amy's description. I suspect she'd actually got in a bit of a state. When asked what she'd said, or what happened next, or did they have a plan to meet up – answer came there none. Myself, I bet that Amy's dad had to save the situation and say friendly grown-up stuff to disguise the fact that his daughter was completely and incapable of saying stuff – friendly, grown-up or otherwise.

'I think,' said Amy with an expression of great seriousness, 'that Charlie scores two Compatibility points and three Suitability points. Plus four Hair points. AND, his jeans were awesome. They were so cool. I think he scores ten on Hips and Bum.'

'And I think,' said Sally, painting her nails purple, 'that you are in lurve.'

Which was the very word to attract the attention of a passing Steve. Or maybe he was just listening all the time – he can be quite a devious brother. As well as one who occupies the bathroom, uses up the loo paper, nicks my bus pass, leaves the fridge door open, puts his smelly socks and trainers in the hall, shoves dirty bowls and mugs under the sofa, uses up all my shower gel... I could go on.

'Who's in love?' he said as he put his quite pustulant (excellent word that, conjuring up the very pus in the pustule) face round the door.

'Not that it is remotely the business of a nosy pustulant,' (I was quietly confident he wouldn't know what it meant) 'but we were talking about Mark Anderson's friend Charlie.'

Oops. I mentioned Mark. I had been trying soooo hard not to think about him, but I couldn't help remembering his face as he looked down at my battered body at the station. I must have been all knickers and bruises and dirt. Oh God, oh God.

And just when I'd discovered that he read proper books. I mean, *Anne Frank* – in touch with your inner sensitive soul or what?

Oh dear.

'Charlie? He's cool,' said my uncool brother. 'He's part of the team organising the Snog Fest. Apparently he's handing out the bar passes.'

'Marvellous,' said Amy. 'So he's handsome, charming, good natured, older, nice – and now powerful too! Soooo out of my league.'

I couldn't really reassure her, so I didn't try.

'Hey, everyone,' said Sally cheerfully, waving her ghastly nails in the air to dry. 'Nearly telly time!'

We sank gratefully into the undemanding, unquestioning, unanything really, cocoon of prime-time Saturday-night television.

I (Still) Hate Mondays

Another day, another dollar, as Karl Marx used to say. Actually, I'm not sure he did. This is something Mr Horriday, our supply History teacher, used to say at the beginning of every lesson. I did once ask him whether Karl Marx actually founded Marxism on this principle, but he just looked a little witheringly at me. I don't think he's cut out to be a teacher.

This particular day was my first back at school after my accident.

I had a rather fetching sling round my arm (in an ironic purple colour) which was meant to support the damaged limb, but was also meant to warn people off banging into me. I was convinced it wouldn't work, so had got Sally and Amy to surround me in a protective shield-like way. It seemed to frighten people off – mostly because I think that what with the sling and

Sally's nail varnish, I was just too purple for people to come anywhere near.

After a couple of weeks lying in bed trying to keep quiet and get better, I'd done an awful lot of catching up on Facebook.

Especially the comments about my accident.

Chloe's head down! LMAO one had said. (Happily no picture, oh lord, so very happily no picture.)

Chloes got uglie legs carted off to hosp, but theirs no point oprating. She still be uglie!!! This one I thought strangely OK. Horrible, but at least you don't need to worry when you know the writer hasn't even got the brains to use spellcheck.

Know your enemy. (Or: No you're enemmy.)

None of it had made me feel any better about coming back to school. But all bad things come to an end, and this bad thing had come to Biology. This is taught by a proper old bat, called Mrs Slopeth. We are all pretty sure that there never was a Mr Slopeth, because you simply can't imagine anyone having 'relations' with the aforementioned bat. This may sound rather cruel, but Mrs S has the unenviable task of teaching us Sex Ed. So it's hard not to let the imagination run away with one. Or not.

Mrs Slopeth was sitting at the top desk looking even

more boring than usual. (I think people *can* look boring. It's to do with the shape of their faces. I realise this is an unusual theory, but I'm happy to put it to the test any time.)

Today we were to dissect locusts. I was dreading this; I'm really bad at blood and guts and the idea of cutting things up. Apparently, having an ironic purple sling didn't get me out of it, so I found myself sitting at the bench, wearing some fetching protective glasses, with a Petri dish and a small sharp instrument in front of me.

I was sitting next to Gemma – we still hadn't got to the bottom of why she'd kept such a low profile lately – who was also looking a bit green.

Moments later the Petri dish was filled with what looked like a short fat stick insect. We were told to cut off the legs and both sets of wings. (For those of you who are squeamish, look away now.) I half shut my eyes and stabbed. That seemed to do the trick, because Mrs Slopeth nodded briefly as she walked by, looking at what I'd done.

Then we had to cut up the right side, then the left side of its thorax. I shut my eyes and gave another couple of stabs. There were little bits of locust all over the bench. I gathered them all together with the aid of a paperclip and the end of a pencil and put them back in the dish. Mrs S came round again and this time her nod was of unqualified approval.

'Girls,' she said in loud (but still boring) tones. 'I want you to come and look at Chloe's work. This is exactly how this dissection should be done.'

With that she took my Petri dish, put it on her desk, and sat down as one by one everyone else had to look at My Work.

Oh how I laughed (internally, of course). Perhaps life wasn't so ghastly after all if it could provide light relief like this.

The three of us gathered round Gemma at breaktime. She looked tired and a bit cross.

Apparently Jezza (I *knew* he'd be at the bottom of it somehow) and two of his mates had called round at her house the Thursday before last to get her to go to The Purple Pig, the new club that has just opened. Stupidly she had agreed. Even though she's way too young to go to clubs, she can make herself look sooo old. Plus Merv never checks up on her.

But she didn't get further than the entrance, where

a bouncer turned out to be not as stupid as he'd looked. He'd insisted on seeing her ID and then insisted her father come and get her and bring her home. Jezza and co. had left her to it and gone into the club. Horrible on every level.

No wonder she was grounded, barred and only allowed out to learn about Marx and locusts' thoraxes.

I decided that this led to at least three more negative points categories on our spreadsheet:

Skanky seduction technique

Bullying by numbers

Abandonment in time of need

And Jezza now had five points in them all.

But I bet Gemma would soon forgive every one.

The afternoon, considering it was Monday, wasn't too bad – especially because the first bit of it was English Lit. We were doing *Animal Farm*, which I was enjoying. Although I had a terrible feeling about the horse, Boxer. I just didn't think it was going to end happily ever after for Boxer.

Our English teacher, Mr Fanshawe, seemed to be suffering from a hideous cold. Usually quite dapper and laid back, today he had little slits for eyes, and a voice so bunged up you could hardly understand what he said. Half an hour of listening to a voice like that and we all began to feel a bit ill too.

He released us early, having given us the task of writing an essay on the topic 'Can violence ever be justified?' (Well, duh, yes it can. Especially against QB Maggie when she's made vile comments about you all over Facebook.)

As we shuffled out of the classroom I felt a tug on my ironic purple sling.

'I've got an idea,' said Sally, still tugging at my sling in what was starting to be rather a painful way. 'Why don't we go to the Shedz gig this weekend?'

As Sally Ideas go this was better than some. Better, for instance, than the idea she'd had last month of hitch-hiking up to London to queue for the Justin Bieber concert. On so many levels that was a Bad Idea. And not just because we couldn't be sure we wouldn't get a ticket. (See what I did there?)

Still, we hardly wanted to show solidarity with the hideous Jezza. Supposing he saw us – the good friends of someone he'd got into trouble and then Abandoned in her Hour of Need?

'Everyone will be there, and we can do lots of

research for our Boy Watching notes,' went on Sally. 'We can get Gemma to come. I bet Jezza will be beastly and have some horrible girl in tow – so she'll see how vile he is and be inspired to start looking for someone nicer.'

I doubted whether this was a sure-fire safe strategy, but before I could say so, Sally went on: 'Rob will be there too, won't he?'

'Very possibly, as he does actually play in the actual band that's actually playing on Saturday.' I was a little sarcastic because I could tell where this was going. I think Rob's KTCA points had majorly endeared him to Sally. Hmmmm. Another thing to think about later, but for now it was important to see if Gemma was all right.

Sally, Amy and I found Gemma outside the gates frowning at her phone. I wasn't surprised she was frowning at it; she'd only just got it back from being confiscated and it had somehow managed to lose all her contacts and most of her music. But now she had a new problem – horrible Merv had texted to say he had to go to Nigeria and she should stay

73

with a friend for a few days.

'So the good news is Merv's out of your hair, but the bad news is you've nowhere to stay,' I said.

Before I knew it, I'd suggested she come back with me. Lord knew what Mum would say, or Ralph, but I was pretty sure Steve would approve. Dreadful pressure on the bathroom schedule, though.

Gemma was grateful. Well, she didn't actually say she was, but she smiled into the distance, tossed her hair and tried to look cool. Although I've a feeling she could just as easily have burst into tears.

We decided to walk home past the sports field. Sally told me she had it on good authority that Year Eleven and Twelve St Thomas's were having a first elevens try-out.

'Which first eleven would that be then?' I asked Sally, strongly suspecting she didn't know the answer. She was always a little hazy about sport. Were there seven in a rugby eleven, or eleven in a cricket seven?

It wasn't the most successful exercise in the history of Boy Watching. We had got to the sports field – and absolutely identified the sport, it was football, surprise,

surprise – but we couldn't get close enough to any boys we knew well enough to score.

Sally excelled herself by announcing this fact out – very – loud: 'We can't score here,' she said. That got her some very dodgy looks.

She'd been reading an article in her favourite magazine (she had a different favourite magazine every week) which was called '10 Ways to Make a Boy Like You' and had determined that we should do some experimenting.

Her two favourite tips of the week (these changed every week, too) were:

Spend the first five minutes ignoring him

And

Use prolonged eye contact so he knows the attraction is mutual

Amy had tried to explain that you really did need to decide on one policy or the other. She also said that trying out flirtation techniques in the middle of a football match wasn't necessarily a brilliant idea.

I'd had a long day, and my arm inside my purple sling was hurting. Perhaps on a normal afternoon the sight of Sally trying to make eye contact with the cute blond boy in goal at a distance of twenty metres would have had me doubled up with the hilariousness (perhaps). But today I'd had enough, and I rounded up our rather bedraggled and fractious team and took us home.

Half an hour later, we hauled ourselves in through my front door. Downstairs, Albert started a big bark, but Sally was too tired to panic, and anyway we had Gemma to worry about.

She'd been totally silent. I could understand this, of course, because commentary on Sally's flirtation techniques was sort of unnecessary, plus I expect she was worrying about being a temporary member of my family.

Mum was at home. I could tell that because there was a loud clattering sound coming from the kitchen – interspersed with banging and humming. (This was Mum's way of emptying the dishwasher. I think she imagined that if she made enough noise someone would come and help her. Poor Mum.)

'Hi, there,' I said with the kind of breeziness I didn't feel. 'We're all here, and Gemma's coming to stay for a few days.' I thought best to get it all out in one go, besides, I felt the accident had left me with a few brownie points.

Everyone muttered their own kind of hello, and we shuffled off into my room, leaving Mum looking a bit shell-shocked and holding four of Ralph's beer glasses, two soup bowls and a carving knife. Ever the multi-tasker.

While she got used to the idea, we settled down on my bed and huddled round the laptop.

'I'm afraid,' I said portentously (this is a new word for me, and probably designed for older people, but I like the *portentousness* of it), 'that we have a lot of negative points to attach to Jezza, who's going to have to do some really good things in the next few weeks to stop us rejecting him for all time.' (I didn't look at Gemma while I was saying this.) 'But on the plus side Rob has climbed into the lead on the Personality front, and Mark Anderson has scored on the Cultural front.'

'How's that, then?' said Sally, a little belligerently, I felt.

'Well. Excuse me. But reading *The Diary of Anne Frank* is a sign of unusual sensitivity.' I thought I'd done very well to get to the stage of actually talking about Mark. I managed to say the words 'Mark' and 'Anderson' as if he were just another boy. 'Even though he is arrogant and full of himself and seems, unbelievably, to like the look of QB Maggie, I think he deserves some credit.'

'What about Charlie?' said Amy. 'Surely we can all

see that he's got to be the nicest person and the highest scorer in the whole of St Thomas's. I mean, even if he didn't look great in jeans, he'd still be the best *person* we're talking about. Right?'

I didn't know. This Nice thing is difficult points-wise. But I could quite see why Amy – who had been the victim of such incredible *un*niceness at the Snog Fest – would think it ultra important. But there was no chance of scoring Compatibility points when Amy really didn't know whether he was interested in her or not.

'We're going to have to introduce an Objective Checker,' I said. 'We need to know if Charlie's just a smiley person, or whether he smiles particularly for Amy,' I said.

'Well, off you go then, Miss Know-it-All,' said Sally. 'Dare you to talk to him at the Shedz gig and find out if he fancies Amy.'

I thought about this for a moment. 'All right,' I said. 'In the interests of Boy Watching research and Amy's future happiness, I will find out what sort of a guy Charlie is. It'll be my mission this weekend.'

I wondered quite how I was going to do this, but at that moment we were interrupted by Steve and Ralph. They'd been sent by Mum to help put up the sofa bed for Gemma.

By the time we'd put the bed up the wrong way, twice, we were all getting a bit tired, and some of us very grumpy. Actually, it was mostly me being grumpy. The warm feeling of doing kind things for friends in trouble was beginning to wear off, and the numb feeling of a bad arm was starting to kick in.

I decided to send everyone home, or out of my room, whichever was the most appropriate. I wanted to have a little quality time playing cards on my phone before bedtime. Playing cards on your phone is one of the most mindless and soothing activities ever invented. I guess it's a bit like the maiden aunts in old-fashioned novels, content to sit by the fire playing Patience all day, only occasionally interrupted by young people wanting either their advice or their money.

This led me to imagining how life will be in years to come, when I'm a prize-winning novelist and very rich from all my international deals but still very single because all the boys I'd ever known grew up into men who lit their farts and had only half a mind to play football, the other half having been rotted by taking vast quantities of hallucinogenic horse pills... And with those cheery thoughts I drifted off to sleep.

Bad Vibrations?

This was the week for getting back to playing with OTTO (Overgrown Throttle and the Tempted Obscurity, for anyone who might have forgotten the unforgettable name of our band). The arm was a bit better, so I felt I could manage a few chords, Sally needed some drumming practice (perhaps she could get lessons from Rob...probably only a matter of time before she thought of that...) and it would be good for Gemma to make loud noises and throw her long, straight hair about.

It had been an uneventful few days for Gemma, unless you counted her nearly getting arrested for shoplifting. She'd been trying out perfume testers in Boots, but after her fifth, the rather bored security man decided she was going to steal it. It took all her hair-waving and trembly-lower-lip expertise to get herself out of that one.

But we'd managed the whole staying-with-me thing quite well, all things considered. Ralph was on best behaviour, which meant a massive decrease in Overt Public Burping, Steve was positively speedy in the bathroom (I *knew* he had it in him. As it were) and Mum even had some help with emptying the dishwasher. (I think Gemma would have been so much happier if her own mum was still around and hadn't run off with her best friend from school. Her mum's best friend from school being a rather racy piece called Juliet... No wonder Merv was bitter, and Gemma a bit adrift.)

Anyway, at the end of a week playing happy families, we were going to celebrate with making some noisy music on Friday night, and heading off to the Shedz gig on Saturday.

I had decided to make the best of a bad job, and to enter willingly into the spirit of a Saturday night adventure. Who knew? I might even meet some extra-special hunky boy with a six pack and a great sense of humour who could quote Shakespeare and make me feel special. (I had tried to add 'Shakespeare' as a category for our file, but it had been my most least popular suggestion ever. We had points for Great Kissing instead – which actually was fine by me,

Shakespeare you can get on the internet.)

But first we had to get through Friday. Which sort of started off OK (getting into the bathroom, enough milk for cereal, got a seat on the train, that sort of thing), but then deteriorated into Biology.

This particular Friday, Mrs Slopeth decided that we should all write up our practical notes in class. This was always a sure sign that she felt even less inclined than usual to actually teach us – the clue was in the little slitty eyes, the pale complexion, the greasy hair, the monosyllabic responses. Oh yes, I haven't reached the great age of fourteen without being able to detect the signs of a monumental hangover.

Still, it was a good opportunity to gather my thoughts for the weekend. Under the cover of my practical book, I started to make the ultimate list of the top twenty things we wanted in a boyfriend. I'd started off with 'likes reading, wants to look after me', which I thought really important, and then moved on to 'knows how to kiss, looks good in a V neck...' Then I scrubbed out the bit about the V neck sweater – tooooo painful a memory; I didn't think I'd ever be able to look a V neck sweater in the face again. I'd just folded it all up and was passing it under the desk to Sally – when I heard the deep voice of Mrs Slopeth. (Useful observation point: people with hangovers always have deeper voices than usual the morning after.)

'Chloe,' said the deep voice, 'I'm sure it isn't just Sally who can benefit from the incisive nature of your notes. Please read them out loud so we can all share.'

Oh dear. We'd come a long way since my great locust triumph. The practical had been all about testing for starch in leaves as part of learning about photosynthesis. All I could remember was that we had had to put a leaf in a test tube with some alcohol. And that the alcohol had tasted really horrible.

Then I felt a little rustling movement near my right hand. Sally was passing me her notes. Feeling a surge of warmth towards my best ginger friend, I stood up and read, fluently, confidently and gratefully, from her notes.

At last it was the end of the day. Art had, if anything, been even more waste-of-timey than Biology. Mr Pampledousse seemed very distracted and did a lot of gazing into the middle distance. Amy reckoned he was imagining he was in his beloved Greece, Sally thought he had just been told he had a secret love child, Gemma thought he was having some sort of pervy fantasy, and I thought he was probably worrying about the gas bill. He dismissed us unusually early, which I thought was a good thing because we had songs to sing and chords to play.

Sally and I headed to the gates to wait for Amy and Gemma, who'd gone to their lockers.

The first sign that all was not quite well in the world was when Sally made a choking noise. I looked at her, looking at the gate. For a moment I thought she'd seen Sunny Side Up, but it was the six-foot boy who had been pestering her at the Snog Fest where we all had such a horrible time. The one in black who had wanted his own little snog fest with Sally. He was still on the outside looking in, but he seemed to be staring at her.

'Chloe,' said Sally in a little voice. 'Let's go back inside.'

On closer observation, I couldn't help but notice that the Six-Foot One bore an uncanny resemblance to the Giraffe. This isn't a random reference to a zoo animal, but the name we – affectionately, of course – call Joanne the v. tall goal shooter in our netball team. There was just a faint chance that the Six-Foot One was waiting for his sister, and Sally was getting her knickers twisted for no reason.

But I decided to humour her. We turned round anyway and, scooping up Amy and Gemma, who were clutching their guitars and coming the other way, headed back into the school. If we hung about in the entrance for a while perhaps the Six-Foot One would just go away.

Meanwhile, it was good sport watching the staff leave for the weekend. Mrs Slopeth walked palely, determinedly and relievedly to the exit, probably to have a lie-down for the weekend.

Horrible Miss Grunbar (she who could make even Isaac Newton loathe Maths) marched off in a business-like fashion, no doubt to make life a misery for anyone who came near her at the weekend. (Perhaps nobody ever did come near her, though. Oh dear. MUSTN'T feel sorry for her.)

Mr Fanshawe, who made us like English Literature despite his seemingly constant cold, walked by, blowing his nose copiously (ugh).

Mr Horriday – History supply teacher who doesn't know his Marx from his elbow (in my opinion) – was gazing around him, and then brightening up when he saw Mr Pampledousse. Together they walked out of the main door.

'Ha,' said Gemma. 'I *thought* so.'

'No you didn't,' I said, 'and anyway, they might just be going off for a manly pint before they go their separate ways to meet their separate girlfriends.'

'Ha,' said Gemma again.

I sighed.

It was now eerily quiet in the school entrance, and I started to feel a bit depressed. 'Come on,' I said with a cheeriness I didn't feel, 'let's try again. And if our tall friend is still there we'll just march on through him and get on the next bus, wherever it's going.'

We walked determinedly across the school yard, looking neither to left nor right, and got on the number 62 bus. As it drew away, we looked back and saw the Six-Foot One still standing by the gates.

'It is just possible he's waiting for someone else,' I said to Sally. She didn't look convinced, but on the other hand we did have something to distract us in the form of: 1. The sight of Miss Grunbar sitting at the front of the bus. 2. The fact that the number 62 went in precisely the opposite direction from Gemma's house.

Tempting though it was to find out where Miss Grunbar lived, we decided life was way too short and anyway we wanted to get started on band practice. So we got out, turned round, got on a number 73 and made our way to Merv's garage and our beloved instruments.

It was freezing cold, and we only lasted an hour or so – my arm wasn't quite as much better as I had thought it was – but I thought it was good therapy for us all to make a lot of noise.

As it was still quite early when we finished, we went our separate ways on our separate buses. No need to trouble Merv and his shifty gear stick.

'See you tomorrow,' we all said, separately and together. Our plan was to set off for the gig the following day from Sally's. After several hours getting ready in her bathroom, natch.

Albert was in fine voice as I opened the door to my house. His enthusiastic barking sounded for all the world as if he'd been waiting for me, which made me feel inexplicably warm inside. I made a mental note to offer to take him for a walk over the weekend. He was young and strong and the handsomest of wire-haired terriers, and who knew? Perhaps he might meet the love of his life in the park the very next day. Perhaps there'd be some ravishing lady terrier looking for romance...with a handsome boy in tight jeans who looked just like Zac Efron on the end of her lead.

As I unlocked my front door, I had a mental picture of Zac and me, sitting on the sofa watching TV together, or, no, wait a minute, we'd probably be on the red carpet in Leicester Square for the premiere of his latest movie. Although then I'd have to have a stellar, knockout designer dress to wear, I didn't think my wedges, skinny jeans and a sparkly top would really do it. Best to stick with the sofa...

Just when I'd got to the part where Zac was complimenting me on my home-made burritos and shyly putting his arm round me (who was I KIDDING? Shyly?), and I was just starting to wonder if he'd notice that my bra was at least a size too big, my reverie was interrupted by a solemn sight.

Ghastly Stepdad, Mum and Steve were all in the sitting room, standing in a rather stiff triangle and looking a bit tense. Ghastly Ralph's little goatee beard (did I mention the goatee beard? It's every bit as hideous as you might imagine, perhaps a bit more so) was quivering with what looked like indignation.

'Hello, love,' said Mum. There was a pause. Her smile was on the watery side, and she didn't ask me about band practice. Something was up.

'What's going on?' I said. 'You look like you've all just been voted out of the Big Brother house.' Although, come to think of it, that should have made them look a lot more cheerful.

'It's Steve,' said Ghastly Ralph. 'He's only gone and applied to join the army.'

I immediately had a vision of handsome officers in camouflage uniforms – the brown and green ones where they're meant to blend in to the nearest hillside, assuming there is a hillside nearby – standing around in our kitchen listening to me telling amusing anecdotes of life as a prize-winning author.

Then I looked at Mum. She looked suddenly older, and rather sad.

'I thought he was going to go to catering college,' said Mum quietly. 'I thought he'd get to be a cook, maybe run a little café, perhaps even a restaurant one day. I never thought he'd want to join up and get himself killed.'

'Now, now, Gill,' said Ghastly Stepdad. 'There's no need to let your imagination run away with you. It might be the making of the boy. Get him fit. Give him something to aim for in life.'

'Stop talking about me like I'm not here,' said Steve, a little belligerently for him. Although I guess 'belligerent' was rather appropriate for an aspiring soldier. 'I've put my application in and that's that.'

He walked out of the room, and moments later we heard the sound of his bedroom door being slammed shut. Ghastly Ralph went after him, and then seemed to change his mind and went into the kitchen. Probably to get a bottle of beer – a bottle of beer in Ralph World was the solution to pretty well everything.

'Oh, Mum,' I said. 'Maybe they won't accept him. Maybe they'll give him a boring desk job for the rest of his life. Maybe he'll join the catering corps.' This was a flash of inspiration, though I say so myself. And it seemed to have the desired effect. Mum smiled at me, a bit more convincingly.

'You might be right, love. You two have got to do what you want with your lives. I mustn't get in your way,' she said.

'Well, at least you won't have to worry about me,' I said with my best encouraging smile. 'They don't send prize-winning authors out to war zones.'

I *think* that was a comforting thought for Mum to go to bed with.

Let's Go Down to the Gig Tonight

It had been a dark and stormy night. I guessed the dark thing was only to be expected, but there had been thunder, and howling wind, and lots of rain bashing against the windows.

One particularly loud thunderclap had woken me from a satisfying dream about Orlando Bloom (obviously Zac had given up on me) where we were having dinner in a very smart restaurant, and he was protecting me from gunfire. Wrapped in his strong arms, I felt no fear as Mr Pampledousse and Mr Horriday ran towards us waving huge machine guns, or even as the walls of the restaurant came crashing down to reveal Miss Grunbar and all the boys from Year Ten standing in a line shouting and waving giant locusts.

But the next bang was a bit closer to home, and

swiftly followed by Albert downstairs having a good Saturday-morning bark. The grown-ups had gone to work.

I wandered blearily into the kitchen, where I saw Steve looking morosely at a bowl of Coco Pops.

'You serious about this?' I said in my best concerned sisterly tone.

'Absolutely,' he said. 'I just need to find some milk and some sugar and you'll see how serious I am.'

Lord, brothers can be tiresome. 'I meant about the army, you dork. You can see how upset Mum is. Shouldn't you at least finish your exams first?'

'Don't need to. Kev and I are going to be soldiers, we don't want to be officers.' Kev was Steve's mate. And, incidentally, also completely hopeless from the Boy Watching point of view. He was a total clone of Steve. He had the same greasy hair, acne, and dorky way of quoting from superhero movies. So even supposing I found that sort of combination irresistible (as if) it would have been practically incest for me to go out with him.

But he was Steve's only mate, so I felt sort of warmly towards him. Clearly they both had their hearts set on becoming macho men-of-arms together. I decided it could well be a passing phase and anyway even if it wasn't perhaps it *would* be the making of them.

So with that thought I/Pollyanna got ready to go out. It was going to be a long day. I needed three possible outfits for the evening (way too early in the morning to make the final decision as to which to wear); all my make-up (probably best to take absolutely everything, including some of Mum's eyeliner and hair straighteners), a clean pair of knickers in case we missed the last train home and had to stay on someone's floor, and my phone charger.

By the time I'd packed up I looked like I was leaving home for good.

'See you later, dork,' I said to Steve as I ran down the stairs past Albert's flat.

As I was walking down to the bus stop, vaguely wondering how Sally was going to feel when she saw Rob the drummer again, and whether he already had a girlfriend, and whether he really was one of the good guys, I felt my phone vibrate. Sally had Instagrammed me a picture of her twin brothers, Harris and Jock. They were obviously in the middle of a huge fight as each one had a finger in the other's ear or mouth, and they appeared to be shouting very loudly. (Interesting how you can tell what somebody sounds like just from the shape of their mouth.)

Clearly things were going to be nice and relaxed chez Sally. Ha.

But as I got nearer to Sally's house everything seemed weirdly silent. Perhaps Sally's mum, Liv, had woken up with another attack of Pinot Grigio flu and decided to silence the horrible twins once and for all.

Or maybe Sally's mysterious father had come back unexpectedly and stolen them. (Apparently he'd been on a secret operation when Sally was about five and the twins not yet born, and has never been seen since. Gemma thinks the secret operation involved a young, pretty woman who lives the other side of the country and has enormous bazookas, an insatiable appetite for sex and a massive private income. She's always one to imagine the best in people.)

I rang the doorbell. It was a piercing, screamy sort of doorbell that I guess you needed if you were Sally's mum because it would have to penetrate the noise of the horrible twins. Though it did sound a bit scary in the eerie silence.

Sally came to the door. 'Mum's taken the twins to the doctor,' she said. 'Harris put his finger in Jock's eye, so Jock hit him in the mouth so hard a tooth fell out.'

I often think that if we all get seriously worried about over-population, we could easily put people off the whole business of having children by parading Harris and Jock all over the country. 'Roll up, roll up! Two little perishers for the price of one! Watch the blighters beat each other up! Horrible sights and sounds guaranteed!' I reckon everyone would go home and back on the pill like a shot.

'Brilliant,' I said unsympathetically. 'Let's have a go with Harry while we wait for the others.'

Obviously Harry was Harry Styles, and obviously 'have a go' meant nothing more than playing 'Midnight Memories'. Maybe it's a cliché to love Harry, but there are some things you just can't help. Sally had hundreds of Harry and 1D pictures which she now played on a loop on her Macbook Air (how come she had one of those? Gemma reckoned it was hush money from her dad's rich mistress, but she would reckon that, wouldn't she?).

'Story Of My Life' was interrupted with the piercing screaming of the bell. Gemma and Amy came in carrying make-up bags even bigger than mine.

I interrupted the flow of Harry photos to bring up my

spreadsheet of Boy Watching. We were still refining our 'Top Twenty Essential Requirements' in the Perfect Boyfriend list, but we also needed to add a definitive Action Plan for each of us. Well, actually the first item was 'Go to Shedz concert, check out Charlie and see if he is what we think he is and good enough for Amy'.

I had been having an awful thought that Charlie – who did seem like really and properly one of the Good Guys – might have heard via the vile bullies of the dreaded Snog Fest that Amy only liked girls. Gemma, who always seems to know more about this sort of stuff than the rest of us, was of the view that this didn't matter because even the nicest boys thought they could convert a lezza to natural gas (as she put it). And anyway, he wasn't part of the vile bullies crowd, and probably didn't even know about it.

So I was feeling quite at ease with the world as I put on an extra layer of eyeliner. I'd read somewhere that it was very important to have as much line on the top of the eye as the bottom or you looked tired. So by the time I'd finished that bit of the operation I looked like a really, really wide-awake panda.

'Jeez, Chloe,' said Sally, looking at me in the mirror. 'You look like something out of a fifties movie – all that curly hair and more make-up than skin.'

'Thanks a bunch,' I said. Then I remembered some of Mum's favourite movies – she was a great one for old black-and-white films – and thought that most of those stars from the olden days were actually very beautiful. I decided not to pursue the conversation and simply imagine myself as, say, Sophia Loren, with (much) smaller boobs.

After about another hour or so of squabble and dither, we declared ourselves ready. We'd all gone the dress and heels route, and looked rather great, though I thought so myself. Still and all, we had thought we looked great when we set out THAT time to THAT party.

We walked to the train station in a good mood with ourselves, though, and got on to the back carriage of the stopping train. We spent the journey taking lots of selfies and singing 'Diana'. I like to think that the rest of the carriage, which seemed to be full of old people coming back from boring shopping trips, looked on our youthful high spirits with tolerance and even affection. But perhaps it's more likely they were thanking God they'd stayed on the pill.

You could hear the crowd a mile away.

'I had NO idea this was such a big deal,' said Amy, looking a bit unnerved. And then we all felt even more unnerved when we spotted the QB Maggie ahead of us in the crowd, surrounded by all her favourite horrible friends. They were screaming with laughter at something QBM was showing them on her phone.

I immediately thought they were looking at a picture of me being laughed at by V neck Tim, or me falling down the station steps showing my knickers. Isn't it amazing how we always think that it's all about us?

Just as I was starting to think quite deep thoughts about how we think we're the centre of the universe, we had to get into our places as the concert was about to start.

Onto the stage he swaggered, that sweaty heartbreaker with the wristbands and the ventilated clothes. Must confess, Jezza did look good, and he did sound great as he lurched from side to side of the stage, seeming to use his mic as a chat-up weapon for every single girl in the audience.

Hey ho. Gemma was transfixed, of course. And it didn't help that QBM and her horrible cohorts were in the front row making themselves look like Jezza's special girls.

I focused on looking around for Charlie. Of course I was looking for *Charlie*, you understand, who might just – coincidentally, of course – be there with his friend Mark A*. Who read *The Diary of Anne Frank*. And who I hadn't seen since what Sally calls The Adventure of the Falling Floozie.

Then I saw him – Charlie. He was just three rows away. He was smiling and bouncing around like he didn't have a care in the world. And now I come to think of it, why should he have a care in the world? I was trying to see who he was with, but was distracted by the feel of a peculiarly still figure beside me. Sally was looking intently into the dark area at the back of the stage. Out of the shadows would occasionally loom the white face of a certain boy who we had officially designated as being Kind to Children and Animals.

Rob's face had on it a brilliant example of the drummer's expression. He looked utterly preoccupied, as if he were trying to remember the theory behind Newton's First Law of Motion. But at the same time he had a sheen of dampness on him which seemed to indicate that he was actually concentrating like his entire life depended on his not making a mistake.

Eventually the whole set came to an end and the shouting and cheering and whistling must have woken up many generations of dead people.

We started to leave the hall. The plan was to skip the second half (we didn't know the band) and go on to Gemma's house unless we were suddenly asked to some cool after-party. But perhaps we were confusing ourselves with Zac and Orlando after a film premiere, because there were no signs of cool after-parties that I could see.

Gemma wanted to go round to the stage door and see the Shedz boys.

'What, and torture yourself with the sight of QBM walking off into the night with Jezza?' I said.

But then I thought we could do some useful Rob Watching – would we see *him* go off into the night with some long-haired, high-heeled Year Twelve, I wondered?

'Chloe? That you, Chloe?' I turned round. Charlie. With the bouncy hair and the crinkly smile. He was on his own, and came over to the four of us with such a nice grin that I had to remind myself that it was Amy we wanted him to fall in love with.

'You OK now? I hear you had a dramatic accident at the station and ended up in hospital.'

Oh. My. God. I nearly passed out at the thought that the only way he could have known about my accident was if Mark A* had told him about it. *He cares!* Then I told myself not to be so silly; the Falling Floozie was all over Facebook, complete with messages about uglie legs.

'Yes, I'm fine now thank you,' I said, a little breathlessly, but I don't think he noticed. 'You know Gemma, and Sally…and Amy, don't you?' I really did do the dot, dot, dot thing. The meaningful pause thing.

Charlie turned his crinkly smile in Amy's direction. 'Yes, of course,' he said. 'I saw you the other day with your dad. Is he going to run the course again next year, do you know?'

'Um, yes, I think so,' said Amy, looking at him with an expression of intense dumb amazement, as if she could hardly believe she was actually standing within touching distance of this amazing human being who, amazingly, was actually saying something to her.

'That's great,' said the amazing human being. 'He's really good. I was going to get some friends to go on it if he's doing it again.'

Some friends, I thought. Which friends? Not the ones who read *The Diary of Anne Frank*… Then I pulled myself together.

'Isn't Amy's dad lovely?' I said brightly, because I

thought there was a distinct danger of Amy not being able to say anything more. 'If all teachers were like him, then I think everyone would like going to school and learning things, and the world would be a better place and there'd be no more wars.'

'You might have a point there,' said Charlie, not the least bit patronisingly. I was liking him more and more. And then when he turned to Amy and said, 'Say hi to your dad from me, hope to see you both again soon,' I thought he was officially perfect.

'Charlie is officially perfect,' I said as the perfect one headed off back in the direction he'd come. 'I think that piece of Boy Watching alone was worth the train fare.'

Amy didn't say very much. She just smiled her sweet smile and seemed to disappear inside herself.

'Well, that's one for your Boy Watching charts,' said Gemma rather bitterly. 'He's absolutely oozing Positive Attribute points.'

She spoke with such venom that the three of us turned in the direction she was looking. Sure enough, there was the vicious, vile, short little Maggie, standing with her vicious, vile, short little friends (well, OK, some of them were quite tall) in a circle round Jezza.

Jezza seemed to be looking in Gemma's direction

and making 'come over here' motions. But if he was, Gemma wasn't having any of it.

'Let's go,' she said. 'I've had enough of this. Let's leave him to the little cow.'

Sally had been dancing about, trying to look over the crowd to see if a certain drummer was lurking about. There wasn't a sign of him.

'Come on, then, everyone,' I said. 'Let's make our own after-party at Gemma's.'

I thought we'd done a good day's work. Charlie and Amy weren't exactly going out together, but then neither were they absolutely not.

With that incredibly positive thought, I followed the others on to the bus for an evening of exotic pizza at Merv's mansion.

A Walk in the Park

Sunday morning. All was quiet. Not a creature was stirring, not even a mouse.

That's a poem. I'd no idea where it came from, but ever since it had popped into my head I'd been lying in bed imagining I could hear a mouse scuttling about in the roof. It was massively distracting me from the serious business of writing my blog.

So there was nothing for it but to get up and see what sort of a state the Ghastly Stepdad and my only marginally less ghastly brother had left the bathroom in.

Yuck to the power of yuck was the answer. Why is it that the male of the species regards the bathroom as a wet room? And leaves it not only awash with water, but also with a smell of stale methane hanging in the air?

Horrid though it was, I took a long time in the bathroom that morning. Not just because there was much to be done – there's always much to be done if you leave eyebrow-plucking till the weekend – but because I didn't really want to face another family discussion about Steve joining the army. I did think that everything that could possibly be said on the subject had been said.

'…beat them to a pulp, and quite right too,' Ghastly Stepdad was saying as I came into the kitchen.

Silly me. I'd forgotten that other sacred Sunday morning ritual: Ralph reading the papers and telling us exactly what he thought should happen to benefit fraudsters. Or Romanian beggars. Or women with ten children by ten different men. Or bankers with seven-figure bonuses and vast houses in Kensington and the country. (Ralph could be quite classless when it came to pure hatred and resentment.)

'Do you want some orange juice, love?' asked Mum. She was obviously keen to get away from the subject of whatever bit of the human race 'had it coming to them' that morning.

I decided to make it an orange-juice-and-nothing-else for breakfast morning. The remains of Ralph's plate of bangers and burgers were enough to put you off food for life. And anyway, I still felt full of banana-and-curry pizza from last night. (I kid you not. Merv's deli had excelled itself. The other option was cashew-and-cream-cheese pizza. Sally reckoned the deli people were 'taking the pizza'. She really is quite the jokester.)

'We were thinking, love,' said Mum as she spread a surprisingly large spoonful of marmalade over her toast. 'About Wales.'

She took another spoonful of marmalade. I was fascinated. Just how much marmalade could one piece of toast carry? Perhaps there was a record for it somewhere in the *Guinness Book of Records*. But I expect there were strict rules as to what counted, and lots of variables. For instance, how liquid the marmalade is, how big the piece of toast is, and whether it is capable of being lifted up to the mouth in one go.

'Whales?' I said, coming to from my speculations. 'Why? Have you been watching them on television or something? Or thinking of going swimming with them, like you do with dolphins?'

'No, love,' said my mother patiently. 'Wales, the country. We were thinking we might have a few days' holiday there at Easter. Perhaps rent a cottage near the sea. It would be a nice break for Ralph. He's been working so hard lately. And you, too. You've got GCSEs starting next year, and you'll have to be serious then, but I think we could all afford some time off now. Especially with all the uncertainty about your brother.'

Lord. A family holiday. I hadn't factored that in AT ALL. I'd imagined the Easter holidays full of band practice, Boy Watching, the odd party, some shopping, fooling around taking selfies, catching up on *Made in Chelsea*, making one drink last all morning in Starbucks, painting our nails, watching *Mean Girls* for the ninety-seventh time... Not going for wet walks on the beach, and having egg sandwiches in the car, and quarrelling over whose turn it was to do the washing-up. Oh dear.

'Is Steve going to come, then?' I asked, still trying to work out the full horror of the idea.

'Course he bloody is,' said the Ghastly one. 'Least he can do after all the upset he's caused.'

There was, clearly, no end to the joys ahead.

I retired to my room and did what I usually do when life throws a sticky one at me, and texted Sally:

NEED RESQ. ALL GHASTLINESS.

That should do it.

I decided we'd take Albert-downstairs for a walk. Sally might not like the idea, but it was time she got over her dog thing, and anyway it would get us out of the house and into the land of real people. Also, there was always the chance that Zac-lookalike walked his terrier on a Sunday morning too.

Sally appeared incredibly speedily. At first I was touched that she had come rushing so quickly to my rescue. But she rather spoilt that by telling me that Harris and Jock had locked themselves in the sitting room and were throwing furniture at each other (rather light furniture, I assumed) '...so it's just brilliant to have an excuse to get out of the house.'

When I told her we were going to have a bonding day with Albert, she looked almost as if she'd rather be back in the film of *The Terrible Twins and the Flying Furniture*. But it was too late by then and moments later we were knocking on Albert's door.

Albert's owner was a crabby old guy of about fifty, who was the leading light of the local English Civil War re-enactment group. Which meant that sometimes we could hear rather alarming clanking sounds from downstairs as he set off in full seventeenth-century battle gear.

When he wasn't wearing a huge helmet and a noisy breastplate, he seemed to favour the string vest and elderly jeans look. Neither made him seem any less crabby.

On this Sunday morning he'd branched out and was wearing a moth-eaten tartan dressing gown. But he gave us what passed for a smile in his world, as he seemed pleased to be getting rid of Albert for a bit.

'Don't forget to keep him away from small children, he's got previous with small children,' he said.

Brilliant, I thought. Albert turns out to be a child-molester. I had visions of him with one end of a child in his mouth, Sally and me holding on to the other end – and a Zac-lookalike looking on with an expression of horror and disgust.

We set off towards the park, me holding Albert's lead, Sally walking so far apart from us that anyone would think she didn't like dogs.

After about half a mile or so, she seemed to get a bit more used to the idea. I was just thinking that all was going terribly well, when I saw a figure in the distance that looked familiar.

Uh oh, I thought, it's the Six-Foot One, the pest from the Snog Fest, the putative Sally snogger. He was heading our way, deeply engrossed in looking at his phone. He looked as tall as ever, but if anything just a bit goofy. Still, I hoped Sally wouldn't see him.

Sally saw him. Suddenly she was back in her nervous mode, clearly convinced he was Coming to Get Her.

'Let's just grab Albert and make a run for it,' she said. This was fine for Sally who was wearing a pair of practical Ugg boots, but I was still struggling to get the hang of my new wedges. We were making slow progress.

'For heaven's sake. He's not even looking this way,' I said in what I intended to be a very reassuring tone. 'But if you insist, we'll just walk quickly round the other way, and head straight for Amy's house. It's only about three minutes from here.'

Sally made a little whimpering sound. I looked around for Albert, and then realised he was trotting obediently behind her, looking up at her with an expression of doglike devotion. I guess 'doglike' was part of the package, but the devotion was most unexpected. For a brief moment I found time to think that maybe this was the beginning of a beautiful friendship.

We headed towards the gate that led to Amy's house. Sally was now speeding ahead, but I was really struggling – I don't think the suedette on my wedges was designed to withstand wet grass, mud and dog poo.

Albert clearly thought all this was great sport, and had starting barking in an isn't-this-fun? kind of way.

Just at that moment my foot hit a particularly large pile of turd. I was sent slithering forward at high speed straight into a jogger coming the other way. Up until that moment the park had seemed almost empty – just us, and Six-Foot One – so it was a bit of a surprise to bump into someone.

'Still sliding all over the place, Chloe?' said a voice coming from the general direction of the navy blue tracksuit my nose was buried in. (Nice smell – new material mixed with fresh soap. Surprisingly pleasant.)

Charlie. He was smiling, but only just. I guess if you're on a quiet Sunday run, the last thing you want is to collide with a high-speed fourteen-year-old.

'It's not her fault,' said Sally breathlessly. 'I think we're being followed. It's that boy over there. I've seen him before. We were trying to get to our friend's house before he caught up with us.'

She was so clearly distressed that Charlie's

expression changed. He saw the Six-Foot One, who had slowed down but was still heading our way, and said, 'OK, don't panic. Where's your friend's house? We can go there together.'

Oh, the relief. What a difference a boy makes. One moment a boy is a mysterious possibly threatening thing, and the next a different boy is the most heroic of protectors and kindest of people. I decided I would write a little essay on the subject on my blog when I got back.

Then I had another thought – amazing how they just kept on coming – we were taking Charlie to Amy's house. Surely now he'd see that they were meant to be together? Who'd have imagined that fretting about the Six-Foot One was making something good happen...?

Well. I hoped it was good. As we walked out of the park, with Albert yapping at our heels (All these new people to play with! All these new smells!) I texted Amy:

HOEP U UIP & DRSSED IN BST. US & CHARLE WT U IN 5.

That was the best I could do at the same time as managing the wedges, holding onto Albert's lead and listening to Charlie and Sally.

'So, you've seen him once outside the school gates and now here?' the heroic one was saying to Sally. 'Let's see if we can find out who he is, he does look a bit familiar. I'm sure there's nothing to worry about, and he was just waiting to meet someone.'

Exactly, I thought.

Amy is an only child who lives with her parents in the smallest house in a street full of small houses. Her father, of course, is the Dad Who You Would Most Like If You Didn't Like Your Own, and the one most likely to teach world peace. Her mother works at the hospital, doing we weren't quite sure what, but definitely good. All this, of course, explains why their daughter is so chock-full of goodness.

There was a little iron gate in front of the house, which gave a nice noisy creak when we opened it.

Hopefully, I thought, that should alert the family to the arrival of their distinguished visitor – their future son-in-law.

Amy's mother opened the door. If she was a little taken aback by seeing Amy's friends with a strange young man and a madly yapping dog, she didn't show it.

'Albert,' I said fiercely to him. 'Behave.' This had no effect whatsoever, but as I was starting to apologise to Amy's mother I was aware of Charlie grabbing him by the scruff of his collar, looking him in the eye and saying very firmly, 'Sit, Albert.' And Albert didn't only sit, he lay. He looked up at everyone, one by one, seemed to decide he didn't have to do any protecting, and with a little snuffly noise settled down for a bit of a rest after all his exertions.

'This is Charlie,' I announced, just as Amy's dad came into the hall. 'He's the voice of common sense, and he tames wild dogs.'

'Hi, Charlie,' said Lovely Dad.

I allowed myself to think that this was all going perfectly. All we needed now was for Amy to waft downstairs dressed in something weekendy but still designed to show off her perfect figure, her wavy hair and her sweet face. Bit like Jane Bennet and Mr Bingley in *Pride and Prejudice*, I suddenly thought. And I started to wonder if Charlie – undoubtedly 'a single man' – was 'in possession of a good fortune'. Judging by the number of times we'd seen Amy's green dress, it was entirely possible that Amy and her family could do with a 'good fortune'.

But before I could finish showing off to myself

my perfect knowledge of Jane Austen, I heard Amy coming downstairs. You could actually hear everything everywhere in that house.

She was wearing jeans, flats and a lacy top with lots of beads.

Brilliant, I said inwardly. Just the thing to appeal to Mr Bingley.

'Hi, Amy,' said Charlie Bingley.

'Hello,' said Amy Bennet.

OK, so it wasn't exactly evidence of a passionate meeting of minds. But definitely promising.

After a lot of peanuts, crisps and Coke at Amy's house (probably a month's supply for them, I couldn't help thinking guiltily) we all went our separate ways. I was *almost* sure I'd heard Charlie *almost* making a plan to see Amy again. I heard them talking at the other end of the room about something to do with the Snog Fest. No doubt we'd find out about it later, but for now I thought we should congratulate ourselves on an excellent morning's work.

The crabby guy downstairs was strangely ungrateful for the safe return of a well-exercised Albert.

'He's late for his dinner,' he said grumpily.

'But on the up side,' I almost said, 'he's had a lovely time away from you.'

I didn't, of course, because I didn't want to spoil the chances of the budding new relationship between Albert and Sally.

No Fire Without Smoke

When I got back home, I found Ghastly Ralph and Steve slumped (there's no other word for it) in front of the TV. There was a colourful and extremely noisy game of football going on.

They both looked up at me and made shushing gestures. Right. So I was going to make a noise that could possibly interrupt or even be heard against the whistling and shouting and rattling and 7000-decibel commentary.

The air smelt stale, as if it had been breathed in and out countless times already. There were empty plates all over the floor with little dried-up chips on them. The table was covered with Sunday papers and rows of empty bottles of beer. Ugh. I hate football.

I found Mum in the kitchen. She looked tired. She had put all her spice pots out on the draining board. I happened to know for a fact that she'd reorganised her spice cupboard only a couple of weeks previously. But I supposed anything was better than being in the sitting room with her horrible menfolk watching all that noise in silence.

She looked up when I came in. She smiled.

'There you are, love,' she said.

Yup, I thought to myself, nobody like Mum for stating the obvious. But I wasn't going to say anything; she looked like she'd had enough of a day already.

'How about some tea, Mum?' Personally, I hated tea (though not as much as I hated football of course) but I knew how much she liked it. The mere act of saying, 'I'm just going to have a nice cup of tea,' seemed to work like a magic cure for everything from a rainy day to exhaustion after dealing with stroppy customers at Happy Hairliners.

'That'd be lovely, Chloe,' said Mum. Something made me stiffen. My name in Mum World was 'love'. 'Chloe' was only for serious moments, like when I'd done something really, really wrong. But I hadn't done anything wrong. I mean, here I was making a cup of TEA for her. That was good, wasn't it?

'What've you been up to today, Mum?' I asked as I wrestled with the kettle. It had one of those curly electric leads that always seem to curl the wrong way, which was almost certainly why they haven't made them like that for the past thirty years.

'Oh, nothing much. The washing. Put my feet up and had a bit of a sleep actually.'

Perhaps she really did need this Welsh holiday, I thought. And I made a New Year's resolution (you can do that in March, can't you?) to be nice to Mum in general and about Welsh Wales in particular.

I gave Mum her mug of tea, and retired to my bedroom with Ghastly Ralph's laptop. I thought I'd update the Boy Watching file with a report on Mr Bingley's amazing qualities. (Note to self: must find out Charlie's actual surname, or Bingley is likely to stick and one day cause embarrassment.)

I was making good progress and thinking deep thoughts, despite being constantly interrupted by Sally pinging through new photos of Harry S on my phone and wanting my comment on each and every one.

My deep thoughts mainly focused on its being such a Good Thing that Amy, who had been so upset by the boys at the Snog Fest, was now being exposed (I think I mean exposed) to such a fine example of boyhood. And a boy who just happened to be a friend of the one who dare not speak his name. Well, I expect he *does* dare to speak his name.

I think Mr Horriday's lost the plot.

Gemma thinks this is because things are going badly between him and Mr Pampledousse. But I think Gemma just has a compulsion to see some sort of weird drama going on, usually sex related, in even the most humdrum of happenings. (Humdrum. I wonder where that comes from. Perhaps it originated with a drummer in the army who had an irritating habit of humming as he drummed, and being a very dull drummer he gave the language a new word. Or perhaps...but I digress.)

The reason I think Mr Horriday's lost the plot is that he's taken to muddling everything up. It's not just that he doesn't know his Marx from his elbow, qv above, but on Monday he started off with the causes of the Industrial Revolution – spinning jennies, coal, enclosures, that sort of thing – but then mixed them up with the Balkans, nationalisation and the assassination of Archduke Franz Ferdinand. It made no sense at all, especially when QBM and co started singing 'Take Me

Out' and banging their desk lids to the rhythm. Mr Horriday looked horrified. And probably not just because he didn't know 'Take Me Out' was one of Franz Ferdinand's greatest hits.

Then everyone on the left-hand side of the class near the window started banging the blinds. And by this stage everyone on the right-hand side of the class was either having a ruler fight or playing with their phones.

The noise was deafening. Mr Horriday had his hands on his hips and was shouting in a strangely high-pitched voice.

'See?' said Gemma leaning over to me. 'Sooooo gay.'

I couldn't really see anything gay about it, in any sense, and had a terrible fear that we were going to see someone actually have an actual nervous breakdown actually right now in front of us.

'That is ENOUGH, girls,' a stentorian voice boomed through the din. (Stentorian! Where did THAT come from? But I know it means booming, and we were definitely talking booming in this case.)

Miss Grunbar was standing by the door looking so furious and so scary that even Queen Maggie's Beeyatches were suddenly silenced.

'You will remain in this classroom, girls, until half past two. You will read your notes from the last lesson and be prepared to answer any question by the end of the lesson. Mr Horriday is coming with me, and there is to be absolute silence while we are gone.'

She swept out of the room, followed by a rather pale-looking Mr Horriday.

There was a rather shocked silence after they'd gone. Even the QBM cohorts seemed a little shaken. It didn't last longer than twenty past two, though. At that point everyone started to shift restlessly about, get up and edge towards the door.

The only thing that lay between us and freedom that day was – God help us – a swimming lesson.

Perhaps we all only have short little spans of attention, because it seemed like only seconds later that we were all en route to the pool, chatting away about our latest method of getting out of swimming, all thoughts of poor Mr H forgotten.

'I've got just the thing this week,' said Gemma. 'I shall tell Miss Dinster that I have a fungal infection Down There and a doctor's note to prove it.'

This was good, I had to hand it to Gemma. Miss Dinster was exceptionally mannish and rather shy. This meant that she could be made embarrassed at more or less any point by the combination of a pretty girl and mention of 'Down There' and wouldn't dream of asking for said doctor's note.

'Well, I have got a HUGE verruca,' said Sally. 'Suck on THAT,' she added, revoltingly and unnecessarily.

I sighed. The hidden advantage of being the sister of Harris and Jock is that very rarely is there a shortage of contagious diseases to get you out of a sports-related activity.

So Amy and I were the only ones who had to go through with it, the whole swimming lesson thing.

I don't know what it is about all that water and being expected to float and generally move about in it. It just never happens for me. I seem to expend the most incredible amount of energy splashing about trying to get from A to B, but nothing much seems to happen, except that I get rather out of breath and go red in the face. I foresee a very difficult situation when I'm on the gold-encrusted yacht of my millionaire lover – which is, of course, the twin of the gold-encrusted yacht I bought from the royalties of my bestselling books – and I have to wear inflatable armbands before I dare lower my gorgeous, suntanned, honed and fit body into the water.

The whole lesson was exactly as horrible as I'd

foreseen. I failed yet again to swim a whole length without putting my feet down, and I managed to be the only one in the class to do an actual belly-flop when we were doing diving.

'Just tuck your arms tight into your head...point down and out...focus on the point of entry...clasp your hands together and look at your hands...keep your toes pointed.' Oh yeah, yeah, yeah.

Thwack.

Eventually it was all over, praise be to whoever is the god of not-swimming, and Amy and I set off to meet lucky old Gemma and Sally back at the school gates.

Sally was there but no sign of Gemma.

'You looking for your friend?' said one of QBM's least nasty friends as she walked out of the yard. 'She's got caught, hasn't she? She's in Mrs Munroe's office.'

Oh lordy lord. What had she gone and done now? Mrs Munroe = ultra scary headmistress. The one you really, really don't want to mess with. She of the piercing eyes who seems to know what mischief you have in mind before you do. She with an enormous brain, who seems to know you from top to bottom, and has unreasonably high expectations of you. And she who has a way of expressing her disappointment in you that makes you want to melt into the ground. She.

Since normally Mrs Munroe would leave the daily grind of disciplining us lot to her lessers, being in Mrs Munroe's office meant real trouble.

We got there just as Gemma emerged. She looked quite white, ashen even. And quite without her usual bravado.

'What on earth's happened? Surely Mrs M didn't find out about your made-up fungal infection?' I said.

'I was having a rollie round the back of the chemistry lab, wasn't I?' said Gemma.

'I don't know,' I said a bit coldly. 'Were you?'

'Well, YES. Course I was.'

'Clever old you, then,' I said. 'And are you looking bright white because you've been frightened by Mrs M or because you feel sick from the rollie?'

Gemma gave me a withering look. At least I think she meant it to wither. I do understand that, because sometimes I can sound a bit holier-than-thou. But then that's really only because there but for the grace of God go I. And just in case all that obscure religious language is a bit confusing, the thing is that I know I would LOVE to smoke. I know I'm not supposed to, but there's a small part of me that thinks it makes you look cool, plus it stops you eating, and it would be a way of introducing yourself to boys who smoke ('Have you got a light?', that sort of thing). But I *think* I've been brainwashed enough with all those lessons about the effect on the lungs and stuff to resist. I think. So no wonder Gemma and I have the odd difficult moment over this issue.

She went. Took her ashen face, and her sick stomach (I just *bet* she hasn't got the hang of smoking yet) home, and to Merv, and their own little gated community.

We headed off too.

Only Monday. It was going to be a long week…

I was right about the long week. Although it could only have been five days long, it felt like twelve. Especially when we were sitting in our Maths lessons.

Miss Grunbar, clearly taking it upon herself to have revenge on us for the hapless Mr Horriday's hideous History lesson, did an excellent job of humiliating us one by one.

If ever you need to show someone a horrible time, make them come up to the whiteboard and, in front of as many mocking classmates as you can gather together, make them calculate the capacity of an irregular cuboid. The more you scoff at their inability to multiply the length by the width, or the depth by the height, or whatever combination of the above your sadistic brain can conjure up...the more you'll addle their brains and confuse them – and put them off Maths for life if they weren't already, and make them *hate* you. Miss Grunbar.

But, oddly, the whole thing had the weird effect of making us all bond together. Nothing like being in the same rocking boat. Thanks, Miss Grunbar.

That was the end of Thursday, a day that had been more or less unremitting in its irritatingness. But more cheerfully, I was off that evening to Sally's – to help her babysit Harris and Jock.

You may think this would be a ghastly prospect. And indeed in some ways it was. But Sally had found a new computer game, called something or other whose name escapes me, except I know it was misspelled (presumably the whole world now thinks 'combat' is spelt with a k?) Sally reckoned it had just the right amount of mindless violence to keep H and J quiet for at least four hours. By 'quiet' I mean, of course, focusing their noise on a machine rather than the outside world.

As we headed towards the bus stop, my eye was caught by a big group of senior St Thomas's boys in the distance. They were looking all golden in their golden uniforms. I was just going to point out their loveliness to Sally, when I realised that at the back was none other than the one who dare not speak his name.

Mark A*, for it was he, was walking more slowly than the others, and oh God, oh God, he was bending down to listen to what the girl walking next to him was saying. He looked utterly engrossed. And she, dammit, looked lively and pretty. She had long dark hair, tied back in a carefully careless style, and was wearing jeans and a yellow sweatshirt that was much too big and looked all the more great because of it.

As I watched, they both burst out laughing at something she'd said.

Why, I thought to myself, had I ever imagined that such a one as he would look twice at such a one as me? He was three years older, rumoured to be brilliant and destined to get a scholarship to university. He was in the first eleven for football (football is OK in this context, of course) and had broken his year's record for running the 200 metres. (Oh yes, I had Googled him to within an inch of his life.) All that and he was sympathetic (qv expression of concern for the Fallen Floozie) and good with literature (qv *Anne F*).

I suddenly felt incredibly depressed. I would probably end up going to the Snog Fest with Sunny Side Up at this rate. Or Purple Anorak, if I was really lucky.

'Come on, Chloe,' said Sally cheerfully. 'A whole evening of *Made in Chelsea*. We can do our nails and eat illegal quantities of ice cream.'

Sally's idea of heaven. Mine too.

If only I wasn't hopelessly in love, life might be worth living.

All went according to plan. We put Harris and Jock in front of the screen, gave them the controls, and then sat back and watched as they electronically beat the crapola out of each other. Excellent.

Next, we found the deep freeze drawer that had all Sally's mum's stash of ice cream. Apparently when Liv is off the Pinot Grigio, she refocuses on ice cream. Never one to do things by halves, that means that the fridge is always full of litres and litres of exotic flavours. Excellent again.

So then we settled down and watched the beautiful posh people make utter prats of themselves. Best sport in the world.

Just as we were laughing our knickers off, a message came through from Amy – Charlie had texted to say that he would come by her house after his Sunday morning jog, and maybe they could go for a coffee.

OMG, I have never seen a text message so full of exclamation marks.

She is so excited.

I am so happy for her.

And not at all sorry for myself. Not. At. All.

Operation Welsh Boy

Someone once told me that someone once said: 'Whenever a friend succeeds a little something in me dies.' Just saying.

Meanwhile, as if oblivious to all the ups and downs and heartache going on around him, Ghastly Ralph was making plans for the holiday in Wales. (Although, come to think of it, of COURSE he was oblivious to what was going on around him. His middle NAME was oblivious. If we had all burst into tears and had epileptic fits on the carpet in front of him, he'd just have grunted and changed the channel on the TV.)

Despite the short notice, he had found a cottage near the sea, in Cardiganshire, which was both incredibly cheap and available in the first week of the Easter holidays. I thought both these things were deeply suspicious, but didn't want to upset Mum by explaining exactly why I thought we were headed for disaster before we even got there.

In fact, not only was it unbelievably cheap but it was also big enough to accommodate another person. I was quite anxious that that person should be Sally. For obvious reasons. But also because I thought it might make Ghastly Ralph and Steve be a bit less odious if there were a stranger watching. It had worked with Gemma, after all.

Fortunately, Ralph and Mum agreed.

*Un*fortunately, I overheard them talking about it as I came downstairs.

They were in the kitchen, and the door was wide open... 'I think it'll make her less bad-tempered if she's got a friend with her,' I heard Ghastly Stepdad say.

'Oh, she's just at that age,' said Mum, not very loyally, I thought.

'Age shmage,' said the ghastly one. 'She thinks she's better than us, and that's a fact.'

I decided to enter the kitchen at this point, and not dignify their conversation with any sign that I'd heard it, though I couldn't help looking a little reproachfully at Mum.

It might be a while before I made her another nice cup of tea.

There was a downside to Sally coming with us to Wales, I realised as we got ready to go a couple of days later: Ralph's car.

This was an elderly Peugeot with a lot of miles on the clock, a reluctance to go uphill if it was full of people, and not a lot of space in the back seat. So for two and a half hours, I would be sandwiched between Steve and Sally. A grim thought, although it did have the advantage of meaning I could see the road ahead and thus be less likely to be sick. Me and feeling car-sick go back a long way.

'You girls,' grumbled Ghastly Stepdad, as we were packing the car. 'Never take one bag if six will do.'

Steve grunted in agreement. Apart from a whole sentence at breakfast the other day, he had done pretty much nothing but grunt for the last three weeks. But he managed to grunt in the sort of way that made it clear that the thought of a week in Wales with his loving family was officially and completely his idea of hell. He already had his earphones in and I was pretty sure they'd stay there for the whole holiday.

At last we were all in the car and pointed in the

direction of Welsh Wales. Three hours later (at least one of which was taken up with Ralph complaining about the tax on petrol) we arrived at the Cardiganshire town that was to be our home for the week.

Ralph hadn't printed off the directions (not his fault of course, somehow it was Mum's) so it took us another half an hour to find a house that looked like the one in the picture.

It didn't look like the one in the picture. Far from being on its own with a sea view, it was in an alleyway surrounded by sheds, an old garage and a launderette. To add to the general cheer, none of the lights worked and the house smelt a bit like an ashtray.

'Let's see if we can get the fire going,' said Mum, in a heroic effort to look on the bright side of things.

With a lot of cursing and muttering, Ralph found some logs and firelighters and eventually got a small fire to flicker in the grate. By some miracle he found a switch to get the lights working.

Not a trace of a signal, though. We were truly left to our own devices – and much good they could do us.

To my utter amazement, the following day was bright and sunny. Mum was even singing 'The Sun Has Got His Hat On' as she clattered about in the kitchen, rearranging the unfamiliar pots and pans. The owners of the cottage had provided a loaf of Ralph's favourite sliced white bread and a packet of bacon, so he was full of the joys of life and a lot of breakfast.

Sally and I decided to head to the beach and go Welsh Boy Watching.

'Who knows?' said Sally, 'perhaps we'll find a handsome hunk to bring home and take us to the Snog Fest. We can get ahead of the others with our research for the file. Or perhaps we'll find One Direction have come to Wales to get away from the plapperizzi.'

'Paparazzi,' I said. I sometimes wonder whether Sally has some sort of oral dyslexia. And I did think that if 1D were determined to get away from it all, they could probably afford to go somewhere a bit posher than west Wales, but I decided not to spell that out to Sally.

Operation Welsh Boy had an unpromising start as we followed a sign saying 'This way to the beach'. We had to go down an alley between the back of a pub and an Indian takeaway, which produced a mixture of smells that was even fruitier than Steve's best efforts in the bathroom.

Sally was tripping over the cobbles as she waved her phone around in the air, hoping to attract a stray signal. 'Hello?' she was saying, 'Signal, where are you? Come on down, signal.'

Not that I wanted to disown her or anything, but I let her get quite a bit ahead of me.

When we got to the bottom of the hill there, all laid out in front of us, was the sea. 'The sea, the sea,' I said rather excitedly and a bit unnecessarily. 'Doesn't it look blue?' Really, I was excelling myself. Truly I am my mother's daughter when it comes to stating the obvious. Still and all, it was a sight, and it did make me think the squashing in the back of the car might be a bit worth it after all.

We started to walk towards the edge of the water. Annoyingly Sally's Ugg boots came into their element again, whereas my trainers quickly became full of sand. Remembering all that stuff about the feel of sand between your toes, and being at one with nature, I took off my shoes and socks and started to run barefoot towards the sea. At one with nature! Revelling in the freedom!

Only to come to a grinding halt – the beach was agony. All those shells and little stones were separately and together piercing every part of my feet. I started to hobble like a very old woman on a hot tin roof. Sally was nowhere to be seen.

Then as I tottered back to the place I'd left my shoes I saw her in the distance, standing on the edge of the caravan site that stood between the beach and the town behind. She was talking to two people. They looked quite big and tall and definitely male.

'Hey, Chloe,' said Sally as I walked their way (I could do that now, what with having shoes on), 'come and meet Hugh and Ya-yan. They're brothers and they're staying in the caravan park.'

'Hello. Nice to meet you,' I said, sounding a bit like I was at a middle-aged cocktail party. Trying to move it all on a bit, I said, 'What does Ya-yan mean?' looking at the one I hoped was Ya-yan.

'It's Welsh for John,' he said. He seemed rather nice. 'It's spelled I-E-U-A-N.'

'Gosh,' I said brightly. 'Four vowels in a row. That's amazing!'

'I suppose it is, but I've got used to it by now,' said Ieuan. At that moment my phone gave a loud squawk, Mum's call sign – we were being summoned back to the house.

'We've got to go, Sal,' I said. 'But maybe see you around?' I said in my best friendly-but-not-too-friendly voice, to Hugh and Ieuan.

'Sure,' said Hugh. 'We're in the games room most evenings.'

'Great,' I said, and we both walked off to start the climb back up the hill.

'Don't look back,' I told Sally. 'Be cool. DON'T look back.'

She did, of course. Because she's Sally.

When we got back to the cottage the sun was going in, and Ralph was going out. It looked like there was going to be a father/stepson moment, as he and Steve were putting on coats in a man's-gotta-do-what-a-man's-gotta-do kind of way. This usually meant going to the pub in Ralph World.

'We're off to the pub,' said Ralph.

'Will you want lunch when you get back?' asked Mum from her tiny new kitchen.

'Nah,' said Ghastly Stepdad, 'we'll have something there.'

Who said we were living in an age of enlightened men and liberated women? Isn't it always the way that a man's gotta go to the pub, and a woman's got to be prepared to have dinner ready, just in case?

I forgave my mum for her comment about it being 'just my age', and said brightly, 'Let's go down to the café at the bottom of the hill, Mum. No need for you to cook anything.'

Mum looked so much more cheerful at the thought that I really did forgive her.

When we got to the café it started to rain. The raindrops were beginning to wear away the letters on the blackboard outside. 'Os gwelwch yn dda dim noethni' it said.

'That must be Welsh,' said Sally, as on the ball as ever. 'It's probably the special of the day. Let's write it down before it disappears so we can order it.' And she tapped away at her phone.

We went inside and sat at a table near the window. Nearly all the other tables were occupied, mostly with the very old and the very young. The very old were couples who seemed to have been sitting together in silence for the past twenty years, and the very young were children who seemed to be little Welsh versions of Harris and Jock at their loudest and shoutiest.

An elderly waitress came up to our table. She had jet black hair and an expression that seemed to say 'I have seen it all, and there is nothing you can say or do that would interest me or make me like you'.

I found her a bit frightening, but Sally was too focused on ordering the special in Welsh to notice her properly.

'Oz gwelch in dada dim nuthny,' she said brightly. Just as she said it, I noticed another board inside with the English translation. Sally had just said to our waitress: 'No nudity please'.

It's very difficult to keep a giggle inside if it's really determined to get out. I thought I was going to explode with a huge snort, but by focusing very, very hard on the veins on the backs of Mum's hands I managed to keep a grip.

'I'll have a toasted cheese sandwich, and what will you have, Mum?' I said, thinking that saying sensible stuff out loud might calm me down. Looking rather puzzled, Sally and Mum said they'd have the same and, without the slightest change of expression, our fully clothed waitress went off with the order.

After she'd gone and I'd explained to Mum and Sally why I'd been making choking noises, we all laughed our knickers off – even Mum. I guess we shouldn't have been surprised that our sandwiches were delivered by a different waitress.

While Sally bent over her phone – there was a full

signal in the café, so all was well in Sally World – Mum told me that her ambition over the holiday was to go to the Welsh Quilt Centre.

Lord, I thought. Good luck with that. I couldn't quite imagine Ghastly Stepdad saying, 'Yes, of course, dear. Can't think of a nicer way of spending an afternoon. Always one for a lovely bit of stitching, me.'

We were interrupted by a cry from the other side of the table. 'Oh, poor Ames,' said Sally. 'Charlie's said he's got to buy his mum a birthday present and has cancelled their date.'

I DID feel sorry for Amy. She'd be utterly miserable. Poor Amy.

And then I felt pleased with myself. I can't be that horrible and jealous if I really do want the best for my friend.

It was food for thought for the Boy Watching, though. Because while Charlie might score for remembering to buy a present for his mum, he got minus points for not organising it so he could keep his date with Amy. Hmmmm. It wasn't a brilliant sign.

Also, of course, we needed a new category for Foreign Boys (Wales IS another country, after all). Perhaps they did things differently Abroad. Not that we really knew how they did things anywhere, as

Sally pointed out helpfully.

Meanwhile, not a word from Gemma. It was always a bit of a worry when Gemma went off the air. She hadn't said anything about going out of signal range, and anyway, she was hardly likely to go off with Merv for a happy holiday in the countryside. Merv and happy holidays just didn't go together. In fact, Merv and 'happy' just didn't go together.

She'd hate me saying this, but I sometimes wondered if we'd ever reach the age where we didn't have to worry about Gemma.

It was still pouring with rain by the time we came out of the café, so we decided to go back to the cottage and watch one of the DVDs there.

Imagine Mum's delight when she saw they had *Summer Holiday*. Well, in order to imagine it, you would need to know that Mum has a bit of a thing for Cliff Richard. Whenever she hears anyone groan and call him a cheesy Christian, Mum gets the closest I've ever seen her to cross. 'You should have seen him in his early days, the *Living Doll* days. He was like an English Elvis. The way he moved his hips. And that pout. Very sexy.'

Lots of things disturbed me about this. For a start, she never HAD seen him in his early days, and for another start my mother talking about someone being sexy made me feel very, very uneasy.

I decided to leave them to it and go to my room and finish reading *Animal Farm*. I know this makes me sound like a bit of a nerd, *Animal Farm* being a set text and all, but I thought it was really good and besides I was getting very worried about Boxer.

Well, THAT was flipping depressing.

I was right to have been worried about Boxer, and I came downstairs in a right gloom. Which wasn't helped by the fact that Mum and Sally, having finished with *Summer Holiday*, had moved on to *Wonderful Life*. The owners of the cottage must be Cliff nuts to have TWO DVDs in the house. (I mean, one you could understand, but two...)

Ralph and Steve still weren't back, which did not bode well.

It was getting dark, but it had stopped raining, so I decided to tear Sally away from Cliff and go down the 'games room' to see if Hugh and the one with all the vowels were as nice in the evening as they had been in the morning.

It was tricky negotiating the cobbles in the dark. I wondered how Ralph was getting on, since it was difficult enough seeing where you were going even if you hadn't had sixty-seven pints of Special. Perhaps Ralph would fall over, and break a limb or two. Not enough to be life threatening, but just enough to pop him in hospital for a week or so to give us all a rest.

I'd been worrying that we wouldn't be able to find the 'games room'. But when we got down to the bottom of the hill, I realised you would have to be deaf and at least partially blind not to find it. There was such a throbbing and a flashing coming from the pavilion-like building at the end of the row of caravans you couldn't miss it.

It got ever louder as we got nearer. I could see that all the little Welsh Harrises and Jocks were still up and were making more noise than ever.

'They should soooo be in bed,' said Sally, in a surprisingly grown-up and world-weary way. Then I remembered that so much of her home life was spent in trying to get dear little Harris and dear little Jock to go to bed that if there was one thing she knew about, it was bedtimes for eight-year-olds.

We made our way to the front of the arcadey bit. The first machines we came to were simulated racing cars. I always rather fancied myself behind the wheel of a Formula One car. (Maybe I'd be the first woman to win a Grand Prix in between writing my prize-winning novels.) I pulled Sally over to a red one that looked a bit less complicated than the rest.

I settled myself into the driving seat, which seemed very comfortable and inviting. It looked easy. Just stick to the road, I told myself, give it some welly with the fast pedal, and let's break some records. Sally wasn't looking the least bit keen on all this, plus I noticed some boys with their hoods up looking at me like I was something they'd trodden in.

I'll show 'em, I thought, as I put in the money. Soon they'll be standing around in amazement, wondering how a 'mere girl' could be so brilliant. They'll be high-fiving me, and queuing up to go on a date with me.

It started off well enough – gentle coast up to the starting line, lots of crowds shouting and cheering. But then nothing much seemed to happen. I heard more shouts, but this time they were coming from behind.

'It helps if you press start,' said a sarcastic Welsh

voice from one of the hoodies. (I had liked the Welsh accent up until then.)

When I did press start we were off at such a pace that I began to feel a bit sick. It was incredibly difficult keeping to the road, which bent in the most unexpected ways. And every time I tried to slow down I drove straight into the crowd. In no time we'd ground to a halt and I'd scored fifteen out of a possible 750,000 points.

The Welsh hoodies were laughing and jeering and Sally had completely disappeared.

I had three more goes left, but by now I was bright red in the face and wanting to run away to sea. As I extricated myself clumsily from the controls, even the seat seemed to be laughing at me.

I saw some cuddly toy tombolas in the distance and headed in that direction. Cuddly toys can't laugh at you. Can they?

'Come on,' said a voice at my elbow. Sally. Where had *she* been in my hour of need? 'There are Hugh and Ieuan over there. Let's go and say hello.'

They were in a big crowd; lots of girls, boys, and boys in hoods.

'Let's go home,' I heard myself say a bit feebly. 'I've had enough for one day. We can come back tomorrow.'

We edged out through the crowds, me with my head down, trying to hide my face, which was glowing, but not in a good way.

Walking up the cobbles in the dark was just as tricky as going down. Although at least if you fell over, you'd fall on your face and stop, rather than roll all the way down to the bottom – ready to be jeered at by every passing hoodie.

Everything got a bit lighter as we got nearer the pub and the Indian takeaway. Which meant that I could see, lurking outside the pub, two familiar figures. Jeez Louise, I thought. If that's who I think it is, it's an all-time record breaker for the plonker stepdad and my dumb brother. Nine hours in the pub. Or, as was the case at the moment, *outside* the pub.

Ralph's eyes were glazed. Unseeing. Blank. He looked much, much more stupid than he usually looks. He peered at us without a hint of recognition, staring fixedly, as if he were focusing intently on some distant ship on the sea. Steve, on the other hand, was just leaning against the wall. He was in the middle of a group of smokers, but without seeming to have the faintest idea where he was. He still had his earphones in – which made me wonder if he and Ralph had actually said anything at all to each other for the past nine hours.

At that moment Sally bumped into me. Even in the dark in a strange town, on cobbled streets with lots of even stranger people around, she was still completely focused on her phone. Incredible, but lucky, really, because it meant she hadn't seen my unseeing shame-inducing relations, so I could just grab her arm and drag her up towards the cottage.

'You're back,' said Mum as we opened the cottage door. As usual, irritatingly and undeniably true, but I decided to let it go, because she looked a bit miserable. I guessed that wonderful though *Wonderful Life* was, it couldn't quite make up for being in an empty house on the first day of her holiday.

'There's no sign of your father and brother,' she said. Since I knew exactly why that was, and was still working out what to tell her about it all, I didn't fly at her about her use of the word 'father'.

My father, my real actual father, died of something sudden to do with his heart when I was three. I have the haziest memory of him – he was dark, and he smelt warm, and I can still remember the pattern of the hairs on his arms. I know that I used to feel safe whenever he was around, and that he had a quiet, gentle voice that I never remember being raised against either of us and certainly not at Mum.

That was my 'father', not this selfish, goatee-bearded, football-loving lump of a drunk who was swaying about halfway down the hill.

'I think I saw them outside that pub on the way to the sea. Ralph looked a bit, er, well…' I said. 'I expect they'll be back soon. How about a nice cup of tea?'

There. Forgiveness must be absolute if I was putting the kettle on.

The three of us had had scrambled eggs, watched the news and were about to go up to bed when the door banged open and in came two wild and wet figures. Steve still had his earphones in (I was beginning to wonder if they did actually come out) as he took off his coat and slumped down on the sofa. Seconds later he was deeply asleep and snoring with the sort of roaring snuffle that I thought only cartoon characters made.

Ghastly Ralph, truly living up to his name, managed to hang his coat on the standard lamp before he stumbled towards the stairs. 'Shtum beds tomorrow full piesh,' he said utterly incomprehensibly. 'Shown go down mersh.'

I had just started to wonder if all this could come full

circle, so that maybe when a Welsh-speaking Welshman is very, very drunk he makes total sense, when I saw Mum's expression. It had been a long day, and she was the one who had to try to go to sleep inches away from the monstrous hulk.

As I shut our bedroom door, I thought almost fondly of the little popping sound that Sally made when she was asleep.

Beach Bunnies

The next day was another bright and sunny one, and made all the brighter by Ghastly Stepdad being very quiet. It was almost as if he were full of remorse, and penitence, and contrition. (We did those words as examples of synonyms in our English language lesson. I knew they'd come in useful one day.)

Incredibly, he seemed to have agreed to take Mum to the Welsh Quilt Centre. Go, Mum! Milk this one as much as you can, I said – to myself, obviously.

As Ralph started the old Peugeot, with a bit of a sulky expression (I did hope the remorse and contrition and penitence managed to last out the trip), Sally and I headed off to the beach.

Almost as soon as we got to the bottom of the hill we saw our targets in the distance. Hugh and Ieuan were by the edge of the water, throwing stones into the sea. They were both quite tall and skinny and had the same thick brown hair that blew about in a really good way in the wind. They both wore black jeans – Hugh with a plain white T-shirt, Ieuan with a green hoodie. I decided that now was the time to get over my fear of hoodies, as we strolled casually up to them.

'Hi there,' said Hugh. 'Didn't see you at the arcade last night.' (Thank God, thank God, I thought.) 'We're going riding later. Want to come?'

'What?' said Sally. 'On a horse?' Sometimes I do think I may have to trade her in and get a new best friend.

'Er, yes,' said Ieuan. 'You can hire ponies at the stables the other side of the hill over there.'

'Maybe tomorrow,' I said, as coolly as I could.

'OK, great,' Ieuan said.

Brilliant. But inside I was in a panic: didn't you have to have crash helmets to go riding? And didn't you have to know how to steer? What if the pony ran away with you? Maybe it would plough into a crowd and kill people. By the time I finished telling myself that they weren't Formula One cars, Hugh was suggesting we went for a walk. Great, I thought. I definitely know how to do that.

So we walked all the way along the beach, past the

arcade and back to the caravan site. We discovered that Hugh and Ieuan were twins, went to school in Pembrokeshire, and that they both worked on their father's farm, but were hoping to go to Cardiff to do Chemistry (Hugh) and Geography (Ieuan). They both seemed nice, and I couldn't decide if I preferred one or the other. (They weren't identical twins, but they were definitely similar enough to be confuseable.) But on the basis that Hugh was the one not in a hoodie, I decided to prefer him.

When they asked us what we were doing for our GCSEs I liked them even more. They must have thought we were at least fifteen. Possibly sixteen.

Once it was time for them to go ('Gweld chi yfory. Welsh for see you tomorrow!' said Hugh), we decided to take ourselves off to the café to regroup. The wind was starting to blow up a storm, so it was nice to get into the welcoming warmth of the café.

Welcoming? Warmth? She of the jet-black hair was in sole command and gave us a filthy look as we came inside. Ooh, er, I wished we had Mum to protect us. We settled down in the corner with Cokes, sandwiches and Sally's phone. Still no word from Gemma, but we made great strides with our report for the charts.

On the whole we decided to award Welsh Boys –

based on a comprehensive survey of two of them – top marks for Suitability, Compatibility (well, there was one each, that was compatible enough for now), Chat-up techniques (a polite and interested exchange of information, surely that was VG), Intelligence, Hair, and Jeans (I vetoed Sally's appeal for a Looks Good in a Hoodie category).

Then we headed up the hill for an afternoon of watching my favourite film, *The Railway Children*. Very girlie, very weepie and very old-fashioned, and I absolutely love it. I reckoned there'd be no squabbles over what to watch, as we'd be pretty safe from Steve for most of the day. There had been no trace of him on the sofa that morning; in fact the only signs that he was still alive were an empty two-litre carton of orange juice and the remains of a packet of chocolate biscuits. You did have to wonder exactly what was swirling away inside his digestive system, but then again, perhaps you didn't.

Ralph and Mum got back just as the credits were rolling. I had a headache from all the crying, and Sally's nose had turned bright red.

There was no obvious sign that anything had gone wrong, so I thought it was probably safe to ask how their day had been.

'I never want to see another quilt again,' said Ralph.

'Actually, he didn't see any quilts,' said Mum. 'He found a gun shop with a pub next door to it, so he was perfectly happy while I looked at the quilts. They were splendid. I'm glad I saw them.'

I wasn't quite sure why Ralph should be so interested in guns, and didn't really want to think about it. But clearly they made him all mellow and peaceful, so I thought it was a good time to ask for some money for riding lessons.

The following day, armed with riding-lesson money (Ralph had been reluctant as ever to part with any money which didn't involve some obvious benefit to him, but in the end he must have decided it was a cheap way of keeping us out of his hair), Sally and I set off for the beach. We'd decided we had enough money to hire crash helmets, if that's what you wore on a horse.

'Perhaps we'll learn how to jump, and go hunting,' said Sally as we walked down the cobbles.

'I think you're confusing us with people who know how to ride,' I said. 'Besides, I don't think you suddenly go hunting on a Welsh caravan site on a Tuesday afternoon.' I wasn't sure if I knew much more about it than Sally, and rather thought we'd be lucky just not to fall off.

When we got to the beach I started to feel a bit nervous. Perhaps we *would* fall off. Perhaps we'd be *carried* off. Perhaps, perhaps…

Then in the distance we saw a group of boys coming towards us on the beach. Hugh and Ieuan were in the middle. All the boys were about the same age and height and were shouting and laughing, and every now and then bending down to pick up stones and chuck them – in a casual, showing-off way – into the sea.

As they grew nearer, we could hear bits of their conversation.

'*You're* the pillock, you pillock…'

'He was just pissing around…'

'When did *he* ever get his rocks off…'

'Just as well he never made a pass at her…'

They were swaggering, and laughing, and Hugh and Ieuan were swaggering more than most.

'Oh, hi,' Hugh said when they got near, only, I felt, because we were so close he couldn't actually ignore us.

'Are we, I mean, are you going riding today?' I said looking at him and Ieuan.

'Riding?' said Hugh. 'Nah, why would we go riding? We're going into town to get seriously off our heads. Aren't we, guys?' He turned to the others.

'Yeah,' said one of the others I hadn't seen before. 'Hugh's got the strongest head in Wales.'

Hugh preened himself, and Ieuan seemed to bask in his brother's reflected glory.

'See ya,' he said as they walked past, heading for the path up the hill into town.

I stood absolutely still, willing myself not to cry. I didn't want another headache like yesterday's. But it looked like Sally had given up the struggle, and big fat tears rolled down her cheeks.

'Come on,' I said. 'Let's walk up to the arcade. We can spend our money on the tombola.'

I felt quite proud of myself for keeping it together. But it was good to be walking into the wind. It was just starting to rain – appropriately enough – and what with that and the cold, our faces were as wet as anything in no time.

If anyone had seen us they'd never know what was rain and what was cry.

The rest of the holiday went by in a bit of a haze of television, the odd outing into town and even, amazingly, all five of us going in the car to go to see a castle. The castle was mega impressive – huge, high walls with big holes in them for guns. There was something for everyone: Ralph was enchanted by the descriptions of pouring boiling oil on your enemies as they approached up the hill; Steve found a sheltered wall to sit under so he could listen to his iPod; Mum, Sally and I had a quality hour or so in the gift shop. (Surely the point of national heritage sites. All those key-rings, penknives, tea towels, handbags, watches, and even replica suits of armour for the man in your life. Marvellous.) As we wandered around, you might almost have thought that we were a normal family.

As for the beach at the bottom of the hill, we didn't go there again.

The last day of the holiday, and it was time to load up the Peugeot. Ghastly Ralph had tried and failed to mend the standard lamp (never the same since he'd flung his coat at it) and the sofa (never the same since it had been collapsed on by a comatose brother). And Mum had washed up everything to within an inch of its life.

Eventually there was nothing more to do, and we started the long drive back.

Sally and I cheered everybody up by singing our two favourite songs very loudly, more or less on a loop. By the time we were halfway home, I reckoned we'd really got the hang of it. It was only when Mum said, 'I think that's enough, love,' in a very weary voice that I wondered if we hadn't been wasting our talents on an unappreciative audience.

We dropped Sally off at her house.

'Thank you, everyone,' said Sally politely as she got out of the car. 'I had a lovely time.'

I think she had, really, apart from, well, the episode that we still hadn't talked about. Perhaps we would when it was all a bit less...*recent*.

There were sounds of Harris and Jock in the background. I realised that I had been quite wrong about the Welsh versions of H and J – they had made NOTHING LIKE the noise of the real thing. Poor Sally, perhaps she *had* had a lovely time – nice and quiet.

As there were two more days of the holidays left, Sally and I decided to invite ourselves round to Amy's. It was always nice to go to Amy's, what with the Dad Who You'd Most Like and her mum being so kind. Plus she (her mum) made the most delicious brownies you've ever had in your life.

A bit later we were all sitting on Amy's bed, which by this stage was covered in brown crumbs, as I typed onto Ralph's laptop. (Ralph had gone for an Easter pint with his good friends at the Jobcentre. I didn't think he'd be missing his laptop.) I'd opened up the page headed Foreign (Welsh) Boy Research, and had been telling Amy about our adventures – we hadn't talked about her and Charlie yet, one disaster at a time, I thought.

Amy, furious on our behalf, had said that Hugh and Ieuan should be stripped of their points for Suitability and all round Good Behaviour, and go straight into a separate category called: Boys Behaving Vilely.

'I think,' said Sally in the thoughtful way she has when she really has been thinking. 'That they should be in both places. After all, they WERE very nice to us, and they DID talk to us as if they were interested in us, and they DID suggest that we met up again. The trouble was pressure peers.'

'Peer pressure,' I said, because I think you need to get these things right, even if you're just among friends. 'And I agree.' Though privately I thought it was a bit depressing to have to have separate points for Not Disowning You When They're With Their Mates.

But we quickly moved on to the subject of Charlie, who despite his recent crime was probably much better boyfriend material, and definitely more conveniently situated.

'Let's just happen to all go for a walk in the park on Sunday,' I suggested. 'And just happen to make it roughly the same time we saw Charlie that day.

'And we'll get Gemma to come too. It's time she came on a proper Boy Watch with us.'

We had a plan. It just required Gemma's OK. And Gemma hadn't been seen or heard of all holiday.

But it was back to school tomorrow, so surely she'd be there.

Midnight Mess

Tuesday was the first day of the summer term. So, most fittingly, it was freezing cold and pouring with rain.

The other not good part was that I found myself walking from the station behind QBM and a whole crowd of her crowd. I couldn't hear what they were saying, but they were laughing and shouting in such a jeery sort of way that I wanted to hide.

But before there was any chance of their turning their incisive wit on me (or the girl walking behind me – she didn't look like she wanted to be there either) two Year Eleven boys from St Thomas's came into sight on the other side of the street. They were both tall and dark blond and looked rather brilliantly colour-coordinated with their gold uniforms.

'You go on,' I heard the QB say to her hordes. And

even from behind I could tell that she was undoing another button of her blouse. Almost without seeming to cross the road she was suddenly standing in front of the two boys, fiddling with her hair and seeming to hold her ankle in some pain. She was leaning over, so that no doubt they could get a faceful of the polka-dot underwired bra that we all knew she favoured, and swaying around like she needed support.

Of course one of the blond ones held her arm as she teetered and tottered about.

Incredible.

In. Cred. Ible.

Then I started to think this was a very important report to add to the Boy Watching dossier. How is it that boys, in a group, want to show off to each other at the expense of interest in any passing girl. But girls in a group stop being part of the group and become helplessly flirty as soon as a likely lad hoves into view. I paused this brilliant thought process for a second to wonder where the word 'hove' comes from, but then re-focused on my first Big Thought of the term.

Yes. This is a very interesting insight, I thought. I shall discuss it with the others. And perhaps together we can decide which sex comes off worse in this analysis – the boys who want to show off at any cost, or the girls who want to pull at any cost.

Our welcome-back-to-school morning assembly was a grim affair. Mrs Munroe, who didn't often come down from the clouds for the mundane business of assembly, was already standing on the stage as we filed in. Behind her the staff looked very strict and unsmiling. Of course they mostly looked strict and unsmiling, I think it was probably part of the job description to look like you never had any fun. Today felt a bit different.

'Girls,' said Mrs Munroe, 'I have some very dreadful news to impart. Our History teacher, Mr Horriday, was rushed into hospital at the end of last term with an extreme case of nervous exhaustion. Three days later he had a complete nervous breakdown. After emergency treatment he is now recovering at home in Newfoundland. His lessons will be taken by Miss Daniels. This is obviously a very terrible occurrence. And I think some of you, and you know who you are, would do well to think about the implications of some of your extremely poor behaviour patterns. That is all. You are dismissed.'

There was absolute silence, even from the disruptive, noisy ones with the poor behaviour patterns. You could definitely have heard that pin drop that they always talk about.

I looked at Sally, she looked at Amy, and we all looked at QB Maggie, who had now done up her blouse and had her innocent who-me? face on.

Terrible indeed. Thank goodness he was recovering. But Newfoundland? No wonder his grasp of Marxism was a little shaky. Not much call for communism in the snowy wilds of Newfoundland. Everybody too busy fishing and keeping warm to think about radical socialism. Then I thought I'd better stop having thoughts like this. It felt a bit disrespectful of someone so very ill.

To distract myself, I had a look round for Gemma. Normally she'd be standing right by us, but normal didn't seem to be happening at the moment. Plus, *normally* we'd have had a whole lot of texts from her over the holidays, if only to tell us what a cool time she was having and what a shame we weren't.

We all rolled into English feeling very subdued. And discussing *Animal Farm* didn't exactly make us bounce around with joy. Poor Boxer. And I didn't think I'd ever be able to look at a pig the same way again.

But at least Mr Fanshawe didn't have a runny nose that day. In fact, he was back to his old dapper self, and was really quite interesting on the subject of the how the book was all about communism. This is a subject on which I'm clearly destined to be quite the expert. At least I thought I now knew enough to pretend to be one. That'd wind up Ghastly Stepdad, who'd always slagged off 'lefties' at the slightest opportunity.

'...Don't you think, Chloe?'

Eek. I reckoned it was time to stop daydreaming about my future career as a communist Member of Parliament and concentrate on Eng Lit.

In no time at all, it was time for Maths. Strange how it so often seems to be time for Maths. Perhaps when you absolutely hate and dread something, it spills over into seeming to be there all the time.

Sally and I filed into Maths class (Amy was in the fast-track class for Maths. Incredible, but true. It was a wonder she was our friend.) There was still no sign of Gemma, but we made for our usual three seats near the back of the class.

Miss Grunbar was already in the room.

'Sally,' she said as soon as we sat down. 'You and Chloe are consistently disruptive and inattentive. You will no longer sit together this term. Come to the front of the class, so that I can more easily have the benefit of your talent for Mathematics.'

Sally got up very slowly and reluctantly, turning her back on Miss G and mouthing the word 'cow' to me she walked up to the front of the class.

I spent the rest of the lesson drawing caricatures of Miss G in my Maths homework book. As I looked at the results, I rather regretted the fact that Mr Pampledousse didn't teach us to actually draw. It was all very well photographing dead bees, but that wasn't of any use if you wanted to do justice to Miss Grunbar's huge nose and scaly skin.

Must remember to tear the pages out before giving in my next Maths homework.

The rest of the day went extremely slowly. Sally was a bit subdued after being picked on by Miss G, and we were both getting more and more worried about Gemma who still hadn't replied to any of our texts. I found myself thinking it would be nice to be back in our beach café or watching DVDs in the Welsh cottage. I was starting to be rather fond of our Welsh cottage.

We trailed home at the end of the day, me to tell

Ralph all about how I wanted to be a communist when I grew up, Sally to the noisy delights of H and J, who she may or may not have to put to bed by herself. (Sally's mum was in a Pinot Grigio period, which meant that the joy of motherhood took second place to the joy of a nice glass of chilled white wine.)

The following morning was a bit sunnier and so was I. Ralph-baiting had gone really well – he'd turned a fetching shade of purple when I told him all about my ambition to be a communist. In fact, I hadn't seen that particular shade of purple since I'd told him I was going to be a gay rights activist. (I hadn't been at all sure what being a gay rights activist would actually involve, I just thought it sounded rather jolly, plus I'd just heard him on a rant about them one Sunday over the papers.)

There were two items of note when I arrived at school. The first was that Gemma was there, waiting to go into assembly, and the second that Sally looked absolutely and completely ill.

I decided to start with the good news item, and rushed up to Gemma.

'What the...where...why didn't you text...how?' I asked, slightly incoherently, because she had worried us after all, but there was also this massive feeling of relief washing over me. (Gemma had a lot of previous on getting into trouble, as we knew.)

'I'm fine,' she said calmly and therefore slightly irritatingly. 'I was away, that's all. And now I'm back. No need to fuss.'

'We're not fussing,' I said rather crossly. I mean, how ungrateful can you be? Honestly, you can go off people. 'We just didn't know where you were, and wondered if you were all right.'

'Tell you about it later,' said Gemma, a little bit more nicely. Perhaps I hadn't gone off her after all.

Then I went to find Sally. She was standing in the corner of the yard, looking like someone had set off a bomb in front of her. Shell-shocked, I think you'd say.

'Whatever's the matter?' I said. 'Are you ill? Have the twins killed each other? Has your mum run off with the boiler repair man?' I don't know where I got that last one from. Perhaps it was the memory of the man who came to mend our boiler once. He was incredibly handsome, and Mum didn't stop talking about how charming he was for at least a week afterwards.

'It's Mum,' said Sally faintly.

Ah ha, I thought, so she HAS run off with the boiler repair man.

'She wrote an email,' Sally went on. I realised there had to be more to it than that. After all, people write emails all the time, and mostly no one's any the worse for it.

'She wrote an email,' Sally said again. She seemed to be coming to a bit of a full stop.

'Yes?' I said encouragingly.

'She wrote an email, late last night…to Miss Grunbar about me having to move desks. She told her that she was a despotic, dictatorial, domineering, high-handed bully, with a totally overblown idea of her own importance.'

I was impressed – not only had Sally remembered all this stuff, but also her mother had come up with so many synonyms for bossy that all began with D.

'Plus,' Sally went on. Oh dear, there was more. 'She copied in Mrs Munroe and all the parents of our year.'

Right. This was really not good. The dread Mrs M would now know that Sally's mum was a crazed late-night emailer and probably guess that it was not unconnected to the drinking of Pinot Grigio. (OK, so even Mrs Munroe wouldn't know what *sort* of wine, but she'd get the general drift.) And everyone's parents would know too. Which meant, no doubt, that everyone in our year would know too.

Plus. And this was the very bad bit. Of course Miss Grunbar would know, on account of being the recipient of the email.

Lordy lord.

But there wasn't that much time to dwell on it all. The bell had rung, and we had to head inside. Amazingly, we didn't have Maths that day, so Sally wouldn't have to confront the hideous Miss G in the first full flush of her wrath.

Also, as I said to Sally as cheeringly as I could, it wasn't actually HER who'd written the email. Also, I thought it was quite likely that some of the other parents might actually agree, and think good for Sally's mum for saying it out loud. Also, well…that's where I ran out of alsos. The rest was still not good.

It was a funny old day, although not in a laugh-out-loud way, of course. In fact, there wasn't much laughing to be done at all. As it turned out, there wasn't a moment to grill Gemma about her mysterious disappearance, and there weren't any terrifying summonses to Mrs M's study.

Or not until half past three, when we were just getting ready to go home. As we were walking down the corridor a Year Eleven who we didn't know came up to us. 'Which one of you's Sally?' she said. When

171

Sally admitted that she was, she was told to follow the Year Eleven to Mrs Munroe's office.

Lordy lord. Again.

I went to a corner of the entrance hall which had a good view of the door to Mrs M's office. That way I could keep an eye without having to get too near the door itself. (The door was big and made of dark wood, and had a brass plate on it saying 'Headmistress'. I think the lettering of that brass plate is engraved (ha) on our minds for ever, it's so associated with scariness.)

About ten minutes later, though it felt like fifty, Sally emerged. She looked a little bit green, but otherwise OK.

'Let's go back to mine,' I said. 'And you can tell me all about it.'

We headed home, and up the stairs past Albert's flat (he was strangely silent, I hoped he wasn't out eating small children) and into my home. There was no one around. Both Mum and Ralph must still have been washing and blow-drying and signing people on respectively.

Sally sat down and took a deep breath and a huge gulp of orange juice. (Not at the same time, of course, that would have been disastrous.)

'Firstly, what's it like in there?' Being either very

good or very careful, I'd never actually seen behind the wooden door with the brass plate.

'Full of pictures and books. And you sit on an old sofa that's got springs that stick up into your bottom.'

I found myself wondering if the springs were operated by remote control, like a sort of torture machine.

'She asked me if I knew why she'd wanted to see me,' Sally went on. 'And when I said yes, it was about the email, wasn't it, she said yes, and it was most unfortunate. But that since she had been copied in she would be telephoning – she actually said "telephoning" just like in old-fashioned movies – Mum to explain to her that if she had some criticism of the school it would be better if she came in and discussed it with her privately. She said she'd talked to Miss Grunbar, who was naturally very upset but had realised that it was not my fault and would try to overlook the incident so far as I was concerned. Then she asked me some questions about how I thought I was getting on, and what were my friends like – I told her about you and how you're going to be a prize-winning novelist, I thought that made me sound good – and then, well, then she let me go.'

I told Sally that I thought it was all fine. We were

never going to have a warm and cuddly relationship with Miss Grunbar anyway, so the worst that had happened was that we'd hate her even more (and probably the feeling would be mutual). Otherwise all that had happened was that Sally's mum had outed herself as a hate-filled compulsive communicator and late-night drinker with a remarkable vocabulary.

At that, we set up the TV in my room to watch *The Simpsons* on a loop. I love the Simpsons, and think that if I were much smaller, yellower and had four fingers I would BE Lisa.

Gemma had messaged us to say band practice was on for Friday, and that's when she'd talk to us properly. The day was ending a whole lot better than it had begun.

It's Just a Party

It was a bit of a low-profile week all round – head down and blend in with the wallpaper, that sort of thing, especially in Maths. Sally and I concentrated very hard in Maths, which it was easier to do since we weren't sitting next to each other. The irony of this was not lost on us, or not on me at any rate. I'm not sure Sally entirely gets irony. Especially after I told her it was the opposite of wrinkly. How I laughed – but I think I also confused her.

By the time we got to the end of the week, we were rather tired. All that good behaviour CAN be very tiring. Also, being bored can be very tiring. And bored is what we completely were by the time we got to Art on Friday.

The project of the day in Art was portraits and the human figure. I got quite excited. At last, I thought,

I shall be taught how to do the perfect caricature of Miss G. And, indeed, of anyone else who makes me cross. So it was very annoying when Mr Pampledousse told us that our project was to create a cubist self-portrait in the style of Picasso. I couldn't see the point of making unrecognisable caricatures of ourselves out of blocks of coloured paper.

But I don't think Mr Pampledousse was really 'engaged with the concept'. (Something everyone keeps telling us to be – even though we have no idea what it means.) Whenever I looked up from cutting up paper, which was quite often as I had got very bored indeed by this time, he was gazing out of the window with his unpaid-gas-bill expression.

Gemma, of course, had the explanation. Mr P was beside himself with grief at the loss of Mr Horriday.

'His heart's not in this,' she said firmly. 'His heart's in Newfoundland. He's saving up for the air fare and then we'll never see him again.'

Eventually we'd made a sufficient mess of enough bits of paper to be allowed to go for the weekend. Phew, the relief.

We hurtled – there is no other word – out of the door as soon as the bell went, Gemma and Amy to get their guitars, Sally and me to wait for them at the gates and do a little Boy Watching.

It was a busy afternoon for the activity. There were hordes of golden creatures outside the gates, mixed with lots of our Year Eleven and Year Twelves. They did look fabulous. But I tried not to look too closely, for fear of seeing someone I knew talking to a girl with a ponytail in a yellow sweatshirt...

I think I did see him in the distance. He was laughing with one of the dark blond boys who'd held QBM's hand while she pretended to have broken both her ankles. Behind him was a girl in red with long dark hair. I decided not to look any longer, and turned back to the school, where I saw with some relief that Gemma and Amy were hurrying towards us.

Since it was still freezing cold we turned up the heating full blast as soon as we got inside Merv's garage. Because of *course* he had heating in his garage (said Gemma) – how else did we expect him to keep his jeep and his training bike warm?

We spent about an hour playing some of our all-time favourites. I thought I was singing brilliantly – must have been all that practice on the way back from Wales

– but I had to admit we weren't in anywhere near the same league as Shedz.

Slightly downcast, we headed into the house, for the barstools and the exotic pizza of Merv's kitchen. We'd already established that Merv was out, so we felt super relaxed as we popped the Cokes and rummaged in the giant fridge. (It really was ginormous. You could put a whole person in there. Quite a large person. Maybe someone the size of Miss Grunbar. And then you could shut the door and if you ever let her out she'd be very contrite – and cold.)

'OK, Gemma,' I said, as we lined up the pizzas for the microwave. 'Time to spill. What's been happening?'

'It's no big deal,' said Gemma as she poured ketchup over her chips. (Did I mention the chips? They were an essential part of our Friday Night Carb Diet too.) 'I was with my mum.'

Well, now THAT was worth waiting for.

'OMG,' Sally said, incredibly unoriginally, but then we *had* had a shock. 'Not the mum who ran off with her best friend from school?'

'How many mums do you think I have, you dingbat?' said Gemma. 'But yes, she rang me on the last day of term, and said could I come and see her. She had been trying to get in touch with me for months, and had only just found out Merv hadn't passed on any of her messages. And besides, she thought that after eight years it was time I met Juliet.'

'And?' I said perhaps slightly over eagerly, because she seemed to have come to a full stop.

'And. I did,' she said. I was right, she *had* come to a full stop.

Then she took pity on us. 'Not what I expected,' she said. 'Juliet comes from the West Indies, and is now quite a well-known artist. They live in a big house by the sea in Cornwall.'

OMG. I'm sorry, but that really was Oh. My. God. How interesting was that? And then I thought, Ghastly Ralph would have a field day, a black gay woman artist. Fantastic! He'd go purple again. Perhaps one day I will be an activist for her rights. Although being a famous person with a big house in Cornwall, she probably didn't need my activating.

'What about your mum?' said Amy. 'Was she like you remembered? Was it OK to see her again?'

'Yes,' said Gemma. 'It was sort of OK. She cried a bit. Quite a lot, in fact. Said she felt so guilty about leaving me, but Merv was impossible. Well, yeah. He is. And she left me to it. I shouted at her. I wasn't going to let her off the hook that easily.' Gemma looked angry when she said this. I guess she had every right to be.

'*Did* you let her off the hook in the end?' I asked.

'I suppose I did. Juliet was so cool that whenever anyone started shouting – or crying – she kind of calmed us down. She's great. Don't get her paintings, though.' She showed us on her phone. It had photos of a series of purple, yellow and black paintings hanging on a white wall.

'That looks just like what we were doing in Art,' said Sally. We told Sally not to be daft. But actually, she had a point.

'I'm going to go there again in the summer,' Gemma went on. 'Dad doesn't know about this yet, so don't say anything.'

I wondered where Merv had thought she'd been over the Easter holidays. But Gemma is a law unto herself, and I sometimes think Merv might secretly be a little bit frightened of her.

We thought we'd better go home before he got back. It had been a long old day and it would be just aaaaawful if one of us gave the game away.

We decided to go shopping the following day. None of us had any money, and none of us needed anything in particular, so it seemed like the perfect plan for a Saturday morning.

Albert was in fine voice as I unlocked the outer door. I remembered that we had to book him for Sunday, our excuse for a walk in the park. Slightly hesitantly, because I was a little bit nervous of his crabby old Civil War Warrior owner, I knocked on the door.

Crabby old owner was having a vest and a pair of jeans day. I tried not to look at the exposed hairy bits.

'Hi there,' I said with a cheery confidence I didn't feel. 'Just wondered if you'd like us to take Albert out on Sunday.'

'All right, then. But you mustn't let him near any other dogs. Especially not bitches.' He seemed to take a delight in saying the word. 'If he gets too close to them he'll get in a fight. And then there'll be hell to pay.'

'Right,' I said, as slowly and as calmly as I could. I was starting to worry about how we'd tell if a dog running towards us was a boy or a girl. And what we should do if it was a girl. And then I looked at Albert. He looked so sweet. It was very hard to believe that he ate children AND fought with lady dogs. Besides, he was essential for our plan, and also to get Sally used to the dog thing eventually.

'That's fine,' I said a bit more cheerily. 'We'll be careful. And we'll pick him up at about eleven.'

'All right,' said crabby old guy, practically shutting the door in my face.

As I climbed the stairs to our front door, I wondered if someone who seemed to hate everyone – especially dogs and people – had any friends. Maybe he didn't have any friends, except the odd Puritan on battle days. I decided to see if Mum could be any help on the subject, after all, she was an old person too so she should know about stuff like that.

There was a lot of clattering going on in the kitchen as I came into the hall, almost as if Mum had gone mad and had started throwing things about. When I went in I saw the most unbelievable sight. Ghastly Stepdad was bent over the dishwasher. And. Emptying. It.

I stood there in amazement. I think if my jaw and the floor were just a little bit nearer to each other, you could honestly say the one hit the other.

'Hi,' I said. 'What's going on?'

Ralph looked up. 'What does it look like? I'm

emptying the dishwasher. Have you never seen someone empty the dishwasher before?'

I had to answer that, just had to. 'Yes, but I've never seen YOU empty it.'

'Don't you be cheeky. Your mother's tired. So I've been cooking supper.'

Unbelievable to the power of five hundred. Out of a sort of scientific curiosity, I found myself asking, 'What did you cook?'

'Sausages and bacon, not that it's any of your business,' he replied.

Ah, I thought, processed meat. The only food that makes sense to a Ralph.

Then I allowed myself to worry about all this, and went off to the bedroom to find Mum.

She was lying on the bed with her eyes shut. I didn't think she'd heard me come in, so for a moment I saw her in a totally unguarded state. She looked weary, and older than I remembered. I reminded myself again that she was probably the same age as the crabby old guy downstairs, although mostly she never looked it or seemed it.

'Mum,' I said.

She opened her eyes, and smiled. 'Hello, love,' she said, getting up from the bed. 'How was band practice?'

'It was fine,' I said, pretending not to notice how slowly she was moving, perhaps it was all that processed meat that slowed her down. 'Amazing, but Gemma's been to see her mum. That's where she was all Easter holiday. Her mum's girlfriend is West Indian, an artist, they live in Cornwall. It all sounds rather cool. Typical of Gemma to have an exotic mother.'

'Well, I think that's lovely that she's back in touch with her mother, love. Very important things, mothers,' she added with a smile.

'Absolutely,' I said really meaning it. 'You're not going to work tomorrow, are you? Seems like you need a rest. I'm off shopping, but I can be back in the evening. We can have scrambled eggs in front of *X Factor*.'

'No,' she said, 'not working. And scrambled eggs sound lovely.'

I left it at that, and went off to play an energetic game of cards on my phone.

A successful day's shopping always starts in the coffee shop. It's where you make one drink last at least an hour and a half, and can plan a strategy. This Saturday was no exception.

Sally and I were there first. I had a half-baked plan to buy some furry boots. I reckoned the first Saturday of the summer term would be just the time to pick up a bargain. Sally was just telling me how cheap they were (I do wonder about the way she seems to have expensive things, and sometimes think Gemma's theory about her dad's mysterious rich mistress might have something in it), when Amy and Gemma arrived.

'Don't look now,' said Gemma. 'But just about to come in the other entrance is a whole load of boys for you to watch.' Quite why Gemma thinks Boy Watching is nothing to do with her, I don't know. It's not as if she isn't watching them too.

All three of us immediately turned round. 'I SAID,' said Gemma, 'don't look now. Goodness' sake.'

We looked back at her. There had just been time to notice that there were five of them, and two girls. And two of the five were Jezza and Rob. No wonder Gemma was trying to play it cool.

'Who are the girls?' said Amy. 'Do we know them?'

'No,' said Gemma who was facing that way, 'but they look Year Eleven at least. Oh God, Jez is making come-here signs.'

'That's great,' I said. 'You go over, and take Sally with you, then she can chat to Rob.'

'Chat?!' squawked Sally. (It really was a squawk. The kind of noise you'd get from a parrot.) 'You can't just CHAT with the Shedz guys, 'specially not with strange older girls there.'

'If Jezza wants to talk to me he can come over here,' said Gemma. 'He still hasn't apologised for leaving me outside the club. So he can go hang himself, for all I care.' It did look a little bit like she cared, but I wasn't about to point that out.

We decided to get on with planning the day's strategy. The others were heavily into checking out new tops, plus Sally had to buy a new phone charger (this must have been the sixteenth I'd seen her buy, I wondered if there was a room in her house entirely filled with chargers that she'd never thought to go into) but I was still firmly fixated on a pair of furry boots.

It had been a long time since we'd bought any drinks, and we were starting to get dirty looks from the staff. We were just getting our things together to go when we heard a voice say, 'Gem.' It was the rock god himself, standing over our table.

'What's with you, Gem? You haven't answered

any of my texts. Wassup?' said Jezza. He looked skinnier and cooler than ever, and covered in torn denim, and quite a lot of silver jewellery. But still I couldn't help noticing his hair was stiff with grease, and not in a good way.

'Nothing's up with me. Or nothing that's anything to do with you,' said Gemma. Sometimes I had to hand it to our friend; she really could do cool too.

'Suit yourself.' Jezza shrugged. And turned back to the table at the back, where Rob and the others were doing a not very good job of pretending not to look at us all.

I thought that was our cue to go. Our work was done. Although what that work might be, I wasn't sure. We got up, trying to look older, taller and skinnier than we were, and walked out of the coffee shop without looking back. That is, I think Sally looked back, but then she would, wouldn't she?

They didn't have expensive furry boots on sale, and they didn't have any tops that the others thought suited them, although we spent many a happy hour making sure. But Sally bought a phone charger, so we did achieve something. Plus we had made a plan to meet up at Amy's the following morning for Albert-walking. Always good to end the day with a plan.

Boys Being Boys

I headed home for an evening of joys with my beloved family. I'd decided my mission was to cheer up Mum and persuade Steve not to sign up for the army till after he'd finished school. I walked up the stairs in a bit of a glow at the thought of my noble, unselfish ambitions.

As I opened the front door all the nobility fell away and I felt instead a huge burst of irritation. Football. Full blast in the sitting room. As I went in I smelt that familiar smell and heard those familiar sounds, made all the worse by there being three of them producing that 'eau de methane' scent. Kev, Steve's mate and clone, was lounging on the sofa too.

Looking at my beloved brother and his friend, I wondered if perhaps they weren't after all related. The same glazed expression, the same glazed hair (yuck) and even spots in the same places on their necks (double yuck).

Shutting the door on the whole scene I headed for the kitchen in search of Mum. She was sitting at the kitchen table doing a Sudoku. (Now what's that about? Why would anyone fiddle around with numbers for *fun*?)

'Hello, love,' she said looking up. 'Did you have a nice time? You look a bit cross, what's the matter?'

'I don't know how you can stand it, Mum. All that noise. And aren't we going to watch *X Factor*?' I said, getting even crosser on her behalf – she always seemed to be in the kitchen, banished from her own sitting room.

'It's OK, love. The boys have promised to stop at seven o'clock, and we're going to have tea and scrambled eggs, just like you said.'

'The boys.' That made them sound rather adorable, like little boys in shorts playing in the park, or the handsome muddy heroes of the St Thomas's first eleven football team, or the young uniformed marines standing to attention in any American war film you've ever seen, or the guys of One Direction, or half of the cast of *Friends*...but not, absolutely not, the slobs in the next room.

I decided to let it go, though.

Seven o'clock came soon enough, and 'the boys' did actually turn off the TV and come into the kitchen.

'Hi,' said Kev-the-clone-of-Steve to me. 'How you doing?'

This was a giant leap forward. I'd only ever heard him grunt, and even then only in agreement with something Steve had grunted. Perhaps he'd been told you had to be able to speak to get into the army, and he was practising on me.

'I'm fine,' I said, because that's how you usually answer the question. Nobody ever asks it and wants an honest answer. 'I hear you're going to try to get into the army too.' The use of the word 'try' was a little unkind, but it made me feel better and I didn't think Kev would notice.

'Yeah,' he said. 'It's going to be great. See the world. Learn stuff.' I thought this was quite encouraging; he was making it sound all rather admirable. 'Plus you pull the birds in a uniform.' Ah. Not so admirable. Just as shallow and grunty as I'd thought. Pathetic, absolutely pathetic.

Then I remembered my vision of standing in that very room surrounded by admiring men in uniform laughing at my anecdotes of life as an international bestselling author. I had to admit that it was all the better a vision for the lovely uniforms they were wearing.

I didn't have to admit any of this out loud, though.

'That's pathetic,' I said self-righteously and hypocritically. 'Sexist rubbish. I bet that's actually the only reason you're thinking of joining the army.'

'Give it a rest, Chloe,' said Steve, pronouncing it 'clow' because he knew how much it annoyed me. 'You should be thinking about how to make our last days at home happy and nice. So we've got good things to remember as we're being shot at in Iran.'

Mum looked a bit sick at this, but I was totally distracted by Steve seeming to know something we didn't. Last time I looked 'we' hadn't gone anywhere near Iran.

'You must have a hot line to Downing Street,' I said sarcastically. 'First we've heard of an invasion of Iran.'

'That's enough, you two,' said Mum in her most stop-it tone of voice.

Behind her back Steve raised his middle finger in my direction. With incredible self-control I ignored him and moved into the sitting room to take charge of the television.

Sunday morning was a distinctly wet one. Ghastly Ralph came back with the papers, rubbing his little goatee beard in disgust.

'Ruddy chucking it down,' he said, shaking out his horrible plastic mac. (I hated that mac even more than it needed to be hated. It was the one Amy had worn on the Day of Horror when we'd ended up on Facebook thanks to the QB Maggie.)

This was v. bad news for Operation Charlie and Amy. Would Charlie still pound the paths of the park if it were raining? After seventeen messages, we all decided it was better to go for it and hope that Charlie was perfectly happy to run about in the wet.

Dressed to kill in my own brand of fluorescent waterproof, I went downstairs to knock on the door of the old and crabby and hairy one.

'There you are,' he said as he opened the door. Even though I was early he made it sound as if I'd kept him waiting for hours. 'Here's his lead, and don't forget about the bitches.' He grinned slyly as he said this.

Albert looked up at me with such a sweet and gentle expression that I wondered again if he really did have these psychopathic behaviour patterns that we kept being told about.

We set off for Amy's to meet the others with a spring in our step. Well, Albert's step certainly had a spring. Between our front door and the bus stop he spotted three cats, a bird, two other dogs, and countless traces of dog pee that only he could smell. All these things had to be inspected immediately and at great speed. I'd nearly been pulled off my feet three times, and was exhausted by the time we arrived at Amy's.

As Amy opened the door I could almost taste the sense of gloom that hung over them all. Albert was bouncing around at my feet – we needed Charlie to take him by the scruff and tell him who was boss, because it sure wasn't us – but the others were huddled over The Dad Who's iPad on the kitchen table.

'It's Jezza's Facebook page,' said Amy. 'He's posted some stuff about a party last night.'

Ah. So maybe that was why Jezza had wanted to talk to Gemma. Maybe he was going to ask her to a cool party. Oh dear. But if that was the worst that could happen – 'Jezza has party and we don't go' – it wasn't the end of the world. Was it?

I went over to the table. It wasn't, quite, the end of the world.

In the middle of the screen was a big group photo. Jezza was in the centre with his arm round QB Maggie (looking, it has to be said, quite amazing, as if she'd had a Hollywood makeover) and a Year Twelve girl who looked suspiciously like the one in leather trousers and fifty-six-inch heels who was 'Tim's' girlfriend. On her left was a tall, familiar figure. It was Mark A*. One of his arms was round the fifty-six-inch-heeled one and the other round another girl I hadn't seen before, but who looked even more like she'd had a Hollywood makeover. And, as if that weren't enough, the girl with the ponytail and the yellow or red shirt was standing just behind her, with her arm round Rob.

Great. Just great. No wonder everyone was so quiet. If Charlie had been part of the frame that would have been all our plans, hopes and dreams dashed in one fell Facebook photo.

Amy clicked to the next photo. There was Charlie, in a sea of girls I didn't recognise, and by that stage *couldn't* recognise because a sort of curtain of hopelessness fell over me.

'It's just a party,' said Amy, in a very slightly quavery voice.

At that moment there was a loud and rather cross-sounding bark from under the table. We could hear Amy's parents opening the front door. Seconds later, they came into the kitchen.

195

'Hello, all,' said the Dad Who. 'Anyone for hot chocolate on this steamy, drenchy, dreary day?'

And Amy's mother headed for the big tin marked 'brownies'.

There was something so reassuring and comforting and altogether NICE about Amy's parents. I think I spoke for us all when I say that it wasn't just the chocolate and the brownies that made us feel better. Although they did help.

Much later on, and full of chocolate in all its many forms, we set off for our walk in the park. Although Operation Amy and Charlie was dead in the water, in every sense, we decided that sweet little Albert needed some fresh air and so did we.

We had told the Dad Who that Sally had got in a bit of a state about the Six-Foot One and – because he was that sort of dad, the one you tell all your troubles to – he decided he'd come with us, just in case.

Progress was slow, probably due to all the chocolate, and Albert was getting more and more impatient. Being held back by a piece of string (the crabby one's idea of a dog lead) was obviously not his idea of fun.

So – and I think I knew this wasn't a terribly good idea at the time – I let him off the lead. He shot off into the distance, heading in a straight line for the children's playground. Fantastic. Absolutely fan-fabbo-tastic. Jeez.

Of course his first move would be to chew off the arms of a couple of toddlers, and, while everyone was screaming in panic, he would bite the ear off a lady Labrador (bitch) and the paw of a small pug (also bitch) for afters. The Labrador and the pug would, naturally, be owned by Zac and QB Maggie's mother respectively. The toddlers would be rushed to hospital in a private ambulance, because one was Mrs Munroe's niece and the other was Mark A*'s little brother.

So, in the split seconds that it took for Albert to cross the park, I had got quite a long way in my fantasy of possible epic disasters. You would expect me to be prepared for anything.

It was still an awful shock, though, when I heard a piercing scream coming from the playground in the distance. It was the scream of a child, but not a toddler – perhaps a child big enough to fight off Albert for long enough for someone to save his or her life. Plus, if a child can scream then at least they haven't been grabbed by the throat. Have they?

All thoughts of digesting chocolate well gone, we dashed towards the playground as fast as we possibly could. Obviously the Dad Who was in the lead, but Amy was hard on his heels. Who knew she could run so fast, I somehow found time to wonder. A sense of responsibility for the whole thing spurred me on to third place, thankful that today was a trainers day, not a wedges day. And then way behind were Gemma (lace-up wedges, really only good for tottering to coffee shops) and Sally (expensive furry boots, but probably slowed down by a huge reluctance to go anywhere near a dog in the process of eating a small child).

I still couldn't see what was happening, even when I was getting closer to the play area. But it was all going on by the swings, and quite a large crowd was building up. Oh lordy God.

By the time I got there, the Dad Who was in the middle of the crowd, and shouting quite a bit. I pushed my way through lots of people of varying sizes till I could see that the Dad Who had Albert by the scruff of his neck in one hand and a large pit bull terrier in the other.

'Whose is this dog?' he was yelling at the top of his voice. 'Whose is this DOG?' Albert was barking his little furry head off, and the pit bull terrier was doing a rather scary barky thing, mostly in the direction of Albert.

Then a man in a hoodie came forward and grabbed the pit bull terrier. 'Webster, shut up, you ----ing little -------. ------- come here, you ------- ****.' (He was a man who clearly spoke mostly in asterisks and dashes.)

'Sorry about that, mate,' said the hoodie to the Dad Who. 'He goes ape when he sees a bitch. Sort of sexual urge, innit.' And he sniggered.

'Brilliant,' said Gemma, who had finally made it to the scene of the crime. 'Who's going to tell him his dog is gay?'

The hoodie went off into the distance, leading his secretly gay dog off to make someone else's life horrible.

None of this had made me any more fond of the hoodie as an article of clothing, nor, I reckoned, had it made Sally any more at ease with the idea of The Dog as such. I looked around for her, to see if she had actually made it to the centre of the drama.

Then I saw her at the edge of the crowd, gazing fixedly at a point in the distance. The focus of her gaze was the child who'd been screaming, a little girl in a red romper suit, whose face was equally red from all the screaming. She did look terribly upset, but she was being comforted by three people, two women and a boy, all of whom, I'm sure, were promising her a lifetime's supply of chocolate and other comforts.

Then I realised what was making Sally quite so statue-like. One of the three people was Rob. This very child was very likely the very one who he had been playing Frisbee with when we'd awarded him those points for being very Kind to Children and Animals.

'Hey, Sally, that's Rob over there,' I said brightly and a bit unnecessarily. 'You could go over and say hello, and ask if the little girl is all right. In no way do you have to admit any kind of acquaintance with Albert.'

'OK,' said Sally a bit shakily. 'It's not as if I can't be sympathetic. That was sooooo scary.'

I watched her head towards the small group. They looked up as she approached. She said something (hurrah), one of the women said something back (OK...), Sally said something else (more hurrah), then Rob said something to her (double more hurrah), then Sally said something again, and so did Rob (lots more hurrahs). There was a bit more of that, and then Sally turned and came back towards me. She looked quite serene, certainly better than she had before.

'Well?' I said. It was very frustrating watching a scene like that without subtitles.

'Well,' said Sally. 'He was nice. He thanked me but said it was OK, they were taking her home for ice cream.'

'And he remembered you, and your name, and all that?' I said.

'Yes, he did. The little girl is his sister. He said he'd let me know how she was. And then he asked for my number. Isn't he amazing?' said Sally, looking a bit... kooky, I think is the word.

I could only agree that Rob was amazing. Although I didn't think she'd heard me. In fact, I don't think she really wanted my opinion at all.

I had never thought of the day being all about Operation Rob and Sally, but if there were a silver lining, then I guess this would be it. I would have to adjust the charts and notes in the Boy Watching records big time. (Our last entries had all been under C for Charlie. Who knew that we'd leap forward to R for Rob so soon?)

At that moment Sally's phone went off like a New York police siren. Liv, queen of the Pinot Grigio calling. (Except apparently, since the late-night emailing to the headmistress and half the school, she was now more Liv, queen of the sparkling mineral water.) Sally was given her shopping instructions and had to head off.

But she headed off as bouncily as if her Uggs were made of rubber.

Meanwhile, the Dad Who was a bit out of breath with all his activities, and I could hear that – under his out-of-breathness – he was swearing a bit. I couldn't quite make out what he was saying – probably not as many dashes and asterisks as the hoodie – but I could tell he was cross.

I thanked him, and then I thanked him again. And then, as I tied Albert back onto his lead, I thanked him again. Just for luck.

Albert seemed none the worse for his excitements, and I decided that on the whole the crabby old guy need never know about all this. It wasn't Albert's fault, and he didn't seem to have suffered any injury. I made a mental note, though, to buy him some super doggy treat next time we met, as he *had* had a bit of a traumatic time of it.

After I'd returned Albert to his home, with nothing but a grunt of acknowledgement from his owner, I headed upstairs to ours. I had a great deal of homework to do.

Generally I try to avoid doing homework at home

(that's what those frantic twenty minutes before assembly are for), but every now and then it just has to be done. This Sunday evening there was some French vocabulary that could do with a bit of a look, plus I also had to learn a speech from *Macbeth* for English and Drama. I was finding this incredibly difficult (surprising, really, in a future bestselling author with an enduring love of literature), so I decided to lock myself in the bathroom and dye my hair.

I'd been preparing myself for this secret mission for some time, and had watched several videos on YouTube which told you how to do it. It looked really easy. Perhaps it was the sight of the Hollywood makeover queens in those dreaded photographs that spurred me on, but I reckoned the time had now come for a little makeover of my own.

One of the advantages of having a hair stylist for a mum (she is a hair *stylist*, not a hairdresser – apparently it is important to get that right) was that there was always plenty of kit hanging around.

I had my eye on a box of amber colouring. I reckoned that streaks of amber would be both subtle and cool. Plus it would be a good contrast to the light brown of my hair. (Which is a shade Mum describes as 'honey blonde', and QBM described as 'on the dishwater side of mousy' in the dreaded Year Nine Ugly Chart on Facebook. Thanks, QBM.)

All was perfectly quiet at home. Not a sound from the living room or kitchen, and the bathroom was looking all empty and inviting.

I went in and locked the door. I opened up all the tubes in the box marked Amber, put on the Marigold washing-up gloves Mum used in the kitchen (a little thicker than the ones on the YouTube video, but a glove is a glove) and set to work.

Some of the liquids got spilt on the towels, because it was hard to hold anything steady in thick gloves that were five sizes too big. And on the whole, it was quite painful whenever I squeezed the stuff on my head, but, as everyone knows, you have to suffer to be beautiful. Eventually the tubes were empty, and I tied a supermarket plastic bag over my hair and went to my room to wait for the magic to happen.

I opened up my *Macbeth* workbook, and took a deep breath.

'Out, damn'd spot!' I cried at the top of my voice. I had decided that the louder I declaimed (I think I mean 'declaim') the more understandable the words would become. 'Hell is murky! Fie, my lord, fie!' – that was a good bit, and the meaning really quite straightforward.

'What need we fear who knows it, when none can call our power to account?' That bit was more difficult, and needed to be thought about properly.

'Yet who,' I was yelling now because I knew this next bit, 'would have thought the old man to have had so much blood in him?'

'Chloe? That you?' Oh lord. The pock-marked brother. Here all the time. Disaster. Although I couldn't help noticing that he'd adopted Mum's habit of asking questions that could only have one answer.

My door was shut, thank goodness, so Steve couldn't see that I had a Morrisons plastic bag on my head, tied up with the shoelaces from my trainers.

'Kev's here,' he said. 'We're making chips. Do you know where the ketchup is?' Perfect. An evening with the brother, his clone and the smell of chips. (Why chips always smelt disgusting when Steve had anything to do with them, I didn't know. Perhaps he cooked them in hair oil.)

'In the cupboard over the cooker. Roughly where it always is,' I said with a wither in my voice. It always amazed me that Steve never seemed to know where anything went in the house or where it came from. Perhaps there was some inner working in his DNA that said knowing about the inside of cupboards was women's work, and it wasn't worth using up valuable memory space recording such information when that space was needed for important things like the latest goal differences in the Premier League.

At least he went away. I turned back to my workbook and the mysteries of Shakespeare, and then got distracted by the Boy Watching records. I realised that if Rob called Sally, then he'd officially outscore Charlie on Suitability points. If he only texted, then they'd be level, except, of course, we really needed Charlie to do something soon for Amy's sake.

I was just starting to hatch a new fiendish plan to throw Amy and Charlie together when I noticed the time. The Morrisons bag should have come off half an hour before.

As I peered hesitantly from behind my bedroom door, I could see the kitchen door was safely shut. There was an occasional grunt coming from behind it, plus the smell of stew and chips. It was safe to creep to the bathroom.

Off with the bag, on with the new me! The bag came off easily enough, although the acrid smell that came with it made me almost pine for Chips a la Hair Oil.

I looked in the mirror.

Right. OK. We have a crisis. Looking back at me

was a shocked white face surrounded by a thick, dry frizz that was a pale orange colour. I touched the frizz hesitantly. My hair was almost completely stiff – almost, in fact, a little crunchy.

Amazing how quickly the human brain can process catastrophe. In half a second I decided I had three options: the shaving of the head (and going into hiding until the hair grew back); the wearing of a wig that was an exact replica of my previous much-despised (though now much longed-for) mousy hair; running away to… well, somewhere a long way away.

'Chloe? We're back.' It was Mum. 'Where are you, love?'

It had to be done sooner or later. Best get it over and done with. A little bit defiantly, I flung open the bathroom door. It slammed against the wall, the handle fell off and quite a lot of paint came off the skirting board.

'Chloe,' said Mum in quite a different tone of voice. 'What *have* you been doing?'

Now was not the time to point out that the answer to her question was, once again, only too obvious.

Ghastly Ralph was looking furiously at the skirting board. Mum, on the other hand, was looking at her beloved daughter with an expression of such total horror that if I'd been in any doubt about the exact size of the disaster I wasn't now.

I did what you have to do in a situation like this. I started to cry. Within seconds Mum had her arms round me and was telling me I was a 'clot'.

And then soon after that I found myself with my head under the shower with Mum rubbing in conditioner, perhaps rather harder than she need have done. Meanwhile, Ghastly Ralph was now on the floor, fully focused on the skirting board. Steve and Steve-clone were still in the kitchen, probably both with earphones in, and, I really hoped, quite unable to hear what was going on.

Once Mum had finished rubbing my head, she popped another Morrisons bag over it and told me to keep it on for as long as I could bear. It wasn't going to solve the Orange Problem, but we'd worry about that part tomorrow, she said.

I think mothers are wonderful things, especially ones who know about hairdressing. I mean hair *styling*.

Some of the World's a Stage

It was going to be a tougher than usual Monday, what with one orange thing and another. But at least my hair was now an orange that didn't crunch when you touched it. Plus Mum managed to tie some of it up in a black scarf so that it didn't look quite so bright, and had promised to look out a treatment colour from Happy Hairliners.

Still, I walked the last part of the journey to school feeling a little bit sick.

The first person I saw was Sally. She was looking quite incredibly cheerful. And then her expression of kooky happiness was interrupted by one of high hilarity.

'You look hilarious!' she said at the top of her voice. I was right about the hilarity.

'I'm not THAT much more orange than you,' I said

209

rather nastily, but needs must. If Sally was going to be horrible, what would QBM and her cohorts do?

I soon found out.

QB Maggie, as extreme bad luck would have it, was just around the corner at the school entrance.

She took one look at me, and an expression of the utmost glee came over her face. 'Hey, hey, hey, you all,' she said to her cohorts (she always had at least one cohort with her). 'What do you call a ginger at a party? Unwelcome!'

They all burst into cackles of witch-like laughter.

I put on my best withering look and walked through the gates as fast as I could.

My lucky day just got luckier and luckier, because the first teacher I ran into as I rushed up the steps to the main door was none other than Mrs Munroe herself. Fan-bloddy-tantastic. I didn't look at her, as if somehow my not seeing her meant she wouldn't be able to see me.

Amazingly, it worked! She just walked on past. I guess she had better things to worry about than bright orange pupils.

Our first lesson was English and Drama. This was my chance to shine with my word-perfect declaiming (I looked it up, I DO mean declaiming) for my Lady Macbeth 'Out, damn'd spot' moment.

Sally and I went into the classroom together, bracing ourselves for ginger jokes. (There's no such thing as a good ginger joke, by the way. Funny that.) But before anyone could say anything we were shushed by Miss Brewer.

Miss Brewer is the fierce English and Drama teacher, the one who doesn't like digression. She is scarcely any taller than her desk, borderline elderly (well over fifty), wears mostly bright pink and purple, has a big nose, and a pair of glasses that cover almost the whole of her face.

But she's fierce in a good sense. Not only can she get QBM to stay quiet all lesson, but she's got a way of making you understand all the difficult bits in some of the set texts. I think she's one of the reasons I'm going to be a prize-winning novelist. (I must remember to include her in my Acknowledgements.)

'Girls. There will be an important initiative later this year with the boys of St Thomas's,' she began.

There were the beginnings of a rustle, some giggling and a lot of nudging.

'At the Christmas end-of-term concert, there will be a joint performance of scenes from *A Midsummer Night's Dream*. We will start rehearsing with St Thomas's at the beginning of next term, and in the meantime we will look at the scenes this term before we decide who will go forward and be in the finished drama.'

Well. *Never* have I seen a classroom full of girls pay such rapt attention to the words of their teacher. Not even the tallest, slimmest most beautiful English and Drama teacher in the world could have had her pupils sooooo in the palm of her hand.

If I hadn't been RIGID with determination to have a part in the play, I would have found it all quite funny.

Miss Brewer announced that the first scene in question would be the last one of the play. I'm sure it's famous enough to be fresh in everyone's minds, but just in case it's not, it's the one where all the mixed-up lovers have got together with their right partners, and they and Theseus the Duke watch Bottom and Snout and co. act the Pyramus and Thisbe play within a play. It's a perfect choice for a joint production with the boys' school – lots of characters, lots of mistaken identities, lots of 'humour'. Although I have never really got Shakespeare's humour – the odd drunk porter, the odd clown, some word play and puns, and that's humour?

'You will see, girls,' Miss Brewer was saying, 'that the scene in question is full of Shakespeare's comic genius, with the humour intensified by the watchers' interaction with the players.'

Right. Comic genius. One of us is wrong, and I expect it had better be me. I decided to focus my attention on which part to try for, perhaps a lovesick Helena or Queen Hippolyta...perhaps Mark would be Theseus, and I could be his queen...we would have to sit side by side looking lovingly at each other...perhaps holding hands and exchanging the odd kiss...

'Chloe.' Miss Brewer again. 'I'd now like you to convey to the class the full extent of your misery and hopelessness.'

For a moment I felt sick, especially when I heard tittering and the word 'ginger' coming from the back rows. Then I realised that it was my big Lady Macbeth moment. As I stood up I saw out of the corner of my eye QBM and her vile cohorts giggling together as they looked at me.

I positively spat the words 'out' and 'damn'd' and 'spot'. I think it was the performance of a lifetime.

My mood of dramatic Shakespearian defiance had worn off by the time we got to lunchtime. By then there was nothing to look forward to except swimming and double Chemistry.

What sort of perverted sadistic timetabler came up with that combo? As if ruining your hair (if you haven't done that already), forcing you to swallow chlorine down the back of your nose, and humiliating you with instructions to do impossible dives weren't bad enough, you then have to go into a lab and do more impossible tasks with smelly liquids, usually wearing a pair of absurd glasses that only go to exaggerate the terrible lank greasiness of your chlorinated hair. Yeuch. Oh, and plus – here was another great thing to worry about – lord knew what chlorine did to dyed orange hair. Perhaps it would just make it turn green and fall out. Marvellous.

Having lunch with Sally and Amy didn't help my mood. Though I suppose Amy was fine, in fact, better than fine because she was subdued by her Charlie-less-ness, and so suitably miserable. But Sally, well, Sally was horribly bouncy and smiley and even more glued to her phone than usual.

'We're here, Sally,' I said slightly coldly. 'So who can you be expecting a message from?'

'Do you think,' said Sally in a slightly faraway, preoccupied voice that made it sound like she was simultaneously struggling with the proof of $E=mc^2$ and the plot of a Dickens novel, 'that if someone says they'll text you later, that the someone means later in the day, or later the next day, or later in the week, or just generally later meaning late at night?'

'I think,' I said, still using my cold tone of voice, 'that if the someone is the someone we think it is, and he's a "he" sort of someone, that you can have absolutely no idea what he means. It may mean today or tonight, or it may mean some time in the next month if he happens to remember.'

This was uncalled for, I know. But I was feeling bitter as well as orange (ha), and anyway Sally didn't seem at all put out.

'OK,' she said slowly. 'So if he texts today or tomorrow that proves that he really wants to see me again. I mean, that's got to be worth some positive attribution points, or whatever, hasn't it? Or maybe he'll call instead of texting, and that would be even better, wouldn't it?'

'I shouldn't get your hopes up even if he does text,' said a quiet voice coming from the general direction of Amy. 'I think boys are just wired differently when it comes to making arrangements and things. They don't seem to realise how much we believe what they say and how we think they'll keep their promises.'

It was a long speech for Amy, and if I didn't know her better I'd say it was even delivered with a tiny bit of venom. But she was looking down at her chocolate brownie as she said it (I love the way that family is never very far from a brownie) so I couldn't really see her expression. But clearly Charlie was going to have to work hard if he was going to re-endear himself to her. We let a bit of a silence fall. There was much to think about here.

'Blimey,' came Gemma's voice from immediately behind me. 'It's the love child of Ron Weasley and Jessica Rabbit.'

With friends like her I'd say the school beeyatch will soon be out of a job.

'Ha, and ho,' I said, pulling Mum's black scarf further over my hair. 'Anyway, where have YOU been all morning? You missed the news about the school play.'

'Plus you missed Chloe's performance of Lady

Macbeth,' said Sally loyally. 'I've never seen so much shouting and hand-waving, not to mention all the spittle.' Maybe not so loyal.

'I had a doctor's appointment,' said Gemma, not very convincingly.

How she gets away with it, I don't know. I think if she just fancies the morning in bed, she forges a note from Merv and nobody asks questions because she's the poor girl with the runaway mother. Hmmm.

'Anyway, that's boring,' she went on. 'What's interesting is that we're going bowling. Merv's booked us a couple of lanes for Saturday afternoon, and as much pizza as we can eat. He's feeling guilty about abandoning me over the Easter holidays, so let's make the most of it.'

There was a lot of information here to chew over. Clearly Merv had no idea that Gemma had been to see her mother or he wouldn't be being so generous. More likely he was feeling guilty about something else...I would make it my mission to find out what.

But in the short term, a night of bowling courtesy of the dodgy Merv Millions was not to be sneezed at. Fantastic Boy Watching opportunities, a bit of a laugh, plus a chance to get my own back on Sally who'd actually beaten me by a hundred points last time we'd played. (Not that I'm competitive. But I've perfected this really professional bowling style – straight down the middle, very fast. And Sally had this lackadaisical approach. A sort of what's-this-ball-in-my-hand-oh-well-I-suppose-I-might-as-well-throw-it-at-the-pins style. And mine seemed to go down the gutters, and HERS seemed to knock over all the pins. Most annoying.)

'Brilliant,' said Amy with a hint of a smile.

'That would be great,' said Sally. 'I'll be there, 'slong as I haven't got a hot date or anything.'

'You can't have a date,' I said going all cold again. 'This is a night out with your friends, you can't just drop them if some boy says so.' There was a very important point of principle here. Plus it would be a long time before I forgave her for the one about the hand-waving and the spittle.

Swimming was every bit as horrible as it usually is.

But at least we didn't have to dive, and at least my hair didn't fall out as soon as it got in the water. In fact, it seemed to rather like the chlorine and even felt a bit softer than usual. I was standing by the edge of the pool squeezing out the water and feeling relieved that it was all still there and actually almost normal, when QBM minced past in her uplifting one-piece.

'Just wait till you use the hairdryer. It'll all fall out. Well known fact with orange hair dye,' she said as she bent down to pick up her towel.

How I longed to fill her pockets with lead and push her into the pool. Impossible, though, on so many levels.

I spent the rest of the swimming lesson absolutely dreading drying my hair, and at the same time wondering yet again what it must be like to be QBM and spend so much time working out how to make other people's lives that little bit more miserable.

In fact, the hairdryer did nothing more unexpected than dry my hair. So I went into Chemistry feeling strangely positive about life. It may be the most boring subject in the world, but at least I still had hair on my head to learn about it with. With my new positive attitude to my hair colour I bent over the test tubes in front of us with something approaching interest.

The test tubes had either oxygen or hydrogen in them. And we were actually allowed lighted spills to find out which was which. The flame either exploded or re-lit itself depending on whether it was oxygen or hydrogen. Marvellous. And probably quite educational if you could remember which gas was which and why it behaved like that.

Our teacher that day was one we hadn't had before: a short, wrinkly person with her red hair in a bun and a broad accent I couldn't identify. She was dressed in a blue plastic uniform that seemed to cover her entire body, and which made her look a little bit like a pre-wrapped muffin with a cherry on top.

I don't think anyone had told her that we shouldn't be allowed to play with fire, but I was definitely distracted from my hatred of Chemistry by the pleasure of waving a flame in front of Sally's nose.

Spittle indeed. I'd give her spittle.

The end of the Chemistry lesson came all too soon – and in a thousand years I never thought I'd write those words.

As we packed up to get ready to go, I found myself rather dreading going home to Ghastly Ralph and a whole evening of being nagged about the skirting board. Then I thought that that was nothing compared to Gemma having to go back to the revolting Merv, or indeed Sally not knowing whether her mother would have cooked her a loving tea or gone to bed with Mr Pinot Grigio.

That was my thought for the day: all families are the same – weird. They are just weird in different ways. I think it is a very good thought, but I'm not completely sure it's original.

Dogs, Doorknobs and Other Obstacles in Life

As I put my key in the front door I heard a little strangulated bark from Albert's quarters. I was anxious to get home because I'd remembered Mum had promised to bring back the cure for orange from work, and I thought the sooner I got going on Project Normal Hair the better. But the bark worried me; perhaps Albert had been damaged after all by his dramatic encounter in the park.

I froze, key half in the door.

'Little ****er,' shouted a voice the other end of the flat. And then a sort of thwacking sound. Like the noise you make when you do a belly flop only without the splash.

And then a little whiney sound from Albert. And then another thwacking sound and another whine.

It was too much. Project Normal Hair would have to wait. Albert needed my help.

I banged on the door.

As I heard the hairy crabby one approach, and as he opened the door I felt a wave of intense blushing coming over me.

I could hear more shouting and thwacking going on…from the TV in the back room. How was I to know that late afternoon soap operas would upset Albert so much? Or be so violent?

'Um,' I said. Then, thinking fast, 'Would Albert like a walk on Saturday?'

'All right,' said the crabby one, who seemed to be wearing pyjamas from circa 2009, with genuine original stains. Yeuch. 'Have to be in the afternoon. Two o'clock.'

'Right,' I said. And without looking back, put my key in our front door and scampered breathlessly upstairs.

It was only when I got to the top that I realised that, irony upon irony, I'd just committed a cardinal sin, and agreed to go out with Albert instead of out with my friends.

And that wasn't the whole muddle. The top of the stairs and all of the hall were covered in dust sheets. There were boxes of tools, wet paint brushes

223

and sandpaper everywhere.

'DON'T!' shouted a voice that came from a large grey bottom bent over the floor. Ghastly Ralph.

'Don't what?' I said, trying to find somewhere to put my school bag.

'Just don't,' said Ralph still rather shoutily. 'There's tools everywhere. And wet paint. I've spent the whole day tidying up the mess you've made and if you make a mark on that wet paint there'll be hell to pay.'

'OK,' I said quietly. Perhaps if I spoke really quietly it would somehow rub off on him and he'd stop shouting. 'Where's Mum?'

'She's in bed asleep, and don't you disturb her. You can make me a cup of tea, and then you can make yourself scarce and keep out of my way,' said the ghastly one.

I put the kettle on. Its curly lead was curlier than ever and had somehow managed to tie a knot in itself. There didn't seem to be any tea bags and the noise coming from the TV in the sitting room sounded suspiciously like that of a large number of people watching a football match. Perfect. Brother Steve doing what he does best. When I opened the fridge I saw there was no milk, just a bottle of ketchup and a big plate of what looked suspiciously like Steve's chips from last night.

More perfect. I reckoned the sooner I met Zac properly and he whisked me away to his famous glass house in the Hollywood Hills the better. I bet the inside of *his* fridge didn't look like this.

But it only helped a little bit to imagine myself in the Hollywood Hills. For now I had to find the tea bags and get some milk. I headed off to Mum's room to ask for some money to go shopping.

She was just waking up when I opened the door.

'Hello, love,' she said a little bit sleepily. There was a strong pattern of crumpled pillow on her left cheek. She must have been having quite a long rest. 'I haven't done the shopping today. Must get down there before teatime.'

'You stay put, Mum,' I said, 'I'll go.' I didn't have the heart to nag her about my need for certain hair products. Perhaps another day of Ordeal by Orange wouldn't kill me.

As I clutched her ten-pound note and clambered over Ralph and his paint pots and sandpaper I wondered if he would ever just for once, just for perishing once, do the shopping for Mum and think about someone other than his selfish self.

The evening was every bit as fun-filled as I thought it would be. When I got back from getting milk and industrial quantities of sausages and potatoes, the flat stank of paint and football. It was, apparently, a big match and a European decider – would England be in or out of Europe? I felt sure there was a subtle political joke to be made here, though it would probably be wasted on my dear brother and the stepdad. Even if I could think what it was.

Mum had promised to bring me some Normal Colour the next day, so at least I went to bed with hope in my heart.

And my tweezers in my hand. I was determined to get to grips with my right eyebrow which seemed to be out of balance with my left. As I looked at myself in the mirror – orange hair and asymmetrical brows – I found myself wondering what I'd have worried about in Jane Austen's day. Life must have been so much simpler before the invention of DIY hair dye and tweezers. I suppose you just had to go with what you were given in those days.

I couldn't decide if that was a good thing or a bad thing.

Mum didn't manage to get hold of the right normal colour till right at the end of the week, so I decided to perform the operation on the Friday night so I could be de-oranged for Bowling Saturday.

I still hadn't extricated myself from my date with Albert, but I thought if the worst came to the worst Albert could just come with us. Whoever wasn't having a turn could just keep him company outside. Not an ideal arrangement, but I couldn't face any sort of renegotiation with the crabby one.

The other big news at the end of that week was that Amy had had a text from Charlie. It was only a 'hi there, how u doing?' sort of text, but it was an olive branch, apologetic in tone, and seemed to hold out hope of a future for them both. Well, that was what Amy reckoned, although how she managed to imbue sixteen words of text-speak with all the meaningfulness of a 500-page Victorian novel, I'm not sure.

I think I mean 'imbue'.

It turned out that Charlie was going bowling on Saturday too. This was incredibly exciting news. In fact, really nerve-wracking. Obviously mostly because I was anxious that he and Amy would have a proper talk and get together again, but also because there was a chance that he might be going with friends. Good friends. At least one of whom might be called Mark.

That Friday we were sitting about waiting for our History lesson to begin. Miss Daniels, the hapless Mr Horriday's temporary replacement, was almost invariably late. We were pretty sure this was because she found the whole business of teaching us History incredibly boring. This would explain why she was incredibly boring and we were incredibly bored. We were meant to be studying the civil rights movement, but we were just as likely to be told about Germany's invasion of Poland or the beginning of the slave trade. It was all very confusing and at this rate very unlikely that any of us would do History for any longer than we absolutely had to.

'What time will Charlie be there?' Sally was asking Amy. She hadn't heard anything from Rob since the walk in the park, and I could detect a little bit of peevishness in her voice. I'd filled in my Boy Watching charts with some marks for Sustainability for Charlie, and now he was neck and neck with Rob. It wasn't a competition, as I kept on saying to Sally, but I knew she was starting to get rather anxious that Rob would have forgotten her charming concern for his little sister by now.

'Not sure, but it won't be before five, I don't think, so we'd better play very, very slowly so we're still there in the evening,' said Amy.

'He didn't say who he was coming with, did he?' I asked with an air of spectacular nonchalance (nonchalant is a great thing to be, much better than cool, I think).

'No, he didn't say if Mark Anderson was going too,' said Amy in a slightly eye-rolly way. Perhaps I'm not as subtle as I think.

'You're so ooooobvious,' said Sally, getting her own back for the Sustainability points. 'Besides, I'm not sure—'

But we were never to know what Sally was not sure about because she was interrupted by the arrival of Miss Daniels, who came into the classroom with a furious expression on her face and a large pile of worksheets.

Banging the sheets down on the desk with an air of deep disgust she took one look at us and barked, 'Why did the French Revolution matter?'

This was a question we were really not equipped to

answer, so not surprisingly she was greeted by a rather startled silence.

'Tsch,' Miss Daniels said. Or at least something like that – definitely a noise meant to indicate scorn. 'Have you girls been taught nothing? We'd better start at the beginning and make it simple with the Three Estates and the Tennis Court Oath.'

And all was confusion from then on, almost as bad as Mr Horriday at his most mad. Those of us who had a vague idea of the French Revolution meaning guillotines, liberty-fraternity-equality and the general impossibility of eating cake were left even more confused. Especially since our homework project had been on the causes of the Vietnam War.

It was strangely exhausting, being taught in this random fashion, so it was more of a relief than usual when it all stopped and we could head off to our last lesson – Art, with the disengaged Mr Pampledousse.

'I wonder what sort of a state we'll find old Pimplemouse in today,' said Gemma as she stalked along by my side. (Gemma does 'stalk', even in flats. I think she pretty much constantly imagines that Jezza and his friends might appear any minute, so she must always be on her guard and at her best, even when she's only in the school yard with us lot. Interesting. I guess it's like models having to walk like models all the time – one slouch and they're out.) 'All this pining for his love is making him dopier and dopier. They should just put him out of his misery and send him to Newfoundland.'

I thought Gemma was just doing her usual dark weird stuff until we walked into the Art class and saw Mr P gazing with an expression of despair at a large picture of piled-up skulls. It was all a bit spooky, a bit like the beginning of the kind of film you had to watch through your fingers.

We all sat down, and eventually he turned to us and announced in a thicker than usual accent, 'Today you will learn about pain, and death, and light and shades. These picture is all darkness. You must learn about darkness.'

Apparently the painting was by Cezanne, who I reckon must have been pretty miserable too, judging by the way the skulls stare at you. The object of the exercise was to copy the picture with all its shadows.

As we sat in a row at the back of the class struggling to imitate the lights and shades of the picture, I found myself thinking that this education thing isn't all it's cracked up to be. I couldn't wait to get home and get started on Project Normal Hair Colour. If we're talking shades, then the only thing I cared about was getting rid of an orange one.

Gemma had told us that Merv was using his garage that evening to perform some sort of operation on his Harley-Davidson. No doubt it involved lots of oil and swearing, but anyway it meant band practice was off.

'See you tomorrow,' said Amy. She seemed to have a little bit of a glow about her as she headed at great speed for the gates. I knew she'd be spending all night planning what to wear to go bowling the next day so I thought it best not to slow her down.

Gemma had melted away to wherever Gemmas melt to on a Friday afternoon, and Sally was just standing there looking balefully at her phone. ('Balefully' is another one that needs some research. If you're full of 'bale' when you're cross shouldn't that mean you're 'baleless' when you're happy?)

'No Rob message, then?' I said, quite sympathetically for me.

'Nope,' said Sally. 'If he's not there tomorrow, I'm going to text HIM. How about that? After all, I'm really worried about his little sister, aren't I?'

'You are,' I said. 'You certainly are. In fact, all week you've talked of little else except your concern for – what was her name again?'

'Rob's sister,' said Sally, a little grumpily. 'You don't have to know someone's name to worry about them, do you?'

'Seems not,' I said. 'Anyway, you've got a plan now, plus who knows who might turn up at bowling tomorrow?'

We headed off for the gates almost good friends again.

I found Mum in the kitchen when I got home.

'Hello, love,' she said looking up from her Sudoku puzzle. 'You're a lucky girl. I've managed to get you the best cure for your condition there is.'

For a second I panicked and wondered what 'my condition' might be, then I remembered: there was only one tangerine person in our family.

Mum held out a small blue bottle that said lots of things like Deep, Intensive, Moisturising, Restorative, Repair, Serum, Protein, Treatment. Maybe it didn't contain quite all those reassuring words, but it looked pretty mending anyway. And then she picked up a bigger bottle, which said 'mild' and 'gentle' and 'sensitive' in small (but also reassuring) letters and 'Honey Blonde' in big bold letters.

'Oh, Mum,' I said, feeling every bit as grateful and slightly tearful as I sounded. 'Thank you.'

'Come on, then,' she said in her best hairdresser – I mean hairstylist – voice and we set off for the bathroom.

The bathroom still smelt strongly of paint after Ghastly Ralph's attentions to the skirting board, but soon it smelt even more strongly of hair dye. Interesting that however mild and gentle and sensitive and all that a dye tells you it is, you still get a sharp stinging sensation all the way up your nose as soon as you go anywhere near it.

My eyes were streaming, I had a crick in my neck from leaning over the basin, and my head was getting very sore. But Mum seemed to be enjoying herself, and hummed her way through pretty much all the Cliff Richard repertoire as she gave my head a vigorous scrub with each element of product.

Eventually we were done, and I was once more tied up into a Morrisons plastic bag and told to go and do my homework.

Hearing the unmistakeable sounds which large crowds of football fans make coming from the sitting room, I reckoned now was a good time to borrow Ralph's laptop. The ghastly one would be otherwise engaged for at least another hour, and I wanted to make a new spreadsheet of Boy Watching lessons. Plus I'd had this brilliant thought that the St Thomas's first eleven were playing that weekend and maybe there were some pictures of the team on the school website.

But strange things happened when I opened the laptop. There seemed to be urgent messages in red popping up in boxes all over the screen.

They said things like: '5 to 1 Nigeria in or out?' '20 to 3 France, evens Italy?' 'Scotland 4 to 5?' 'Final chance, Tuesday'.

Most peculiar.

I clicked quickly to the more familiar sight of the site of St Thomas's School For Boys. To be honest, it was very familiar indeed, especially at the end of term. That was when there were usually lots and lots of photos of the open days, the sports days, the winning teams, the prize winners... Sometimes there would be general photos of Mark and Charlie's year. So, obviously, that meant having to enlarge the pictures to see Mark close up. I'd done that quite a lot, since I'm being honest. Really quite a lot. Sometimes I'd magnified the photos so much that all you could see was some black and pink pixels. But they were beautiful black and pink pixels.

This time I was in luck. There was the first team in all their golden glory, and in the middle of them all was the very Mark A*. He looked incredibly perfect and perfectly handsome.

I was gazing so intently that I almost didn't notice Mum come into the room.

What a wonderful thing the laptop is. In the olden days it would have been only too clear that I was staring at pictures of boys and not learning my French vocab, but now – well, you just flip the lid and look innocent, don't you? And I expect that a Morrisons bag on your head makes you look even more innocent. Or even more something.

'Right then, let's get that bag off your head and see if it's worked,' said Mum.

I thought her choice of words a bit worrying.

'What do you mean IF, Mum? IF I'm still orange and crispy I will have to kill myself, you do realise that, don't you?'

'Don't joke about things like that, love,' said Mum.

So I felt told off as well as nervous as we trooped into the bathroom.

Quite a lot of rinsing and towelling later I was allowed to look in the mirror. I don't think anyone anywhere has ever been quite so glad to see a reflection of themselves with completely unremarkable brown hair. More dishwater than honey blonde – as no doubt my old friend QBM would say – but no orange, and no crunch.

'Thanks, Mum,' I said. And I really meant it.

Bowling Along

Saturday morning dawned bright and breezy. Although, to be accurate, it was a little overcast and rather still, it nevertheless felt bright and breezy because I was *honey blonde* and not at all orange and crispy. All was well in a world that was honey-blonde-coloured.

Or at least it was until I went into the kitchen that morning and saw my beloved family.

There was Ralph standing over the kitchen sink, gazing out of the window and picking his nose with a ferocity that made me fear for its inner tube, or whatever you have in a nose. And there was Steve, jeans hanging onto his bum by a whisker (yeuch), standing at the fridge door drinking OJ straight from the carton and somehow managing to grunt even between the slurps. And there was Mum, looking tired and puzzled as she sat at the kitchen table, pencil hovering over her Sudoku.

It wasn't a great start to the day, and made me think, yet again, that it was high time Zac came and took me away from it all. But meanwhile, Sally had announced she was coming round at one, and then we had to come up with an Albert strategy for the afternoon. So I had less than four hours to shower, decide what to wear, and do my nails. Busy, busy.

Eventually everyone had gone: Mum to a half day at Happy Hairliners (she once told me she was very much in demand there, everyone always asked for her. She must have been very good at her job for them all to put up with her choice of tunes to hum), Ghastly Ralph to do whatever he did at the Jobcentre on a Saturday, and Steve to – well, probably have some grunting practice in the park with Kev-the-clone.

Sally arrived early, and wearing jeans and a white top that said 'Gingers Have Souls' on it in orange (what else?) letters.

'Oh,' she said, her face falling when I opened the door. 'So much for that, then. I was showing solidarity. And now you've gone all brown again.'

'That's sweet,' I said. 'I mean about the solidarity. But for your information, I am not brown, I am honey blonde, and I've still got the bottle to prove it.'

Sally was wearing an incredible amount of eyeliner, which made her look borderline sinister. Her nails were a fetching shade of orange, and her hair was tied up in a fluorescent scrunchie (orange, natch) that wouldn't have looked out of place in a bad eighties sitcom. The overall effect was really quite scary.

'You look brilliant,' I said. After all, what else could I say? Too late for her to rethink the orange theme, and what are friends for, if they don't support each other? I found myself having a fierce internal debate about where the benefits of the white lie began and ended.

'It's all in the colour coordination,' said Sally. 'Plus you've got to define your eyes more than you think you should. That's one of the top tips for the weekend.' Sally had been at the magazines again.

And whenever she came up with a top tip there was always more where it came from. 'Although,' she was saying, 'you mustn't overdo the lips if you're overdoing the eyes. So I'm not going to use much lip gloss.'

Then she followed me into the bathroom to supervise my eyeliner technique.

What with one thing and another we were running late by the time we'd analysed every line and shade, but on the whole we reckoned we both looked pretty good as we got ready to leave the flat. All denim and trainers but with touches of sparkle. Just the right side of dressed up, but still cool. Any random boy who just might be bowling that day would think we'd made an effort, but not so much that we looked like we really *cared*.

I'd broken the news to Sally about our having to double date with Albert as we were debating the pros and cons of glittery eye shadow (con, in the end). She hadn't been impressed, but wasn't as horrified as I'd thought she'd be. I think she'd developed a sort-of fondness for Albert, who had, after all – though he didn't know it – been responsible for her Rob-bonding in the park.

We knocked on Albert's door at half past two. Silence. I knocked again. Perhaps the crabby one was putting some clothes on (that was an encouraging thought) or perhaps he was in the loo (not such an encouraging thought). But I was surprised Albert wasn't making his presence felt. Sally and I looked at each other with one of those what-do-we-do-now? expressions that the heroes in films always adopt just before something absolutely terrifying happens.

I was getting a bit spooked by this time. Then suddenly there was a thumping noise and the door was flung open. The crabby one, face stubbly and wearing the same 2009 pyjamas, glared down at us.

'What?' he growled. (It really was a growl, all rumbly and threatening.)

'We've come for Albert,' I said, trying not to sound scared or revolted or anything that might wind up the crabby one.

'He's gone missing, hasn't he?' said his owner, like he didn't care one way or the other. And not as if we might possibly be able to answer his question.

'Oh no!' I couldn't keep the gasp out of my voice. What had happened to him, why had he run away, was he all right…were all things I didn't say out loud.

'He just b******* off, little ****, didn't come when I called. **** him, anyway,' said our charming neighbour, sounding more and more as if he was closely related to Webster's owner in the park the other day. 'He'll be back. He always is. Got his collar on, someone will find him.' And he shut the door on us.

I looked at Sally, daring her to say that at least that was one problem solved, as we wouldn't have to bowl and Albert-sit at the same time. But instead she said, 'Oh, that's awful. Poor Albert. I do hope he's all right.'

'Me too,' I said, feeling warmly towards my friend, and worried for Albert in equal measure.

But there was nothing for it: we had a date at Best Bowling (somebody was on fire when they came up for that name), and we were already late to meet Amy and Gemma.

As we walked up from the bus stop towards Best Bowling, there were loads of cars picking up and dropping off: lots of parents delivering tiny noisy children, and lots more parents picking up tiny tired children. (So I guess it works if the object of the game is to quieten down your small child.)

Fun4U is a complex that caters for every known form of exercise – or 'fun' as it's known here – for the younger generation. To the left is a vast swimming pool, with little swimming pools coming off it. You can watch from the gallery as mothers hold their tiny children in the water, and bigger ones (children, not mothers) splash about in the shallow end of the big pool. The smell of chlorine is right up there with hair dye, and you can't help wondering what other smells lie behind it.

'Come on,' said Sally, interrupting my speculations about the exact contents of all the swimming pools (probably just as well). 'The others have already gone in.'

We walked past the viewing gallery of the skating rink – there were some brilliant skaters there. I must try skating one day, I thought – and on to the entrance to the bowling. Amy was standing by the bit where you hire shoes, looking really great in her best denim and some of the beads she was wearing the last time she'd seen Charlie/Mr Bingley.

'You look brilliant,' I said for the second time that day, only meaning it this time. 'Where's Gemma?'

'She's over there,' said Amy pointing to the bar area at the other end of the alleys. Gemma was standing by a line of plastic chairs shouting at someone who bore more than a passing resemblance to Merv. I don't know why I hadn't computed that the price of going bowling with the Merv Millions was having the actual Merv there.

Merv, dressed top to toe in his trademark black, came over towards us, Gemma trailing behind him looking angry.

'OK, girls,' he said with that sort of horrible jollity that only people who are never truly jolly have. 'Let's book some lanes and get bowling, shall we?'

'He's going to pay and then leave us to it,' said Gemma, with real ice in her voice. Phew. I was reminded yet again how you probably don't ever want to get on the wrong side of Gemma.

Merv tried to pretend he wasn't at all bothered by his daughter's steeliness, and not for the first time I wondered which of them was really in charge. He went up to the bored-looking man at the till. The music was pretty loud and I could see Merv was having trouble hearing what he was being told.

'Gosh,' said Amy in a slightly horrified tone. 'So expensive…'

'Don't worry,' I said, 'He's rich. It's not expensive in his world. Besides, the more he's spending the longer we can play, and that's a good thing, isn't it?'

Merv had booked one lane for four games, so I reckoned we'd definitely still be there when the boys arrived.

We went off to our lane and entered our names in the machine. This was almost as competitive as the game itself – we had a tradition that the person with the best name got free pizza.

Sally went first, and typed in: 'Oddball'. Very good, and really quite appropriate, especially for someone wearing a T-shirt saying 'Gingers have souls'.

Then Amy: 'Pin Head'. Even better. Nice bit of self-deprecation, but also sounding a lot like the top dog.

Then me: 'Gutter Fingers', I typed. How I laughed.

'I think you've shot yourself in the foot, there,' said Gemma. 'I don't think you'll find any winners' names rhyming with butterfingers.'

And with that she typed: 'Gemma'.

I gave a little sigh, which couldn't, of course, have been heard above the blare and beat of the music.

I guess Gemma is just always going to be that bit cooler than the rest of us.

Half an hour later, and I'd almost forgotten that there was a strong possibility of Charlie and a less strong possibility of Mark A* appearing any time soon. Sally was eighty points ahead. She, her favourite orange ball and her oh-might-as-well-throw-it style were cleaning up.

I, meanwhile, was hurling the ball faster and faster with seemingly less and less success. Once, it seemed to miss the track altogether and just went straight to the gutter at the end – not troubling a single pin on its way. Grrr.

Amy was way ahead, too, just behind Sally. This didn't annoy me quite so much, because what with being very good at Maths and running, Amy was clearly designed to be unnecessarily successful at things that involved sportiness and calculation.

Gemma was doing even more badly than I was, but it seemed to bother her not one bit, especially as she spent more time looking at her phone than anything else.

'Strike!' A jubilant cry from Amy. The clatter of pins put her into the lead, and she danced about in what might have been a rather endearing way if circumstances had been a bit different.

My turn. I turned towards one of the really heavy balls. I had a new theory that it must be about speed and weight. If you had a big enough mass hurtling straight down the middle as fast as you could possibly hurl it then how could you not knock everything down? It was just about science. I was sure there was a formula for it – the Bowling Theory of Moving Mass. Or something.

I put my fingers in the holes of the heaviest ball I could find. It really was alarmingly heavy. But then smashing those pins was all about greater mass and weight.

I lifted it up and started to run – all the better to get the speed of the ball up – towards the top of the alley. Drawing my bowling arm back with all my might I suddenly realised it was all too heavy and my fingers were losing their grip.

Half way through the curve of the throw I lost my grip completely and the heaviest ball available came crashing down on my right foot. Ow to the power of ow.

'Jeeeeeeeeeeez,' I gasped, and sank to the floor with the sheer pain of it. Thank goodness it's just us, I managed to think, so my humiliation isn't going to be photographed or seen by people.

I thought.

As I looked up and saw Charlie two lanes away and heading in our direction.

Just. My. Luck.

Amy was bending over me in a concerned kind of way and hadn't seen him.

'Are you going to be all right?' she was saying.

'I'm fine,' I managed to gasp. 'Just need…to…get…breath…back.'

'Poor Chloe,' said Charlie, as he came up behind

Amy. 'That's quite a lot of falling over you do, don't you?' He was laughing as he said it, but not in a nasty way.

'Charlie!' said Amy. And I could almost see the blush steal up on her. Fortunately the lights were quite dim, and anyway I've always believed that boys don't spot a blush in quite the way that girls do.

'I was just coming over to say hi, and congratulate you on your strike. But then everything seems to have got just a bit more dramatic,' said Charlie. 'Are you really all right?' he said, looking down at me.

I struggled to my feet. I tried to look cool and feel no pain, because I'd happened to glance at the group of people that Charlie had come from. They were looking over at us and talking and laughing together and, yup, in the middle of the group was a tall dark figure who was surrounded by people but still half looking in my direction.

I couldn't see whether He was actually looking at me, so I tried to focus on Charlie. 'Yes,' I said, looking into his greeny-blue eyes – he really did have kind eyes – 'It was my own stupid fault. I thought the heavier the better, so it would sort of bounce into the middle, but I didn't factor in the actually throwing it part of the theory.' I was babbling.

'So long as you're all right,' said Charlie, looking at Amy. 'Are you going to come over and get some drinks with us when you're finished?' he said, still looking at Amy.

'Oh yes, that would be lovely,' Amy sounded a little bit goofy and breathless, but her smile was lighting up her face and making her eyes go all kind and crinkly rather like Charlie's. I couldn't help thinking ahead. They will make a lovely couple, I thought.

Meanwhile, it was my turn again. Although my foot was throbbing like mad I was determined to get at least one strike. Not that it all mattered in the least, it was only a game, but Amy was now ahead of Sally who was way ahead of me and even Gemma was ten points ahead of me. As I say, this sort of thing really doesn't matter, it's not about winning, it's just about not letting yourself down. Actually, I think it's not so much letting yourself down as coming last. Coming last is really not a good look.

I gave myself a good talking-to as I lifted up one of the lighter balls. I could see out of the corner of my eye that Charlie's group were now focused on their own game, so no distractions, no excuses. I drew my arm back and pushed the ball gently down the middle of the lane. Perfect. And then just at the last minute it veered off to the left, knocked one pin over and disappeared.

You can go off bowling.

The others looked at me in a trying-not-to-laugh kind of way. 'It's my foot,' I said. 'Very difficult to balance properly with a painful foot.'

'Poor you,' said Sally. 'So you've had a bad foot all afternoon, have you?' Which I think was really beneath her.

Eventually, we were all done. The machine was lighting up the name 'Pin Head' and making it dance about and congratulating it and generally making lots of noise to indicate that 'Pin Head' was the winner. I was happy for Amy, and, of course, that had nothing to do with the fact that she'd beaten Sally. I was last, but, hey, it's just a game.

We gathered our things together and headed off towards Charlie and his group. They were heads down, bowling, but Charlie looked up as we approached.

'Hi there, come and have a drink,' he said, gesturing towards a table full of brightly coloured bottles and tins. I went up to the table and chose something bright and yellow and chilled looking. I couldn't help thinking that there was probably enough sugar and caffeine on that table to keep us all buzzing for a week. I'd even started to make a calculation based on each can of Monster Mountain Red V or whatever equalling two extra hours of buzz when...

'Hello, Chloe,' said a voice behind me.

It was Him.

He looked just as tall and dark and handsome close up as ever he did in the distance. His white T-shirt made him look slightly tanned and his jeans were just the right degree of torn and skinny. I looked into his eyes. They were the darkest brown and seemed to be drilling deep into my soul.

'Hello,' was absolutely all I could manage.

'Hope you haven't been falling head over heels again,' said Mark.

Oh God, he could read my mind. Was it so, so obvious? But did he think that I fell head over heels in love on a regular basis? Perhaps I was the talk of school, the one who falls hopelessly in love every week?

'That was a nasty accident you had,' he went on.

Of course! My accident! I felt an enormous blush coming on, and, in an attempt to stop it in its tracks, I said, 'I'm fine, now, thank you. Actually it wasn't all bad, as it meant I'm the first person I know to see the inside of an ambulance. Although I was unconscious at the time, so it was all a bit of a waste, really. Next time I must try to stay awake. Although, obviously, I rather hope there won't be a next time.'

I was burbling. Lord, I was burbling.

'I think perhaps you should save your natural curiosity for something a bit less life-threatening,' said Mark.

I was just about to try to change the subject, and talk about *The Diary of Anne Frank* so he could see what an intelligent reader and all-round sensitive soul I was when he turned to the girl with the ponytail I'd seen him laughing with. She had come up behind him, and was looking just as lively and nice and funny as she had that day when they were deep in conversation. I felt a bit sick.

'This is Georgie,' said Mark. 'She's going to be a rare girl in the sixth form at St Thomas's.' Oh no. It was all officially hopeless. She'd practically be living with him if they were going to be actually at the same actual school.

'She's my sister,' said Mark. Just at that moment the scoreboard at the nearest alley belted out incredibly loud music and flashed its lights in every direction.

I beamed at 'Georgie' in what I hoped wasn't too obviously an ecstatically relieved sort of way.

'Hello,' she said. 'Are you any good at this bowling thing? I'm useless. I practically miss the lane, never mind the pins.'

'Me too,' I said, suddenly incredibly glad that I was hopeless. If it meant I could bond with Mark's sister, why, I could be hopeless at anything. 'I've decided bowling is for boys,' I said. 'I think it just matters to them more than it does to us.' I felt a small twinge of guilt when I said this.

'Quite. Look at them...' she said. I needed no encouragement.

Charlie and two other boys I didn't know had been joined by Mark and they were all gazing intently at either the scoreboard or the pins, and the expression of determination on the face of the tall blond boy whose turn it now was had to be seen to be believed.

He belted the ball fast, and right down the middle, everything went flying.

'There,' said Georgie. 'He's won. Now we can go home. Nice meeting you.'

'You too. Bye,' I said, in as cool and casual way as I could manage, although inside I was exploding with pleasure. I looked over at Mark who caught my eye and waved, and then I went to grab Amy. She was deep in conversation with Charlie, but came towards me as soon as she saw we were going.

Gemma and Sally were already heading to the exit, so the four of us walked out into the fresh air together.

I thought I'd wait till I got home before I burst into song and dance.

Living the Dream

We had decided to spend some of Merv's Millions at a pizza restaurant next door to Sally's house. It was a new place, and we thought it important to support somewhere that could be incredibly useful to us for years to come – always assuming that Sally's mother didn't move, and we all stayed friends.

It did mean that, even though Sally could walk home, the rest of us would have to be driven home in the Mervmobile, with its jerky driver and his jerky driving. But I decided to worry about that later, because for now this was a celebration.

The Italian waiter who greeted us was young and very handsome. He had blue eyes and a lot of black curly hair. 'Signorinas!' he cried when he saw us. Although he made it sound like a scene from an opera – 'seen-yor-*eeeeeeeenas*' – and definitely one of those operas where it all ends happily and the (handsome) Italian hero gets the girl.

He guided us towards a table in the middle of the restaurant and made an enormous fuss of getting us a jug of water. By the time he had danced back with some menus, I had decided that I definitely wanted to do Italian A level. And then probably go to Italy, find myself a villa either in the middle of Venice or on a hillside in the middle of nowhere, which would be full of beautiful Italian men making pizzas for me at all times of the day and night. In between eating pizzas and speaking fluent Italian, I would write my bestselling novels, and everyone from Zac and Orlando Bloom to Dame Judi Dench and the Prime Minister would be falling over themselves for an invitation to my famous weekend parties. Mark, of course, would be by my side throughout all this. We would sit on the terrace, admiring the view of Venice, or the hillside in the middle of nowhere, and remember the moment when our eyes met across a crowded bowling alley...

'What are you going to have, everyone?' it was Amy, still looking flushed and happy. Sally, who was staring grumpily at her phone, as if the more she stared the more likely there was to be a message from Rob on it, announced that she was going to have a salad. The rest of us plumped for pizzas with a variety of meat and dairy on them.

'What's with the salad?' I said to Sally.

'Pizza's happy food,' said Sally with the air of someone wise beyond her years. (Not an air that you often associate with Sally.) 'And if you're not happy then you might just as well have something that's incredibly good for you and makes you live for ever.'

I couldn't quite see the logic of this. Surely if you're not happy you don't want to live for ever. But I felt so bouncy inside that I decided my job was to cheer Sally up.

'Well, sensible old you,' I said.

'Yes,' she went on. 'And at this rate, by the time we get to Snog Fest I'm going to have just as horrible a time as last year.'

'There's ages to go till then,' I said trying to be comforting, but also finding time to worry that perhaps it should have been 'there ARE ages', 'all sorts of things can happen in the next few weeks. Plus I bet if you text Rob next week he'll come straight back and suggest a date. Don't think about it for now, and have some dough balls.'

I generally find that dough balls are the answer to most things (IS the answer?) And indeed once Signor

Handsome Waiter had delivered a large bowlful, Sally perked up, and I was able to go back to feeling like a million dollars. Inside, of course. I didn't want to say anything out loud to the others about Mark A* or even his lovely sister for fear of jinxing it all. Supposing they all laughed, or said I'd imagined my conversation, or they hadn't seen us talking, or didn't believe me... No, I had to keep this all inside.

'I've taken a great photo of you and Mark,' Gemma's voice cut straight into my dreaming. 'I thought the caption on Facebook might be something like "Bowled away – is this what love looks like?"'

I felt myself going red. Which was odd because inside I was white with fury. She mustn't, she mustn't, how *could* she? 'If you do that,' I said slowly and carefully and trying not to shout or cry or hit her, 'I will never, *ever* speak to you again. I will hate you always, for the rest of my life.'

There was a bit of a silence. The others were all looking quite surprised.

'Okaaaaay,' said Gemma. 'Keep your hair on. Joke.'

'So you won't put anything on Facebook?' I said. I wanted it said out loud, in front of witnesses. This was serious.

'I won't put anything on Facebook, or any other

form of social media or mass communication. Do you want that in writing?'

I didn't care if Gemma was being cross and sarcastic, I had my promise, and that made me feel better.

I almost couldn't wait for pizzas to be over, so I could go home to my room, shut the door and just rewind the internal video of my afternoon at the bowling again and again and again.

The following morning was eerily quiet *chez nous*. (As I thought this, I couldn't help wondering what the Italian was for '*chez nous*'. After all with my newfound love of Italy and the Italians I would need to start to think in Italian soon.)

I had got home late but safely, as I'd managed to sit in the back away from Merv's attentions to the gearstick (Gemma had sat in the front, which ensured a very frosty atmosphere in the Mervmobile). There'd been nobody around when I got home, so I was able to go to my room and start rewinding without having to talk to anyone. Plus I amused myself by rearranging the Boy Watching chart – Mark and Charlie were now neck and neck, with each having three new Sustainability and Suitability points.

I did have time to notice that there'd been no sign of life as I'd passed Albert's door, but I decided to worry about that later.

I imagined myself back in the noise and glare of the alley, I saw Mark A* coming towards me, looking deep into my eyes as I stuttered through the story of my multiple accidents, the whiteness of his T-shirt and the deep brown of his eyes burning themselves on to my retinas for ever. And then his sister! It was only his sister! And she was so nice, too. Perhaps she would turn out to be the sister I never had. And we'd be friends like Elizabeth and Georgiana Darcy...

But now it was later, in fact very late, as it had taken me ages to go to sleep – what with all the rewinding – and I didn't wake up till there was the sound of a door being slammed. This could mean anything *chez nous* – or '*a casa nostra*' as Google tells me I must now learn to call it in Italian – so I rolled over and had another little rewind. I even found time to fantasise about going to St Thomas's for the sixth form years myself, though I knew Ghastly Ralph would never approve, and Mum probably wouldn't like the idea either.

When I next opened my eyes, there was Mum herself standing by the bed.

'Hello, love,' she said. 'You've had a good sleep haven't you?' For once, Mum stating the obvious was wide of the mark. But I wasn't going to explain about the internal video just at that moment. 'Ralph's just gone out to get the papers, but then he's going to take us out to lunch. That's nice, isn't it?'

Of course it wasn't and of course I didn't say so. Mum looked so tired, like she could do with a good sleep herself, that I thought anything that cheered her up had to be worth cheering.

I made my way to the methane gas chamber, sometimes known as the bathroom, with a slight sense of uneasiness. It wasn't just that I didn't know quite what I'd find behind the bathroom door – although that was usually something I was right to be uneasy about – but I just didn't like the way Mum had looked at me. As if she were worried about ME. I mean, there wasn't really anything to worry about when it came to ME.

The methane gas chamber was just as I'd feared. Little drops of smelly moisture seemed to hang in the air, and covered the mirrors with a thin sheen of mist. I decided not to wipe them. If I couldn't see me and my eyebrows in the mirror, then I wouldn't have to pluck them. I'm sure women in the public eye – supermodels, Hillary Clinton, famous actresses – don't have this problem. I mean they can't afford to be photographed in high definition with uneven woolly eyebrows, so they must just get on with it and tweeze. Perhaps you have to have a high pain threshold if you're going to be a supermodel, presidential candidate (?) or famous actress. As I wondered how you could test this theory of the Celebrity Pain Threshold, there was another loud slam of the door. The Ghastly Stepdad must be back with the papers.

There was silence when I went into the kitchen. Not a silence as in they'd all been saying horrid things about me and suddenly had to stop when I came in the room (in my family they'd just carry on saying horrid things), more of a haven't-got-anything-to-say silence. Ralph was halfway through a plate of grease and sausages, frowning over the sports section of the paper, Mum was brooding over her Sudoku and a cup of tea, and Steve was just starting in on the most enormous bowl of cereal I'd ever seen in my life. The usual leads were dangling out of his ears, and there were little hissing noises coming out of them.

My family. For a moment I wondered what Mark A*

would make of them. Perhaps just as Elizabeth Bennet never apologised for her mother, I should never apologise for my family. Just as Mr Darcy never held Elizabeth responsible for her family, then surely Mark wouldn't hold mine against me. And anyway, Ghastly Ralph wasn't even a blood relation.

'What?' Steve was actually saying something, even if it was only a monosyllable. He was looking up at me slightly aggressively, and had taken the leads out of his ears.

'Nothing,' I said, feeling a little ashamed of how ashamed of them I was.

'You've got that superior look on your face, missy,' said Steve.

'No, I haven't,' I said. Not one of my best responses, but I was a bit taken aback at the thought that Steve might have a view about me as well as me having one about him. Perhaps in between the grunting he and Kev-the-clone had actual conversations. Ones where they talked about me and how I was...

Best not go there. Best, perhaps, not to spend too much time worrying about what other people are thinking about you. That way madness and insecurity lie.

With this great thought I reached into the fridge for

some refreshing, brain-repairing orange juice. The carton was suspiciously light and had no lid. Both these things were easily explained by the fact that the carton also had no orange juice in it. Feeling a massive wave of irritation at Steve, whose work this had to be, I also felt relief that things were back to normal.

My brother was a selfish, lazy dork and yes, I *am* superior.

The Ghastly Stepdad's choice of venue for the day's lunch from hell was a new discovery of his, a pub called the Bear and Chipmunk. His old favourite, the Hand and Arm, had apparently served him one short pint too many, so the ghastly one had taken his business elsewhere.

As the four of us got ready for our ordeal – lunch seemed to happen very soon after breakfast on a Sunday – I wondered whether anyone had ever seen a bear and a chipmunk in close proximity. I reckoned that the one was more likely to eat the other than hang out and pose for the pub sign artist.

I also prayed quite hard that there wouldn't be anyone we knew in the pub. I was pretty sure that Mark and Georgie and their parents (what were they like? I bet they were charming, and beautiful and successful and wise) wouldn't be going to a Ralph-like pub. At least I hoped they wouldn't. No, they'd probably be driving out to the countryside somewhere, to have lunch in some rustic inn near a babbling brook.

Tearing myself away from yet more fantasising, I realised that Ralph was leading us into a sort of cobbled mews off the main shopping mall. Under a sign featuring a small bear and an enormous chipmunk (so maybe I was wrong about who was going to eat who), was one of those formica-filled pubs that served Scandawegian lager out of enormous Alpine-looking pumps that pretend to be made of china.

As if my heart wasn't sinking far enough, I spied a group of people in the corner who looked a bit familiar. At one end of the table were two adults I didn't know and at the other two girls I didn't know and two girls I did. One of these was short, and showing off, and cackling with mocking laughter as only the Queen Beeyatch could. The other was Sally.

In that split second all that Shakespearian stuff about jealousy and anger and betrayal suddenly made sense. HOW could Sally be having lunch with QB Maggie? After all we'd been through together. All we meant to each other. Were all my years of support and unquestioning loyalty for nothing?

I stood there open-mouthed. I knew my mouth was

open because Steve said, 'Sis, you look seriously deranged with your mouth open like that. Shut it.'

I did, and meekly followed the others to a table the other end of the pub. Perhaps if I could just hide, Sally and the rest of them would go soon, and all this would never have happened.

But I kept looking over at the other table. QB Maggie was howling with laughter again, and everyone else was looking at her and laughing too. But you could just tell that if she stopped laughing so would they.

Ugh, I thought. They're just sucking up. They're just weak losers. HOW can Sally be one of them?

'...and mushy peas,' Ghastly Ralph was saying. Food. We were ordering food. How could one eat when one was being betrayed by one's closest friend? How could one pretend to be interested in battered cod when a scene of such treachery was being played out before one's very eyes? And to think, only moments ago I had been floating around on a cloud of Mark-shaped wonderfulness.

'Chloe?' Mum was looking at me with a puzzled expression on her face. 'They've got your favourite. Scotch egg. Would you like that?'

Now normally, there's nothing like a Scotch egg to put a smile on my face. No, seriously. The Scotch egg is one of the world's greatest delicacies. If I could only eat one thing for the rest of my life it would be one of those hard-boiled numbers encased in sausage meat (this is the only time when the sausage is king) and breadcrumbs.

But today I knew it would taste of ashes. Ashes.

'Thanks, Mum, that would be lovely,' I said, not wanting to disappoint her.

The waitress headed off with our order, and we toyed silently with our drinks. Or as silently as the extremely noisy Bear and Chipmunk allowed. The ghastly one was on the third slurp of his second pint, and some of it was running down his T-shirt.

I made the mistake of looking away from the horrible sight, and in that second my eye caught Sally's. I'm pleased to say that at that moment her mouth had exactly the sort of shocked openness that mine had had. She looked so caught in the act, so *guilty*, it would have been funny if it hadn't been infinitely tragic.

I looked away and started to talk animatedly to Steve. 'Did you order the fish and chips?' I said brightly with an amused smile. I made it look like I was the life and soul of the party, one who couldn't care less about certain ex-best friends having lunch with my sworn enemy, the class beeyatch.

Moments later my phone started hopping around on the table. Sally. Well, I sure wasn't answering it. Wasn't even going to look up. I was having SUCH a great time with my lovely, amusing family. Chat, chat, chat, there was so much to say.

Surreptitiously I checked my phone.

ITS NOT WAHT U THIKN

Sally's guilt had obviously brought on her dyslexia.

There was no way I was going to reply – my ex-best friend had a lot of sweating to do yet. Besides, my Scotch egg had arrived. And one thing you could say for the Bear and Chipmunk is that they did know how to make a Scotch egg.

I won't even reply to Sally, I thought. In fact, I'll never speak to her again. That'll teach her. And with this punishing thought I started to feel better, and realised that Steve was saying things. I'd obviously forgotten to listen to my lovely family's fascinating conversation, what with thinking about my ex BFF and appreciating the Bear and Chipmunk's food.

'...come and stay over half term,' he was saying.

'Who?' I said brightly.

'Kev, that's who. Haven't you been listening?' Steve

was in surly mode. I could tell.

'What, you mean come and stay with US?' I couldn't believe it. As if the bathroom methane levels weren't bad enough with two of them, to have a third would send us into orbit. It was all very well having Gemma to stay, but she was at least capable of being clean and quiet, and plus she was a good friend. Apart from when she was annoying.

'Yes, dingbat,' Steve said. 'Like I said. His dad's got this secret security job in Hollywood for two weeks, so he's going to be away.'

I'd seen Kev's dad on a couple of occasions, and he was huge. And not in a cuddly way. I think if he sat on you it would certainly kill you. Plus his head was enormous and very shinily bald, and his mouth seemed to be permanently fixed in a snarl shape. All in all it was amazing he'd spawned such a scrawny, spotty son like Kev. But there wasn't any sign of a mother, or any brothers or sisters, so I suppose they were all each other had. I found myself starting to feel a bit sorry for Kev-the-clone.

'We'll have to be quite strict about the bathroom, Steve,' Mum was saying. 'If there are going to be five of us, everyone's going to have to think about other people a bit more.'

Yeah. Go, Mum. And that includes your unlovely husband.

But it was a pretty horrific thought, even if one was sorry for Kev. Perhaps I could run away for half term. Perhaps Mum and I could go back to Wales with Sally. Ah. Sally. That brought me down to earth.

As the others carried on with voicing their various theories about who exactly was the worst at hogging the bathroom, I looked over at the table the other side of the pub. There seemed to be bill-paying going on, the Queen B was looking over in my direction and saying something and laughing, and there was a general gathering of things. Sally had her back to me, but it looked all sort of stiff and awkward and I knew it was looking at me.

I decided to go back into full life-and-soul mode, and started to tell my favourite pub joke. 'Listen, everybody,' I said with my best happy smile on. 'A sandwich walks into a bar.'

'And the barman says, "Sorry, we don't serve food in here,"' said Steve.

Well, that put paid to my happy smile. There's nothing more irritating than someone else delivering your punchline.

As I turned back to look at the other table, everyone

had gone. I suddenly felt incredibly deflated, and slightly sorry for myself.

The crowd had thinned by now, and eventually Ralph stopped buying pints, and we were all allowed to go. I made myself think happy thoughts about Mark, his family, and how and whether I might see him next.

For once, there was much happiness to be found in the thought of The Boy, and none in the thought of the BFF.

It was a strange turn of events.

Mean Girls

I was beginning to think that Mum's little lecture about being considerate might have struck home with the menfolk of *casa nostra*. Sunday night was spent watching a television programme that had not a trace of a ball in it. Not one single ball. And all the men in it were dressed not in shorts, with muddy knees, but in ruffles and waistcoats and knee-length tailored coats. And they all behaved beautifully, and didn't swear, and didn't hit each other. Though I can scarcely believe it, even as I write this, the family Bennet sat in front of a television costume drama for a whole hour and a half.

Admittedly the Ghastly Stepdad was slumped in the corner of the sofa snoring off his four pints, and Steve had his leads in his ears, but at first glance we might almost have looked like a normal family having a normal Sunday evening.

Mum and I enjoyed it, anyway. There's nothing like a lot of frocks and flirting to make you pine for gentler times. I could feel the old familiar yearning for the days of Jane Austen coming on, and had to tell myself to get a grip. After all, the agonies of not knowing who you would dance with at the Netherfield Ball would have been just as bad as those of the Snog Fest. But I bet Lizzy Bennet and her sisters had a secret Boy Watching list that Jane Austen never tells us about.

And then I remembered what was really gnawing away at my insides. My old friend Sally, greasing up to the horrible QB Maggie, she who never missed a chance to be vile to and about me.

I went to my room and looked at my phone. Nine missed calls from Sally and five messages. They all said 'call me', except the last one which said that her phone was running out of juice and she couldn't find her charger so please call her on her home phone.

If we'd still been friends, I'd have gone round there and personally searched every inch of the house for that room that was full of all her phone chargers. It must be somewhere, as Mum would say.

She'd also say, 'Never let the sun go down on your wrath.'

So I decided to grit my teeth and steel all the rest of me and ring her. I called the landline and wondered what sort of a Liv I'd find the other end on a Sunday night.

'Helloooooo,' said a voice. Ah, that would be the Liv who'd clearly made up with Mr Pinot Grigio.

'Hello, it's Chloe,' I said, speaking slowly as if to someone hard of understanding, which Liv probably was at this point. 'Is Sally there? Could I speak to her?'

'Sally?' said Liv, speaking rather slowly herself. 'Oh, yes, I'll get her.'

We were making progress.

There was then quite a long silent time, although I could hear bangs and muffled cursing in the distance.

Then: 'Chloe?' It was my ex-best friend.

'Yes,' I said. I wasn't going to give her any help by making small talk, was I? She was soooo in the wrong, and besides she was the one who wanted us to speak.

'Chloe, don't be cross. I can hear you being cross,' said Sally.

I didn't say anything.

'Listen,' she said. (I always find it so odd that people say that when you're on the phone to them. I mean what else are you going to do when you've got the phone right up against your ear, and aren't actually saying anything yourself?)

'Look,' Sally said. I wondered what her next instruction would be. Perhaps it would be: 'Learn.'

'The thing is,' said Sally, and it sounded as if she really was going to get to 'the thing', whatever the thing was. 'She said we were going to watch Shedz practise. She said Jezza and Rob and everyone were going to be playing in the hall, and she said we'd go for coffee after, and she said not to tell you because there were already way too many girls, and she said she knew I wanted to talk to Rob, and she said if I told you about it I couldn't come. And then when I got to her house she said it was all off, they weren't playing after all and anyway let's go to lunch with Vic and Lilly and Vic's parents instead. And I thought I couldn't just go home, and I don't like Vic, or Lilly, but I couldn't say no, and then they were all laughing about everyone in the class and all the teachers and Mrs Munroe, and Mr Horriday, and Miss Brewer and it was all horrible, and then when I saw you there I thought I was going to die, and I'm so sorry, and please don't be cross with me. Chloe?'

I left it a little bit longer before I said anything.

'Chloe? Are you there?' Sally sounded a bit desperate.

Just about desperate enough. She was on the path to being forgiven, but I wasn't going to tell her that just yet.

'So what we have here,' I said slowly and with great emphasis, 'is you wanting to see A Boy sooooo much that you take the side of someone you know we both hate, and who almost certainly hates us, or at any rate certainly hates your friend, and you don't tell that friend because A Boy, even the possibility of seeing A Boy, is more important than your friendship. Have I got it right?'

'No,' said Sally even more desperately, and also inaccurately. 'It wasn't like that, and I'll never do anything like it again. I'm so sorry. Please say you'll forgive me one day. I'll always be your friend for ever. I'm so sorry. Please.'

I reckoned that was enough.

'All right,' I said. 'I'll try to understand how you could do such a thing. And we won't mention it again because it'll never happen again. Is that right?'

'Yes, Chloe, yes. Never. And I'll make it up to you. And—'

I heard a loud cry of, 'Sally,' at Sally's end, and a general noise of Harris and Jock activity. Obviously it was way past their bedtime, but Harrises and Jocks didn't take much notice of bedtime.

'You'd better go,' I said. 'See you tomorrow.' And that was the nearest she was going to get to forgiveness for now.

I went to bed determined to rewind the internal video of bowling alley happiness. Mark A* was, even apart from his great beauty, a good guy. He was grown-up and intelligent and, probably, way out of my league. But hope was springing away eternally. He was, for every reason, a much better person to think about than my flawed friend.

I'd think about Sally tomorrow.

Monday morning, 8.00 a.m. and I was running late. Somehow it seemed rather ordinary to be going to school, after such an exhaustingly up-and-downy weekend. But I guessed that wasn't really a good enough excuse to miss registration. I could just see the dreaded Miss Grunbar smiling understandingly as I explained my lateness with the story of Love in the Bowling Alley, and the Great Betrayal in the Bear and Chipmunk. Not.

As I rushed down the stairs past the crabby one's

door, I spared another worried thought for our furry friend. Albert could always be relied on for a barky greeting of a morning, but once again there wasn't a sign or a sound. Perhaps his horrible owner had given him away, perhaps Albert had fallen under a bus or been stolen, perhaps Webster had turned up and fatally bitten him...I decided to knock on the door if there wasn't a bark in the next two days.

Turning the corner on the road to the school, I could see the very QBM who I'd been trying not to think about standing with her horrible cohorts just by the main gate. It was almost as if she were waiting for me, to mock me.

I marched on, telling myself I was being paranoid.

I was not being paranoid.

'Here she comes,' cried the beeyatch of beeyatches. 'Little Miss No-Mates. Nobody wants to see her at weekends, so she has to go out with that fat old monster of a dad of hers. Poor old Chloe. Everyone, let's give her a *poor old Chloe*.'

And, as one, the horrible cohort turned towards me and started to chant, 'Poor old Chloe, poor old Chloe.'

I could give you a list right now of who they all were. Their shouting faces will be imprinted on my mind for ever. Some of them looked like they meant it, a few looked like they were a bit embarrassed and couldn't catch my eye, and the Queen B herself looked like she loved every minute.

I would have crumpled into bits if I hadn't felt so furious. Maggie had called the Ghastly Ralph my father, and I bet she did it on purpose, anything vile she did was usually on purpose. But it's amazing how fury can stop you crying.

I stopped walking. I vaguely remembered that they say that if you should find yourself in a field full of cows and they're all looking at you and starting to trot menacingly towards you, you mustn't run. You should just face them down, and tap the leading one on the nose.

I'd have so loved to have tapped the Queen B on her nose, but I knew that would only end in tears, probably mine. But I stood there, quite still, and looked them all in the eye. I got out my phone and took a picture of them one by one.

The chanting got quieter and they started to turn away from me as if they'd got bored.

How I hated that girl. When I write my first full work of fiction you can be quite sure that there will be a loathsome central character called Maggie.

Sally was waiting for me in her usual waiting place

by the main entrance. She somehow managed to look anxious and sheepish, and apologetic and eager-to-please all at once.

'There you are,' she said.

'I suppose I am,' I said, not having the spare energy to pick her up on the obviousness of her comment. It took a lot of concentration, not crying.

At that moment Gemma and Amy seemed to appear out of nowhere. Gemma had one of her I-know-something-you-don't expressions but Amy had one of her happy faces on, which made me feel quite a lot better almost immediately. I remembered that she would have had Bowling Alley Dreams all weekend too.

'What's up?' said Gemma to me. 'You should be bouncing off the walls now you're practically engaged. What's with the sour face?'

'Maggie and co. Had a go at me on the way in,' I said. 'And I'm here to tell you that one day that vile, mean little cow will get what's coming to her.' I had no idea what that was or how she'd get it, but I felt better saying it.

'Oh *her*, forget her. Life's too short,' said Gemma.

All easier said than done, but walking towards our English lesson with the three of them I thought the mean little cow was wrong about one thing – I did have some mates.

Someone with a sadistic sense of humour had slotted in a different lesson that Monday morning. Instead of English and Drama – where I was all set to do my next bit of Lady Macbeth, all part of my plan to be chosen for the joint *Midsummer Night's Dream* production with St Thomas's – they had scheduled PSHE. This usually consisted of watching some informative film made by the University of the Completely Obvious – things like: don't text and drive, and don't drink and drive, or there'll be a terrible accident and your friends might be killed. They were usually rather upsetting films, and stayed with you for ages. As I said to Mum, 'I know this stuff already, why do they have to make a horrid film about it? It's not as if I'm ever going to be so stupid as to drive like the people in the film.'

'Maybe the stuff works then, love,' Mum had said.

Mothers can be quite tiresome sometimes.

Our teacher for today was Mrs Pikestaff. She was just as plain as you would hope from her name, which was probably why she was also known as BUG, the Big Ugly Giant. Today's lesson was surprisingly amusing; in part of it we had to rearrange a list of alcoholic drinks in order of their strength. It was a lesson that Gemma turned out to be extremely good at. I couldn't work out whether this boded well or badly for her future.

At the end of the morning we went into lunch together and managed to find a table as far away as possible from the Queen of Mean and her hangers-on. Sally, whose expression of contrition and devotion was almost embarrassing, was following me so closely she trod on my heel.

'I expect,' she said, completely unaware of the heel-treading, 'that we should see where we are with our Boy Watching charts, shouldn't we? I think Mark has got a Compatibility point or two now, and Charlie is probably right up there for Suitability.'

Sally was well on the way to getting her own minus points for sucking up.

'I'm so happy for you and Amy,' said Sally. Now she was really overdoing it.

'What are we all doing for half term?' said Gemma, who had a history of being impatient with Sally when she was at her most Sally-ish.

'Well, I'm the lucky one,' I said. 'I'm going to have unrivalled Boy Watching practice, because there are going to be not one but two of them bunging up the bathroom.'

'I'm guessing that would be your lovely brother and his equally lovely friend Kevin,' said Gemma, in full-on sarcastic mode.

Over the years, I had sometimes had the fantasy of my brother growing up into a non-greasy, six-packed intellectual with a ready wit and perfect manners. And that when this transformation was complete he and one or other of my three close friends would fall deeply in love, live happily ever after, and I would have a dream sister-in-law.

At the moment it looked very unlikely that that was ever going to be Gemma.

'Yup,' I said. 'That's good guessing. Apparently Kev's father has a secret VIP security brief which means he has to go away for two weeks to Hollywood.'

Sally and Amy looked impressed. Gemma not so much.

'Are we seriously expected to believe,' she said, 'that Kevin's father is employed by some superstar in LA to protect them from the hoi polloi when they go clubbing?'

'I dunno,' I said, 'but he sure looks the part. I think I'd want him on my side in a punch-up. Anyway, wherever he's going, we've got to have his son to stay. Gawd. All that hair oil and football...'

'Well, I'm going to Cornwall,' said Gemma. 'Juliet's got some exhibition opening, and they want me to be there. It'll be great to get away from all this.' And she made a dismissive gesture towards the whole dining room, up to and including QB Maggie – who happened to look up at that precise moment.

For all the world it looked like Gemma had made a very rude sign to the class cow. I froze in horror.

Maggie looked daggers at Gemma and started to get up. Gemma looked back at her with her best icy glare and ran her fingers through her hair very slowly and with the same gesture. Maggie sat down again.

She may not be my future sister-in-law, but there are times when I do love Gemma.

'But band practice,' Sally was saying as we walked towards our French lesson. She'd been blissfully unaware of the battle of the rude signs. Sometimes I think life must be a lot simpler if you're Sally. 'What about band practice? Aren't we going to be playing over half term?'

'We can do that any old Friday,' said Gemma. 'But this exhibition of Juliet's is a one-off. You guys could always come too.'

What a great idea – no Bathroom Hell with Kev and Steve, plus I'd get to meet Juliet and Gemma's mum (fascinating, whichever way you looked at it), *and* go to Cornwall. I was just starting to wonder if Cornish Boys constituted Foreign Boys, like Welsh Boys did, and whether I could afford an all-body spray tan or whether I'd just buy a tube of self-tan, when we arrived at our French lesson.

Given that Paris, France, the French, are all supposed to be so romantic, you'd think that learning the language would give you a bit of a – frisson, I think is the word. A bit like Italian should. But learning French at Queen Mary's is just an unromantic matter of loads of grammar and lots of trial and error. Mostly error.

Our teacher called herself Madame de Bellaire but, from a letter we'd seen lying on her desk, we knew that her real name was Doris Bracegirdle. Somehow, knowing that meant we could never take her seriously.

Today's lesson was all about learning the French for describing a holiday in the present, perfect and near future tense. Amazing. Like a sign.

'It's like a sign,' said Sally, leaning over towards my desk. That got us a detention point for talking in class. Quite annoying, really, as no actual information was exchanged.

Eventually the lessons stopped, and we emerged blinking into the school yard. There's something extra tiring about a Monday, especially after all the positively Shakespearian drama of this particular weekend, so I reckoned that what with one thing and another, we needed a treat. Also, we needed to take stock of where we were all at with the Boy Watching charts.

I decided that Sally, who was so morally on the back foot that she was practically lying down, owed us ice cream and anything else delicious we could find in Liv's fridge.

'We might have to manage Harris and Jock,' said Sally. 'Mum's out tonight.'

'That's fine,' said Gemma, 'we'll just make them run round the garden 150 times and then they'll be so tired they won't notice we've locked them in their room.' Gemma was a bit zero-tolerance when it came to children. And so was I when it came to Harris and Jock.

Amy was first to the front door and rang the piercing

doorbell. There were some bangs and thumps in the distance and then the door opened to reveal Liv in shocking pink lipstick and false eyelashes, huge dangling earrings and a tracksuit. It looked like she was either going out and had forgotten to get dressed, or was going to the gym in last night's make-up.

'Hello, darlings,' she said in that drawl that could so easily be mistaken for someone either very bored or very drunk. Although I actually didn't think she was either. 'I'm late for Patrick, so there's tea in the fridge and don't forget to feed the boys. If I'm not back by nine, make sure they're in bed.'

'Nine's too late, Mum,' said Sally, with her world-weary hat on.

While they negotiated the best time to put the twins away, I was wondering who Patrick was. Was he Sally's real-life actual father, back from living with his rich mistress? Or was he a new super-hunky personal trainer who insisted on all his clients wearing full make-up? Or perhaps he was…

'Who's Patrick?' asked Gemma. Sometimes you had to hand it to her for sheer…chutzpah, I think's the word. Cheek beyond her years, anyway.

'Patrick, darling?' said Liv, drawing out the drawl as much as she could. 'Patrick? Oh, *Patrick*.' You'd almost imagine she was playing for time. 'Patrick is the gardener. We go jogging together.'

Amazing. And not at all what I expected. Especially not since my image of a gardener is someone gnarled and wizened, wearing an old straw hat and leaning on a rake while he tells you all about what sort of manure goes with a clay soil.

'Patrick is very handsome,' said Sally rather innocently and also unnecessarily. I think we'd all got the picture by then.

'Right,' Liv was saying. 'I must dash. Have a nice time, and help yourself to whatever you'd like, but just don't go into the larder.' And she gathered up her keys and her phone, slamming the door behind her.

Obviously the first thing we had to do was find out what was in the larder.

'We mustn't,' said Sally, 'Mum will kill me.'

'Don't worry,' I said, 'We won't tell her if you don't.' What with being on the moral low ground, Sally wasn't in a position to fight back.

The larder door was locked, but after a five-minute search we found a large pile of keys under a shelf in the kitchen, and one of them was labelled 'Larder'.

'What do you reckon?' I said as I lifted the key. 'Dead bodies, drugs, illicit alcohol or stolen goods?'

I unlocked the door. Piled floor to ceiling were boxes and boxes of designer handbags. Every label you'd ever heard of. Each had at least three boxes and some many more, none of them brand new, and all with eBay labels; there must have been two or three hundred.

'Gosh,' said Amy. And I couldn't have put it better myself. So this was how Sally had the latest laptop. Her Mum was a secret eBay handbag dealer. Scratch the surface of any grown-up, I thought, and you didn't know what would just come tumbling out.

'Lock it up again,' said Sally, a bit nervously. 'Now I've got to forget I know about that. Honestly.'

'I guess we know what you're going to get for Christmas when you grow up. For the rest of your life,' said Gemma.

Time to focus on us, we decided. We gave Harris and Jock a large slice of pizza each, and put them in front of their favourite war game, got out an industrial quantity of ice cream from the freezer and settled down with Sally's giant yet lightweight state-of-the-art laptop.

I opened up all the charts and lists and felt quite impressed with our work so far. There was so much information and analysis, I felt sure that in time we could sell our research to Year Sevens and Eights, or at least write a bestselling book about it all.

There were plenty of boys with points for Hips and Humour, Random cuteness and general cool, but I thought we were getting cleverer at the implications of bad behaviour points. Things like not communicating, or not doing what they said they'd do. We'd learned valuable lessons from Project Wales (that is to say, mostly that the bigger the gang of boys, whether they're in an amusement arcade or on the beach, the more likely they are to be horrible to girls), and also from our observations of all the nice things about our great hopes for the Snog Fest.

'Look at Charlie,' I said to Amy. 'He's right up there, you know. What with the Compatibility and Suitability and Sustainability points he almost doesn't need the Hips and Humour points.'

'Oh, but he does!' said Amy. 'He's all-round lovely. And it's only fair you should record that. Just because he's so nice, doesn't mean he can't be beautiful, and funny.'

I thought Amy was overdoing it a bit, but I had to agree that Charlie was a bit special. And one shouldn't be prejudiced against good-looking people: they weren't necessarily vain or shallow. In fact, on the contrary, if anyone knew it was possible for a boy to be intelligent and thoughtful as well as handsome, it would be me…

'And my big news,' Amy was saying, 'is that he's asked me to a party at his on the Saturday of half term. Apparently it's a Night Off Revision Barbecue. I've said I'd go.'

A party? That Mark A* might be at? Versus going to Cornwall? Why was life so *difficult*? Then I reminded myself that I hadn't actually been invited.

'Well, I can't stand it any more,' said Sally. 'I'm just going to message Rob. I know I shouldn't according to all the rules, but I am. So there.' And she bent over her phone, her right thumb already a blur. All this Boy Watching talk had clearly tipped her over the edge.

'I notice,' said Gemma slowly, 'that you don't seem to have allocated too many points to my ex-friend Jezza.'

'Well, that would be because he's been nothing but trouble,' I said, sounding a bit like my mother. 'Does he actually deserve any points?'

'Of course he does: he's talented, and he's hot. Plus he fancies me,' said Gemma.

'But I thought…' I started, but I didn't finish.

'You're right, though. He doesn't deserve any points because he spends too much time following that little cow about. Besides, he's unbelievably selfish,' said Gemma.

'It's hopeless,' said Sally, curled up in a corner of the sofa and frowning at her phone. 'He's read it but he hasn't answered. He's ignoring me. Why didn't you TELL me not to message him?'

I wasn't going to answer that one.

We were coming to the end of our third huge carton of ice cream, so I thought it was time to move on.

Time to get the fourth one out and settle down to a movie. Not *Mean Girls* again, that would be silly, we practically know it by heart...

Moments later we were back in high school with Regina George.

Friends and Family

I woke up the following morning officially worried about Albert. There hadn't been a sign of a snuffle or a hint of a bark when I'd come back the previous night and it wasn't as if we hadn't made enough noise to wake him if he'd been there.

Liv had come back from her jog looking really healthy and well exercised. Gone were the shocking pink lipstick and the dangly earrings, and gone, in fact, was one of her false eyelashes. Obviously Patrick was a keen jogger, and hard to keep up with.

She was in a very good mood, and insisted that she drove us all home and saw us safely to our front doors. I was first on the list, which meant that everyone had to come up the stairs with me to see me into my flat.

It was all a bit embarrassing, especially as I could

hear Ghastly Stepdad shouting in the living room.

'Useless waste of space,' he was bellowing. 'Can't do the simplest thing. Just get in there, you *******—' He was sounding more and more like Webster's hooded owner in the park.

'Goodness,' said Liv. 'Doesn't your mother mind being spoken to like that?'

Just then my mother had come out of the kitchen carrying her favourite mug. (It had a picture of a crown on it and the words 'Mum Rules'. In the circumstances, probably one of the most ironic mugs in the world.)

'Hello, Liv,' she said. 'Thank you for bringing Chloe home. Sorry about Ralph, he gets very over-excited when he's watching football.'

I did say embarrassing, didn't I?

'I'm going to set up an Albert search party,' I announced over the breakfast table.

'I think Mr Underwood might have something to say about that,' said Ghastly Stepdad. 'It's his dog, after all. You interfere too much, that's your problem.'

Of all the people who might have the right to talk about my problems, my revolting stepfather was definitely not one of them. Also, I wasn't interfering, I was trying to help.

'She's only trying to help, Ralph,' Mum said. Mums are the best. In fact, Mums Rule.

At least I now knew what the crabby, hairy one's name was. I decided to use it when I talked to him, it would make me look more respectful.

I headed down the stairs, school bag banging against my leg – it was PE on a Tuesday in the summer term, which meant a heavy bag as well as something else to dread – and took all my courage in my hands and knocked on the door.

The door opened. Mr Underwood, as I must now learn to call the hairy, crabby one, was, for once, fully dressed. Although there were still vast expanses of hairy stomach in between the bottom of the T-shirt and the top of the jeans, at least most of the flesh was out of sight.

'What?' he said.

'I was just wondering, Mr Underwood,' I said in my best I'm-only-a-humble-schoolgirl kind of way, 'if there was any news of Albert.'

'There isn't, since you ask,' he said, 'he's still missing. Though I don't know what you propose to do about it.'

He was being sarcastic, but I took it as a cue.

'Perhaps I could make some 'Lost' notices to hang on trees and things, perhaps I could email all the offices around here, and the council,' I said. 'Have you got a picture of him?'

'There's one his previous owner had. Here,' he said, reaching for a framed photo on the shelf by the door.

There was Albert, in all his glory, in a beautiful frame. I think his previous owner must have just *cared* more.

'Thanks,' I said quickly before he could change his mind. 'I'll bring it back.' And I rushed off to the joys of Tuesday's timetable.

Sally's waiting place by the main gate was empty when I got there. I instantly felt a rush of hurt and betrayal, imagining that she was somewhere inside the school standing in a circle with the QB's cohorts, laughing at all the short, vile one's jokes. As I stood there, thinking the worst of my friend, I thought it would be such a good subject for my next blog. Loss of trust. And when it's lost, how hard it is to get it back.

'Chloe?' it was Sally, out of breath from running up the path to the entrance. 'I thought I was going to be late… Why are you looking so cross?'

I didn't think now was the time to tell her my theory of lost trust. After all, she wasn't *actually* standing in a circle with the QB's cohorts. I made a non-committal sort of noise, and together we headed off to English Lit with Mr Fanshawe, which was all that stood between us and the horrors of PE.

It was clearly another bad cold day for Mr Fanshawe, who was pale of face and red of nose. He was also croaky of voice. I could feel a sore throat coming on just listening to him telling us to sit down and be quiet.

It turned out to be a very good lesson to take our minds off PE, though. We'd moved on from the sad story of Boxer and all the pigs of *Animal Farm*, and were now getting to grips with the beginning of *Jane Eyre*.

We'd got to the bit where Jane's at Lowood School having a horrible time, and her only friend is Helen Burns. Helen is rather saintly, so, as all saintly people in works of literature seem to have to do, she contracts a fatal dose of tuberculosis. Eventually Jane is cradling the dying Helen in her arms. (This is where you want to jump in to the book and tell Jane to be careful. Not many people survived tuberculosis in those days, and it was incredibly contagious. But then you tell yourself that you wouldn't be reading a book called *Jane Eyre* if Jane Eyre herself dies of TB fifty pages into the book.)

Still, it's jolly well sad enough when Helen dies, and as I snuffled my way through the chapter (this was sad snuffling, not the Mr Fanshawe allergic snuffling) I thought how lucky we were to be alive and healthy and have lots of friends. There's nothing like a spot of tragic literature to put your troubles in perspective.

Plus, what with the Lost Trust theme, my next blog was shaping up to be a bit of a masterpiece.

'So, should I send him another message, do you think, or should I leave it till this evening?' Sally was saying as we headed off to PE. I was still thinking big thoughts about life and death and loyalty, the importance of friendship and making the most of things. So I obviously wasn't going to snap at my friend for banging on about Rob not having texted her.

'I think,' I said in my most patient voice, 'that you should leave it till this evening.'

At that moment we both had to put our

preoccupations aside for a while because we were approaching the chamber of hell. Or the gymnasium as it is occasionally known. I realise it is a cliché to call a gym a torture chamber, but how else would you describe a large room full of ropes and bars and pulleys and pieces of equipment designed to stretch you and generally inflict pain?

Amy was the only one of us who enjoyed this sort of thing. Because she was so agile and speedy she could climb things and jump over things and generally get from A to B incredibly efficiently. It was lovely to watch her do cartwheels and handstands because she was just so good at them.

It's a measure of how nice she is that nobody hates her for it.

Sally and I would cower in the corner, trying to be the last in the queue to do anything, and usually hoping to sprain our ankles within the first five minutes. Today, though, Sally was looking suspiciously smug. She went up to Miss Dinster, who presided over the whole gym torture thing as she did over the whole swimming torture thing, as soon as we arrived, and whispered in her ear.

Moments later, as we all emerged, changed into our gym kits, there was Sally sitting on a bench with an exceptionally self-satisfied expression on her face and all her proper clothes on.

I went up to her and hissed – it really was a hiss – 'What, just *what*, have you gone and done this time?'

'Warts,' she said, still with the horrible smug expression. 'All over, just like Harris. I told Miss Dinster she could check if she didn't believe me.'

Sally had played another Harris-and-Jock blinder.

The rest of us lined up to jump over some piece of apparatus or other, and as I fought my way to the back of the queue I determined to Google 'Infectious Diseases Caught From 16-Year-Old Boys'. Steve had to be good for something.

In the interests of my new rapprochement (a good word that, although weirdly like 'reproach' for something that is meant to mean the exact opposite) with Sally, I suggested she came back to mine and helped me prepare some Albert posters. Also, there'd been a St Thomas's sports day on Saturday, so there should be plenty of photos of the golden creatures to examine on their website.

When we got home – still no sound from Albert's flat

– we found Ralph out and Mum in. Definitely the best way round.

'Everything all right at school today?' asked Mum, wrestling with the curls on the kettle lead.

'Yes, it was great, thank you, Mrs Bennet,' said Sally in her best sucky-uppy voice. (I supposed she *had* had a great day, given that she'd spent gym sitting on a bench secretly playing with her phone.)

'Oh that's good, dear, it's nice to enjoy school at your age,' said Mum.

'We're going to take Ralph's laptop into my room to do some work, Mum,' I said. I wanted to break up this rather sickly love-in between Mum and Sally as soon as possible. I grabbed a bottle of lemonade and left Mum to watch her kettle boil (usually an extremely long process, probably something to do with the curliness of the lead).

'Right,' I said when we'd shut the door behind us. 'First we'll check out St Thomas's, then we'll make a poster for Albert.'

I opened up the computer, expecting to see the usual home page, but there were all those weird messages again. 'Liverpool 5 – 2'; 'Evens Arsenal and Spurs'; 'Newcastle 4 – 10'; 'Both Teams to Score'; 'Win/Draw/Win'. Most peculiar.

'Looks like your stepdad's got a thing going with betting on the football,' said Sally. Of course! Why hadn't I thought of that? But it looked so home-made... very puzzling.

'Here,' said Sally, rattling away at the keyboard. 'This is what we want.' And indeed it was.

The first pages had photos of all the under-sixteen and under-eighteen athletics teams in action. They were in the yellow St Thomas's strip, and they seemed to glisten all over as they jumped over hurdles, passed relay batons and hurled javelins. There were pictures of runners jumping over hurdles and into the water, and of triple-jumpers landing in the sand. It was like a sort of Extreme Day Out at the Seaside.

'Look, there he is,' Sally said as she pointed to a shot of four runners racing to the finishing line. The one in front was Rob. As he leant forward into the tape, his face was frozen into a leering grimace. He looked a little bit like a psychopath.

'Doesn't he look handsome?' said Sally.

It must be love, I thought, if you can confuse the rictus grin of a serial killer with handsomeness.

'I think I'm going to text him and say well done on winning the race,' she went on.

'And I think you're not going to do any such thing,' I

said. 'Do you *want* him to know you're stalking him on the school website?'

'OK,' she said, 'but I'm still going to text him.' And her right thumb was off before you could say, 'Better not.'

I left her to it as I went off to Ralph's scanner to scan Albert's picture so we could make him into a proper Missing Person poster. It took a bit of doing because he wouldn't come out of his photo frame. And in the struggle he got a bit torn. The scan was going to look as if there was already no hope for Albert, on account of him having been cut in half.

I was worrying about who we could get to Photoshop him as I went back into my room. Imagine my surprise at seeing a broadly smiling, utterly jubilant Sally grinning and gurning at her phone.

'Whatever's happened?' I asked, although I had a bit of a suspicion.

'He's only replied straight back,' said Sally looking up with such an expression of happiness that it would be difficult (though not impossible) to be cross with her. 'He says his sister's much better as they've bought her a puppy and she's got over her terror of dogs, and did I want to watch Shedz practise the weekend after half term.'

'Well, that's great. Really great,' I said. So she'd got her invitation to see Rob after all. She hadn't needed the Queen Beeeyatch to make that happen. Despite the fact that I was glad for her, I couldn't help thinking that she *needn't have betrayed me*.

But we had to spend at least ten minutes talking about the when and the what and the exactly how she would say, 'Yes please, I'd love to.' Which was all fine except it was getting late and Albert was still torn in half and we hadn't written his appeal.

MY NAME IS ALBERT. PLEASE HELP ME GET HOME I typed, in between listening to Sally tell me how Rob's Kind to Children and Animals points far exceeded anyone else's, and that now surely he had Suitability and Compatibility points to add to them.

'Also I think we need points for sporty things, don't you?' Sally was saying as I went on to type, I AM LOST AND UNHAPPY.

'After all, being good at sport and things is part of being Fit in every sense, isn't it?' she went on.

AND HUNGRY, I typed.

'Chloe? Don't you think?' Sally must have realised that just for once my attention wasn't fully focused on her. 'What are you doing?'

She came round to my side of the laptop and saw

my poster. Somehow Albert looked even more appealing with his back half not quite matching his front half.

'Aww,' said Sally. 'Poor Albert. That's a lovely poster, I do hope he sees it.'

'It's not really for Albert to see it,' I explained patiently, 'the point is for anyone who's seen him to see it.'

'Well, it's very nice, anyway, I'm sure he'll love it.'

I wasn't sure if Sally had really got the point, but I finished the poster by typing, PLEASE CONTACT MR UNDERWOOD, and his address. Then I added my phone number. That way I'd be the first to know when he was found.

'We'll get Ralph to print some of these at work,' I said, 'and we can see if the school will print some for us too. Then we'll go round the streets and stick them up on street lamps and things. The four of us. We'll do it tomorrow after school.' I felt a bit better now I had a plan of action.

Sally headed off back to Liv and the warty twins, and I closed the laptop and put it back in the sitting room.

Time for bed, and dreaming of Mark. And Albert.

Missing Links

Our last lesson on a Wednesday was Maths – another cruel joke from the Queen Mary's School timetable, saving the worst till last.

The hideous Miss Grunbar still barred Sally and me from sitting next to each other, so for every lesson she had to go to the front while I could cower at the back with Gemma. Poor Sally. I don't think the fact that her grades were getting better was any consolation.

Today Miss G was teaching us about probability: the probability of two coins both landing heads side up, and how there was only one way of them doing so until you added the probability of one head and one tail where there were two ways. By the time she added another coin and another set of probabilities the inside of my head was starting to make a strange buzzing noise.

Trying to distract myself from the buzzing, I started

to write Gemma a note about who was going to be in charge of putting up posters on which street lamps.

By the time I'd drawn a map of the area surrounding my house and the park, and divided the number of street lamps by the number of us, taking into account the distance between them, the buzzing noise was getting a lot louder.

'Perhaps Chloe can answer that.' Suddenly the buzzing noise wasn't the problem. 'How many options would there be?' Miss Grunbar was asking. Utterly unable to imagine what she was talking about, my mind flashed forward to being kept in detention for writing essays about street lamps, and yet another day going by without finding Albert.

Then out of the corner of my eye I could see that Sally had turned round from her front-row seat and was pointing in my direction. She seemed to be mouthing the word 'five'.

In for a penny, in for five pounds. 'Five,' I said confidently and boldly.

'That is correct,' Miss Grunbar sounded distinctly disappointed.

And I felt a warm glow towards my mathematical genius of a friend over there, learning stuff in the front row.

I gathered everyone up as soon as the bell rang, and went to the office to collect the pile of posters they'd let us print. Then we headed off to Ghastly Ralph and the job centre to collect the rest – Mum had persuaded him that it was all in a good cause and the least he could do was pay for some photocopies.

'We can stop at the coffee shop on the way,' said Gemma. 'That one the Year Eleven guys go to.'

I had a feeling Gemma's heart wasn't in Project Albert, but I told her every second counted, and we must get on to the job centre, and to the ghastly one.

The Jobcentre was strangely silent when we got there. I couldn't work out whether that was good or bad news – perhaps everyone already had a job, or perhaps there weren't any jobs to get. Either way, there was no sign of Ralph.

I went up to an elderly lady in glasses and grey hair sitting behind a computer. 'Excuse me,' I said, my best humble-schoolgirl voice coming into its own again, 'but I think Ralph, the manager, has left some posters for me.'

'For a start, young lady,' said the grey-haired lady, with a very cross look behind her glasses, 'Ralph is *not*

309

the manager. And for another start he no longer works here as of this morning.'

I was so shocked I felt a blush coming on. With a slightly sick feeling in the pit of my stomach, I could only stammer, 'But, what, what, did he, I mean, what happened?'

'I expect you'll find out soon enough, and in any case it's not for me to say,' she said. Then she seemed to take pity on me. 'But we did print your posters for you, they're out the back. Wait here, and I'll get them.'

'Blimey,' said Sally as we watched her disappear into a door at the back of the centre. 'Whatever's happened, do you think?'

'Probably been sacked for swearing at the punters,' said Gemma hard-heartedly, though I couldn't help but think it was a pretty good theory.

'There you are,' said the grey-haired lady, coming back with a big pile of Albert sliced in half, in full colour. Her expression softened a bit. 'I hope you find him.'

We headed out of the door, rather subdued. At least I was subdued, because if something had happened to Ralph it would upset Mum and...I decided to think about it later. For now we had to get postering.

Gemma volunteered to do the high-street lampposts, because, she said, it was on her way home. So, I realised, was the café where the St Thomas's Year Elevens go. That would be the last we'd see of Gemma, then, I thought, as she set off with her look-at-me-except-I-couldn't-care-less-if-you-don't   walk. (It consists of a kind of sub-catwalk stalk, a bit of nose in the air, and a bit of running your hand through your hair. So long as the expression is haughty enough, it doesn't look like you're actually seeking attention. Except it does. And you are.)

Then Amy said she'd do the lampposts round the park with the Dad Who, as they were going for a run together anyway.

'This running thing,' I said. 'You seem to be taking it rather seriously. Or is it that there's a good chance of bumping into Charlie if you go for a run in the park?'

'Don't be mean, Chloe,' said Sally, 'Amy's just brilliant at running. Not everything is about boys, you know.'

I almost gasped. This was mighty rich coming from Sally, who was still on very shaky ground anyway after the Great Betrayal. I was just about to round on her when Amy said, 'Actually it's a bit of both. I'd love to get into the under-fifteen team, but I'd also love to bump into Charlie.'

Sally and I were saved from having a terminal falling-out by the calming effect of Amy. In some ways, she's just more grown-up than us. Actually, in most ways.

Leaving Amy to head for her trainers and the park, Sally and I set off for the bus stop. Sally was chattering away about there being a good chance of Albert being recognised by someone in the park as he was probably famous there now, what with the fight with Webster and everything.

I was still seething inside and didn't say a word. I'm not as grown-up as Amy.

I had a bad feeling as I put my key in the lock. And not just because there was silence from Albert's flat. If something had happened to Ralph at the job centre, he'd be angry and Mum would be worried.

'That you, love?' came Mum's voice from the kitchen when I opened the door. Without even stopping to wonder who else it could be I just said, 'Yes, Mum, back now. We've put the posters up—' I stopped short as I came into the kitchen, seeing Mum and Ralph and Steve sitting round the table looking solemn.

Steve didn't even have any leads in his ears, it was that serious.

It was just like the Steve Joining the Army Bombshell evening, only this time the Ghastly Stepdad was looking uncharacteristically sheepish.

'It's Ralph,' said Mum. She turned to him and said, in a rather harsh voice for her, 'Tell Chloe what's happened.'

He looked up from his study of the pattern on the kitchen table, little goatee beard trembling very slightly. 'It's the Jobcentre. They found out about a little thing I had going on the footie. And now they say I'm surplus to requirements. Bloody unreasonable. What someone does in their spare time is none of their business.'

'It wasn't in your spare time,' said Mum, 'and it was illegal.' Her voice really did have a hard edge to it.

'Ralph's been operating a bookie scam on the office computer,' Steve said to me. 'Been taking bets on the football results. Surprise, surprise, they found out. Brilliant.' There was a note of triumph in Steve's voice. How satisfying he must find it to be in the right, and to have Ralph so utterly and completely on the back foot. Especially after he'd been given such a hard time about wanting to go into the army.

I looked at Mum. She looked weary, and angry and

shocked. There was no triumph in finding out that Ghastly Ralph was a scumbag – we knew that already.

'So what happens now?' I said. 'Can you appeal or something?'

'They're having a disciplinary hearing in four weeks' time. Till then he's suspended without pay,' said Mum in the same weary tone of voice.

Unbearable. So we'd be broke AND have the Ghastly Stepdad under our feet all the time. That did it. I was SO going to go to Cornwall for half term. Having the house full of testosteroned Steve and Steve-clone, and a grumpy, bored stepfather was too horrible to contemplate.

Poor Mum, though. In the middle of all my selfish thoughts I almost wondered if I could smuggle her down to Cornwall too.

After a long pause when no one said anything, Steve announced that he was going to watch the Match. Needless to say, Ralph followed hard on his heels.

(It is amazing how often those who love 'the beautiful game' refer to 'the Match' as though anyone and everyone should know which particular match they're talking about. I had very much wanted to have a separate category in our Boy Watching index which awarded loads of bonus points to any boy who had no interest at all in football. I was shot down, of course. After all, even supposing such a boy exists, he wouldn't admit to it. And I knew, in my heart of hearts, that Mark A* almost certainly loved watching football – you couldn't play it and not be interested in it.)

I sighed.

Not realising that I was sighing over the state of our nation's boyhood, Mum said, 'Try not to worry too much, love. I'm sure they'll let Ralph go back, and in the meantime he will get some part-time work.'

'I should jolly well hope so. Just so long as you don't have to work any harder, Mum,' I said. I got up and started to unload the dishwasher. I loathe emptying the dishwasher, almost as much as making a cup of tea or watching football. But somehow that evening I could almost see the point of housework as therapy.

It took me ages to get to sleep that night, what with worrying about Albert trapped in a cellar somewhere, our family about to go bankrupt, Steve getting killed somewhere indeterminate in the Middle East, Sally being best friends with the QB Maggie, and my probably never seeing Mark again because he'd joined a Premier League football team... So I guess I shouldn't have been surprised that I overslept by nearly an hour.

I rushed towards the bathroom, nearly knocking over my doomed soldier-brother on the way in ('God's SAKE, Chloe!') and pushing past a sleepy pyjama-ed stepfather on the way out ('Watch where you're going, can't you?') and barged into the kitchen to gulp down some orange juice ('You're going to be late, love').

As I tore down the stairs, I reminded myself that – in among all the other things I had to worry about – I must make sure that Gemma really meant it about going to Cornwall. A whole ten days with my beloved family would almost certainly end in tears, as Mum would say.

The bus stop was strangely quiet. For a moment I thought, That's great – the bus will be nice and empty, then I realised that I'd missed the bus and there wasn't another one for fifteen minutes. Fantastic.

I sat down to assess the damage. Missing registration and the first half of French could get me some proper black marks, but unless I could flag down a supercar to drive me to school there wasn't much I could do about it. I wished I'd taken a bit more time to clean my teeth...and have some breakfast...and put the right books into my school bag...

Just as I was sinking into self-sorryness, my phone rang. An unknown number. Having nothing else to do, I answered it. 'Hello,' I said in the sort of voice you use when you expect something mysterious and/or unpleasant.

'Is that Mrs Underwood?' said a man's voice. For a moment my imagination ran riot. Supposing I WERE Mrs Underwood – what a horrible life I'd have, washing the old crabby one's T-shirts and pyjamas, watching daytime TV with him, going to endless freezing cold Civil War re-enactments, listening to his sexist comments... But before I had time to answer the voice went on: 'I saw your notice about the border terrier. I think he might be the one we've got here. He doesn't have a collar, but he looks a bit like the one in the poster I saw this morning.'

'Oh, that's wonderful,' I almost cried down the phone. 'He's been lost for a week, and we were so worried.'

'Is that Mr Underwood's daughter?' said the man, obviously realising that I sounded way too young to be a Mrs. That only made me imagine myself as Miss Underwood. Probably living on a diet of processed meat and football on TV and deeply ashamed at the thought of anyone meeting my dad, especially when he was in his helmet and breastplate. Just as I realised that that was pretty much what life was like as Ralph's stepdaughter, without the helmet, I heard the man go on, 'Should I speak to Mr Underwood himself?'

'No, it's fine,' I said quickly, relieved at not having to lie about the being-his-daughter thing. 'Perhaps I could come and get him? I could come now if that's all right?' It was a little bit reckless to abandon all thought of trying to get to school. In that second, though, I reckoned I was going to get into fearful trouble for being late for school anyway, but if I could find Albert it would all be sort of worthwhile.

'Well, OK. That would probably be rather a good idea. He's a bit of a handful. I don't think he was listening in his obedience training classes.'

'I'm sorry,' I said, somehow feeling that Albert's bad behaviour must be my fault. 'If you tell me how to get to you, I'll come and pick him up straight away.'

Albert's rescuer started to give instructions. Get the number 15 bus to the second stop after Jubilee Road, turn right past the school gates, and go into the big house next to the school.

I almost let out a little scream. That was only Mrs Munroe's house. The fearsome headmistress, she who must be obeyed, if not hidden from. I was being told to go to school after all, and not just school, but straight to the headmistress's house; an even more terrifying prospect than the headmistress's office.

I thought of going back home but Mr Underwood wouldn't be there, nor would Mum, and I hardly wanted to send Ghastly Ralph to Mrs Munroe's house, even if he was around (and not having a 'flutter' at the bookies' or a 'sharpener' in the pub).

'So, see you shortly. I'll be around all morning,' said Albert's rescuer. 'Bye, then.'

What a fine pickle. What an astonishingly huge and rich pickle – the biggest, hugest, richest pickle that I'd ever come across in all my life. Though even as I hyperventilated in my panic, I found myself wondering about the origins of the pickle, and how it could be both a disaster and the thing you ate with cheese.

My inner ravings were interrupted by the arrival of a number 15 bus.

The doors slowly opened with their familiar long-drawn-out ssshush noise, and as I stepped up into the bus and they ssshushed shut behind me I felt like I was hearing the noise of my fate being sealed.

Needless to say the bus drove at terrific speed towards Jubilee Road – buses always have a way of getting you there quickly when you don't want to get 'there'. (Traffic jams only happen when you're very late and desperate to get to your destination. Bennet's Law of Travel #34.)

I got off the bus a stop later than the one near the school. I reckoned I could travel backwards to the school with less chance of being seen.

Creeping along the school railing side of the street I must have looked rather suspicious. I suppose I thought being bent double and trotting along quite quickly would somehow make me less conspicuous and recognisable, but I expect I just managed to look like a character who thinks they're being followed in a comedy film, played by a bad actor.

All too soon I was standing in the imposing doorway of the headmistress's house and ringing the doorbell. As I heard its deep buzzing noise I realised that being dressed in the Queen Mary school uniform was a bit of a giveaway, but too late to worry about that now…

There was the sound of distant slightly hysterical barking as the door was opened by a very tall man of about thirty. He had a long face and brown curly hair – just like his mother's.

'There you are,' he said. Clearly stating the obvious was in the Munroe genes as well as the Bennet ones. 'Shouldn't you be at school?' Still with the obvious theme, then. Plus I couldn't help wondering whether he shouldn't be at work. Fortunately I managed to resist saying this out loud.

'Not till this afternoon,' I said brightly, quite pleased with this half-truth. I followed him into the hall and past a huge wooden staircase and an ancient painting of a stern-looking man in a pointy hat (he looked a bit like a Puritan; it wouldn't surprise me if Mrs M was descended from Oliver Cromwell).

We went into a brightly lit, ultra-modern looking kitchen at the back of the house, where the sound of hysterical barking got very loud indeed. A large and noisy ball of fur with legs attached came hurtling towards me. I was half delighted that Albert was so pleased to see me, and half terrified that he'd break some irreplaceably expensive electronic gadget en route.

'We've had to shut him in here because of Hortense,' said the tall one. 'She's our poodle, and rather nervous of terriers. Has your dog been done?'

As I was meant to be Albert's owner I guessed I should have known about whether he'd 'been done'. But I was still reeling at the thought of calling a dog Hortense, and, not having the faintest idea whether Albert could spawn a little brood of Alberts or not, I played it safe. 'Oh yes, I'm sure he has,' I said, now really anxious to get out of this thoroughly grown-up and frightening house and away from this thoroughly grown-up and frightening man – who by now was looking at me rather suspiciously through narrowed eyes.

'Well, thanks, then. Thanks,' I said. 'And, er, bye.' I dragged Albert, who was wearing a collar and lead I'd never seen before, and which probably would have to be returned to Hortense, towards the bus stop.

There was no sign of Mr Underwood when I got home, but the Ghastly One was at home all right, fast asleep in front of a programme about the breeding habits of the ring-tailed lemurs of Madagascar.

I told him he must look after Albert for the rest of the day till Mr Underwood came back. There was a lot of harrumphing, which was still going on as I went downstairs and let myself out of the flat.

Once again on the number 15 bus, I looked at my phone. It was lunchtime by now and I'd collected sixteen messages from the others, which ranged from 'Where u? U late' (Sally, 9.01 a.m.) and 'Hope you ok Xxx' (Amy, 9.23 a.m.) to 'Now worried. U all rite?' (Sally,

11.21) and 'U R in DEAD troubs dork! X' (Gemma, 12.46 p.m.).

The first lesson after lunch was English and Drama – the most important lesson of the week, partly because, obviously, of my love of language and literature and partly because it was when our acting skills were assessed for the all-important joint play with St Thomas's. I really didn't want to miss it.

I marched boldly through the main entrance and headed towards our form room to try to find Mrs Slopeth, who was taking the register that week. She was just coming out of the room as I approached.

'Chloe,' she said slowly and sternly.

I steeled myself. 'Yes, Mrs Slopeth. I'm very sorry I'm so late, but I felt so ill this morning, with a temperature and everything, and a bit sick, and there was no one to write me a note, but now I feel a lot better and I think I'm going to be all right, and I'm very sorry I'm so late. Very sorry.'

A part of me felt that I was being suspiciously apologetic for someone who was so ill and had only just managed to struggle in to school. But it was too late to change my strategy now.

'If you have been feeling so ill, Chloe, we need to get you to the nurse. You could be harbouring a

Hazardous Infection; you could be Highly Contagious. We don't want you spreading Nasty Diseases.' Mrs Slopeth managed to make me sound truly Capital Letters Dangerous. She grabbed me by the elbow and steered me firmly towards the nurse's office.

Hellfire, I was going to miss English and Drama, on the very day when I knew they were going to be reading through bits of *A Midsummer Night's Dream*. Just my luck if the QBM gave some brilliant reading of the queen, and Mark was cast as her husband.

'Open wide,' Nurse Watkins was saying. After a full inspection of my tonsils, and a bit of temperature-taking, she deemed me fit to go back to classes – too late for English and Drama, but just in time for Chemistry. I think that is known as a (capital letters) Double Whammy.

'So now you've got Albert back, you can stop worrying and start planning half term,' said Gemma as we headed out of school at the end of my very short afternoon. (The good news was that nobody was going to be cast for the play till after half term, so I could yet be Queen Chloe to King Mark...) 'Amy's got her big date on Saturday, but Sally's not having her Shedz moment till the next Saturday, so you two can get on a train and come down to Cornwall.'

'Brilliant,' said Sally. 'I asked Mum about it and she said it was OK because she could get Patrick to help look after the twins.'

'He's a bit of a renaissance human being, this Patrick, isn't he?' I said. 'Not only skilled in gardening and cross-country running, but also childcare.'

'Yes, that's true,' said Sally. 'Also, of course, he's incredibly good looking.'

'Like I said. No end to his skills...

'It would be great, Gem,' I went on, 'But what with Ralph and the joblessness I don't know where I'd get the train fare from.'

'Not a prob. Merv still owes me. I've told him I'm going to see Mum, and he's said he'll pay my fare and a friend's. I'll just tell him that'll be three train fares.'

'I want to come too!' said Amy. 'But I guess I want to go Charlie's party even more...'

'Course you do,' I said. 'But you've got to promise to give us full reports. You're going to have responsibility for all Boy Watching, with special emphasis on any Mark or Jezza or Rob activity. After all, you're probably the only one of us who doesn't have to panic about having a date for the Snog Fest.'

'We've still got eight weeks, though,' said Sally. 'That's eight weeks for Rob to get to know and love me after I go to his Shedz practice.'

I couldn't decide whether her self-centred optimism was more endearing or irritating.

Going West

By the time I'd got home, the Albert handover had already happened. He and Ghastly Ralph hadn't bonded at all – perhaps Albert simply wasn't interested in the breeding habits of the ring-tailed lemurs of Madagascar – and so as soon as Ralph heard Mr U put his key in the door he'd rushed downstairs with the errant Albert in his arms. Apparently Mr U had just grunted, taken off the Hortense collar and lead and given them to Ralph ('That's not his. Don't want people accusing me of stealing stuff.') and shut the door in his face.

'Effing needs to be taught some manners, that one,' said Ralph later. This was rich, I couldn't help thinking, but it takes one rude fat slob to know another... Was what I thought, but didn't say.

But meanwhile, the news of my trip to Cornwall had

gone down very well – even with Mum, who said she was going to miss me but it was nice that I was going to have a bit of a holiday, and perhaps it was just as well that there'd be one less person on the bathroom rota.

Kevin-the-clone was due to arrive on the Friday night of half term, and my escape to the sea was booked for first thing that morning. Everything was working out perfectly.

'Don't forget to bring me back some Cornish ice cream,' Steve instructed me two weeks later as I was packing. Before I could tell him what a dork he was, he added: 'Gemma got a boyfriend down there, has she?'

Ah ha. From that little remark, I realised that my oily older brother had a bit of a crush. Poor Steve. I didn't have the heart to tell him that the chances of him making me Gemma's sister-in-law were nought to minus five hundred. 'Yup,' I said, 'and one here too.' Best to exaggerate to make a point and put him out of his misery quickly.

Sally and I arrived at the hideous electric gates of Merv's mansion at exactly the same time. Merv was going to drive us all to the station. I suppose being shut up in a car with acres of splitting black denim and Merv's awkward conversation was a small price to pay for getting to the train on time.

Except we very nearly didn't get to the train on time.

Merv's job was a simple one, to get us to the 09.45 to Penzance, but he had a habit of commenting on the colour, size and shape of pretty well every passing car. And every time he said something he slowed down to about thirty-five mph. It was as if his Merv-shaped brain couldn't manage the two tasks at once – talking and driving.

It made for an incredibly stressful journey. I saw the clock click through…8…8.30…9.00…and still we were twenty miles away. We absolutely had to catch the 09.45 – it was the only train our tickets were valid on, plus Gemma's mother was meeting it the other end.

'You'd better step on it, Mervyn,' came Gemma's voice from the back (I was in the short-straw front seat again), 'or we'll miss the train.' The steely tone had the desired effect, and we drew up to the platform entrance at 09.39. Phew.

We had three seats together at a table; plenty of space for Sally's magazines, Gemma's iPad, and me to relax back while looking out of the window. The other seat was occupied by a blond boy of about eighteen who was deeply engrossed in something that was playing on his own iPad.

When he looked up at us for a second – only a second, clearly whatever was on the iPad was a lot more interesting than we were – you could see he had dazzling blue eyes. Plus he was very tanned. And fit. In every sense.

But I was distracted from this particular piece of Boy Watching by Sally. As she settled into her seat, she took off her jersey. Underneath it she was wearing one of her thin T-shirts. It was quite a fetching green colour and was mercifully free of any instruction to love people with ginger hair. So far so good. What really wasn't so good was the fact that her arms and neck were an eye-poppingly bright shade of orange.

We both looked at her. Aghast, I think is the word.

'Sally,' I said slowly. 'Have you been exposed to some form of radiation? Is it actually safe to sit near you?'

'What do you mean?' said Sally defensively. 'I only put on some Glorious Bronze to top up my tan.'

'Tan?!' we chorused as one. If there was one thing you'd have to say about Sally, after you'd said she had red hair, was that she had skin that was naturally the colour of the brightest gloss white paint you've ever seen. Tan, indeed.

'I'm rather hoping,' said Gemma, 'that the rest of you isn't that colour. Because if we go to the beach, and I'm now thinking that might not be such a good idea, you are going to glow like a beacon. We will attract attention in a way I hadn't really reckoned on...'

Out of the corner of my eye, I could see Blond Boy – whose real tan was looking even more super rich next to Sally – give the slightest of smiles. His eyes were still fixed on his iPad screen, but I had a feeling he'd turned the sound down a bit.

'I think you're being horrible,' said Sally. 'Mum said it'd probably come off in the sea, anyway. Actually, I think most of it came off on the sheets last night. She was quite cross, now I come to think about it.'

'We might pop you in the shower when we get there, then,' said Gemma. 'Juliet likes bold colours but more in her paintings than on her sheets.'

Sally buried herself in her magazines and her phone at that point. Gemma turned back to her iPad, and I got out my copy of *To Kill a Mockingbird*. It wasn't a book we actually had to read, but Miss Brewer had said it was remarkable and important so I thought that – being a future prize-winning author with a Love of Literature – I should read it.

Scout was just about to get into a fight, despite Atticus Finch telling her not to, as we drew in to Penzance. I'd been so engrossed in my book that the train manager's announcement gave me a jump.

Blond Boy was getting off too, so we found ourselves heading to the exit door together. 'Great book, isn't it?' he said to me as I struggled down the passage with my heavy suitcase (I'd read that Cornwall's got an unpredictable climate, so I'd packed for every kind of weather).

'Oh yes, it's wonderful,' was all I had time to say in the scrum for the door.

As we all jumped off the train I thought how one day everyone would just read books off screens, so you'd never know if someone was reading *To Kill a Mockingbird* or, say, *The Diary of Anne Frank*. I thought that was a shame. And a missed opportunity for getting to know members of the opposite sex...

The sound of seagulls was almost deafening as we got out of the train. And there, almost immediately next to the platform, was the sea.

'Look!' said Sally. 'The sea!' It was rather exciting to see it, so I thought that I'd resist the temptation to point out to Sally that she sounded like the text of an early learning picture book.

The three of us headed towards the exit barrier, all a little bit nervous in our different ways.

It wasn't difficult to spot Gemma's mum and Juliet. Standing by the ticket office was a large flamboyant-looking lady in a bright orange dress. The orange – clearly this was going to be a bit of an orange half-term all round – contrasted brilliantly with the deep black of her skin. Next to her was a tall, slim, rather terrifyingly elegant-looking woman in a black trouser-suit, with thick blond hair pulled back from her face.

Catching sight of Gemma, they both smiled and waved. The smiles and the waves made them look less terrifying, and as we got nearer I realised they looked older and nicer close up.

'Gemma, darling,' said her mother hugging her close. She turned to us as Gemma was enfolded in Juliet's ample embrace.

'It's lovely that you're here. Chloe, isn't it? And

Sally? I'm Marianne.' Her voice was sort of soft and unexpectedly gentle, but she had an air about her. The kind of 'air' of a person who wouldn't suffer fools at all gladly.

I decided to try very hard not to be a fool.

They led us to a giant, mud-spattered four-by-four. It smelt of dogs and was quite unlike the shiny sheen of Merv's new-car-smelling jeep.

After twenty minutes or so we arrived at a big stone house perched perilously near the edge of a cliff just outside a small town.

'Gosh,' said Sally brightly. 'It's huge. But it looks like it might fall in any moment.'

'It's been like that for 150 years, so I'm rather hoping it'll stay like that for a bit longer. Or for as long as we're staying around, anyway,' said Juliet. She led us into the sitting room, with its huge, panoramic view of the sea.

I was so bowled over I made a gasping noise. Which sounded a bit babyish, so I just about managed to change it into a cough. It was only the second bit of sea I'd ever seen properly. And it looked unspoilt and beautiful – quite unlike the built-up beach in Wales.

Just off the other side of the room was the doorway into Juliet's studio. I could vaguely make out big splashes of bright colours on the walls beyond. A real-life artist. I had the fleeting thought that perhaps she could teach us to draw caricatures of Miss Grunbar. But I let it fleet away. It was a foolish thought...

Juliet took us up to our room – which was the whole of the top floor, a kind of open-plan dormitory with a sea view if you climbed up on the bed and looked out of one of the tiny, high windows. It must have been the maids' quarters in the olden days – when the poorer and more servanty you were the less view you got.

The sun had come out, so we decided to go straight down to the beach to see, as Gemma said, if Sally's orange would wash off.

As we walked past the cluttered kitchen on our way out, I could see Juliet and Gemma's mother – who one day I might have the courage to call Marianne, but probably not until I am about forty or fifty – chopping a lot of vegetables that seemed to come in shapes and colours I'd never seen before.

'Have a nice time, but don't be late back,' called out Juliet. 'We're having my special green curry tonight.' As I followed the others outside, I tried not to look nervous. A curry was something I usually associated with Ghastly Ralph, beer and burping.

But once we got down to the beach there were

plenty of things to worry about other than curries. For a start the shingle was agony on my feet, my swimming costume lay hideously flat on my chest, and I realised I'd forgotten to put nail varnish on my toenails. Plus I could feel my fake tan make-up dripping down my face in the heat, and my hair was starting to go frizzy in the sea air.

As I tried to hide all this ugliness with my towel I watched Sally run at high speed towards the sea. She was not so much orange all over as splodged and dappled all over. I really hoped for her sake that the salty sea water would have fantastic exfoliating properties.

Gemma meanwhile looked absolutely fabulous. The I-don't-care-if-you're-looking-or-not stalk walk was ideal for the beach, especially as her bikini fitted perfectly and her hair was staying immaculately straight in the slight breeze. Obviously she is a good friend, and we were only here in this lovely place because of her. Otherwise I think I could find it in my heart to take a violent dislike to her.

'Hi,' came a boy's voice behind me. I turned round. It was Blond Boy from the train. He was looking browner and blonder than ever in a black surfer wetsuit, and was dripping wet and carrying a surfboard.

'Oh, hello,' I said, trying to drape my towel over my flat chest, wipe the make-up drips off my face and pull my hair straight, all at the same time. 'Have you been surfing?'

Brilliant, brilliant, brilliant. A hundred out of ten for genius conversation. That will really knock 'em dead in the aisles. I should sell my advice on the internet. How to Dazzle Men and Win Friends With Witty Sayings and Wise Words. Oh yes.

'Can't deny it,' he said with a nice smile. I immediately gave him full Boy Watching points for Humour and Kindness. (He'd already scored heavily in the Hips, Bums and Fit categories. Did he but know it. Which I rather suspect he did.)

We were walking towards the sea and by this time had caught up with Gemma. 'Are you all going to try some surfing?' he asked, looking towards Gemma.

I was beginning to see a little bit of how the land lay.

'I'm Jack, by the way. Jack Harrington,' he said, now definitely looking towards Gemma.

'Hi,' she said coolly, but not unfriendlily. 'I'm Gemma, this is Chloe, and the one in the sea is Sally. But no, we've only just got here, and I don't think any of us are really equipped for water sports.'

'A friend of mine could teach you…I could lend you

a board,' said Jack, by now making no pretence of talking to anyone other than Gemma.

'Maybe tomorrow,' said Gemma, still coolly. 'Might rain. Anyway see you in the morning, perhaps.'

As I watched Jack Harrington smile goodbye and head off up the beach, I realised that it was always going to be Gemma who was the one who should sell advice on the internet.

Fortunately Sally distracted us at that point by coming pounding up the beach looking pleased and excited. 'See!' she said. 'It's all gone a lovely even colour. I expect it's designed to go all smooth when it comes into contact with salt water.'

We didn't have the heart to tell her she looked exactly as splodgy and dapply as she had before.

The dreaded curry turned out to be delicious; slightly burny on the mouth, but generally almost as good as a Scotch egg. It was altogether a nice evening; looking out over the sea, eating strange food and listening to Juliet and Marianne talk about the exhibition. I felt I'd entered a whole new world.

And the next morning was another whole new world.

We spent the morning on the beach while Juliet and Marianne went to St Ives to supervise the hanging of Juliet's pictures.

We'd had a flurry of messages from Amy, who was worrying about what to wear to Charlie's party. (Jeans and a lacy top, like she was wearing when they met after the park, or favourite green dress, or something else entirely. We all gave her different advice, which is what friends are for.) But otherwise we focused on having a great day on the beach.

To my surprise – not – we saw Jack Harrington as soon as we got near the sea. He was with two other surfer boys, but came over towards us as soon as he saw us – or, rather, saw Gemma.

I had my hair up, my toes painted, no dripping make-up, and a swimsuit with a halter neck that almost gave the effect of almost having a cleavage. But I think I might as well have been wearing Ghastly Ralph's ghastly plastic mac for all the notice Blond Boy was taking.

As he started to talk to Gemma about the joys of surfing, I turned to Sally – who was looking a bit less splodgy after her morning's hour-long shower – and suggested we went for a swim. I know. Radical behaviour when at the seaside, but the sea looked rather inviting (so different from a swimming pool) and, who knew, perhaps there were other boys who might want to explain the joys of surfing.

As it turned out, there weren't other boys who wanted to explain the joys of anything to us. By this time Sally and I had skin like prunes from being in the sea so long, and we'd decided we'd extracted all the fun we could from beach-time. Besides, it was time to get ready for the preview of the exhibition at the gallery.

Gemma and her new admirer were sitting at the bottom of the steps going down to the beach. As we approached she got up quickly, nodded to Jack, and came towards us.

'Well, that was awkward,' she said.

'Which bit of having an incredibly handsome boy *obviously* slithering over you is awkward?' said Sally.

'I think you mean "slavering",' I said, because you've got to get these things right, even when you're on holiday. 'But, quite, Gemma. Didn't look very awkward to me.'

'Turns out he used to go to St Thomas's when he was little, and he knows *all* of them. Mark, Jezza,

Rob, everybody. He's threatening to go up and see them all.'

'But that's good, isn't it?' I said. 'That way Jezza gets to see that a boy a lot more handsome than he is has got a thing for you. Might make him concentrate.'

'Too complicated,' said Gemma. 'I like to keep these things separate.'

Goodness, she's sophisticated. A boy in every port, isn't that the phrase? Something to indicate too many, anyway. Or more than the rest of us, that's for sure.

By the time we were de-sanded and dressed in our best going-out-to-something-grown-up clothes (mostly jeans, crop tops, high heels and loads of eyeliner – plus huge dangly earrings if you were Gemma) we'd had twenty messages and pictures from Amy. I think she was getting excited, and from the selfie of her – looking great in a red dress we'd never seen before – we decided she was going to be OK.

Juliet was strangely stiff and silent when we got back to the house. No smiles, no chat – all a bit puzzling. I must have looked as confused as I felt, because Marianne caught my eye and said, 'First night nerves. Always like this. Having your own show is like putting on any performance, the spotlight's on you and you hold yourself up to criticism.'

We all got into the car promptly at 6.00 p.m. 'Don't forget we've got to pick up Sue Baroo on the way back,' said Marianne.

'She's our dog,' said Juliet, addressing us via the rear-view mirror. 'She's got four-by-four energy, and came from a Japanese friend of ours. Sue Baroo, geddit?'

I didn't, but I smiled politely. I've come to the conclusion that most problems in dealing with adults who are much cleverer than you are can be solved by staying quiet and smiling politely.

'Subaru is a make of Japanese four-by-four car,' Gemma said, who knew me well enough to know I'd want to know. 'And Sue Baroo's been staying at St Ives so she can be impregnated by some large and expensive dog or other who gives good puppy.'

Somehow that piece of information made me feel sick. I couldn't think why – it wasn't that we were driving jerkily, or the curry was having some kind of belated bad reaction. Then I realised it was because deep down I had an absolute conviction that Albert hadn't 'been done'. And that with him being young and strong and very enthusiastic it was more than likely that – even as we drove – Hortense was carrying five, six, or maybe more little Albertenses or Horberts.

'How long does it take for puppies to come into being?' I asked in a carefully idly-curious sort of way.

'About eight to ten weeks,' said Juliet. 'It depends on the breed. We'll know if Sue's pregnant in two or three weeks.'

Gawd. What a splendid thing to worry about when I got back.

But for now we'd arrived at the gallery, a big round, white building overlooking the sea. There were lots of people standing on the steps, and when Juliet got out of the car she was immediately surrounded by them. Several pushy-looking men in the front row had huge cameras and were calling out Juliet's name.

So this is what it would be like to be famous, I found myself thinking. This is what it would be like to be walking up the red carpet as I arrive for the premiere of the movie based on my prize-winning book. 'Chloe, Chloe, look this way,' they'd be saying. And I'd have my hair up and my nails done professionally, I'd be wearing the latest couture – and my eyebrows would be immaculate.

'Gosh,' Sally was hissing in my ear, 'she's really

famous. Do you think we'll be on the news?'

'She might be. We won't,' I hissed back as we followed Juliet and the photographers up the steps.

The exhibition was packed, but we could just about see the pictures that everyone was making such a fuss about. Juliet's paintings were big and bold and mostly of people and faces – but often distorted and sometimes unrecognisable.

I wasn't really sure what to make of it all, so I started listening to what people were saying. 'The divide between abstraction and representation... 'She diagrams a full engagement...' 'Mixture of radical and conservative forces...'

No wonder Mr Pampledousse looks so worried and puzzled all the time, I thought. He probably doesn't understand all this stuff either.

But everyone seemed very pleased with how things were going. Juliet and Marianne were drinking champagne and smiling at the people who were queuing to talk to them, and Gemma was somehow the centre of attention too.

Sally and I went outside to check our phones for reports of Charlie's party. They started with two more Amy selfies. The first in her green dress, the second back in the red dress. It looked like the red dress had won in the end.

Then there was a gap. And then a bit later:

Gr8 BBQ. Charlies bn lovely.

And then another gap and:

Theyre all here!!!! Mark Jezza Rob!

And then nothing.

How annoying was that? I wished Amy could stream a video of what was happening at the party, but perhaps she had better things to do than film everything that was going on. I hoped so, anyway.

'Well, that's great,' said Sally. 'Leaving us in suspense like that. But s'pose we'll just have to wait till Amy calls us tomorrow.'

I thought she was being amazingly phlegmatic (I think I mean phlegmatic – calm, anyway) until I remembered that she was the one with the date next Saturday. She actually had an arrangement to see Rob and Shedz, which he'd actually confirmed in an actual message before we'd got on the train.

But she was right, there was nothing we could do about it, so we went back into the noisy inside where people were getting ready to go.

Later that night, as we settled back in to our attic dormitory ('Just like Enid Blyton,' said Sally, 'we should have a midnight feast.'), we could hear Sue Baroo barking downstairs.

'She's clearly over-excited,' said Gemma, 'and therefore almost certainly pregnant.'

I went to sleep and dreamt of little Albert-shaped puppies crowding round the barbecue as Amy and Jack Harrington glided overhead on an outsize surfboard which was being held up by Juliet and Mark A*.

Drummer Boy

I'd just got to the bit where Mark was photographing me in full evening dress swimming up the steps to the art gallery, when a seagull landed on my head with a loud squawk. I opened my eyes to see that the seagull was real, and really squawking outside the window, and that Sally had just thrown a pillow at me.

'Time to get up,' she said. 'Gemma's gone off with her mother somewhere, so let's go to the beach café, do some Boy Watching, and ring Amy.'

What a little bundle of energy my BFF can be. I was still sleepy, and tired from all the swimming and surfing I'd been doing all night, but before I knew it we were sitting outside the café with large glasses of fizzy, icy drinks in front of us. Delicious.

'Oh no!' Sally was hunched over her phone.

'What's the matter?' I said. It sounded serious.

Perhaps the twins had been hospitalised again, or perhaps Liv had had an accident under the influence of Mr Pinot Grigio, or...

'This glass contains the equivalent of fifteen teaspoons of sugar,' said Sally, with a worried frown.

'Well, you sure know how to spoil a good time,' I said. 'Honestly, we're on holiday, do we have to count teaspoons?' But it was too late. Sally had a new app that told her how much sugar was in everything she ate. We were going to be martyrs to her battle with a sweet tooth for the rest of the week.

'Let's call Amy,' I said, partly to distract her from her joyless calculations, and partly because I was now desperate to know what had happened at Charlie's party.

We put her on speakerphone and dialled. Amy picked up on the first ring.

'It was so great, you wouldn't believe how lovely Charlie was, he introduced me to all his family, they're lovely too, and the barbecue was just beyond fab, with this huge garden, and it went on very late, and you'll never guess what happened at midnight, only Charlie put his arms round me, and he said I was adorable, and did I think I might like him as much as he liked me, and he's properly asked me to the Snog Fest, and it was all so amaaaazing... How's Cornwall?'

'That's so brilliant about Charlie. Cornwall's lovely – Juliet and Gemma's mum are very nice, but a bit scary, and the house is great, and a handsome boy is pursuing Gem. Did you talk to Mark – and Rob – and what happened?' I said, by now really wanting to get to the nub of the matter.

'Well,' Amy was sounding a bit less bouncy now. 'Rob was sweet – he came over and said wasn't I with the dog who nearly got bitten to death in the park, and we had a nice chat, and he mentioned seeing Sally on Saturday.'

The squawk that came from Sally at that nearly drowned the real squawks from all the seagulls circling the café. Hurrah for Rob and Sally, but...

'And Mark?' I said. 'He was there too wasn't he?'

'Yes, he was,' Amy was sounding quite a lot less bouncy now. 'But the thing is, Maggie was there too, and she seems to have forgotten she's supposed to fancy Jezza because she was, well, she was sort of all over Mark. I mean, I don't think it was coming from him or anything, but she was sort of hanging on his every word and doing her Gosh You're Funny And Clever And I'm So Looking Up At You act.'

Great. Of course if you're as short as QBM you

pretty much look up at everyone, but I knew what Amy meant. That admiring, adoring upward-gazing expression. Yuck. And double yuck. Surely Mark of all people wouldn't fall for it...

'Which meant,' Amy was going on, 'that Jezza looked a bit put out. And he twice came over to us and asked where Gem was and why wasn't she there.'

So much information to process here. For a start there was the 'us'. Amy was talking coupley already. And then there was the inescapable conclusion that the beeeeyatch had turned her attention to Mark. Which was good news for Gemma, if she wanted it to be, and horrible news for me.

I puzzled over all this as I finished my fifteen teaspoons of sugar and watched the surfer boys doing their surfing thing in the sea. Sally had abandoned her sugar and was taking artful pictures of the sea and putting them on Instagram for all sixteen of her followers.

We walked back to the house to find Gemma. She needed to know that Jezza was pining, plus we had to take Sue Baroo for a walk.

By the time we got to the end of the week, Sally's

skin was a glorious even bright white, mine was perpetually wrinkly from all the salt water, and Gemma's perfect smooth tan had attracted at least three more surfer boys anxious to introduce her to the joys of the surfboard.

The news of Jezza being newly available and keen to see her had been given a pretty frosty reception, but I was sure that deep down Gemma was a little bit pleased to hear that her absence seemed to have made his heart grow fonder.

Friday came all too soon and it was time to head back home. We packed up the dormitory and squeezed ourselves into Juliet's car. Sue Baroo was in the back barking like crazy – perhaps that's just what you do if you're full of puppy – but otherwise we were all a bit quiet and sad that our Cornish holiday was over.

We got out at the station entrance and said our goodbyes and thank-yous. Marianne's expression as she hugged Gemma goodbye was so loving and pained that I had to look away. But otherwise it was all light-hearted laughing and lots of 'see you next time', which I found very cheering.

It was a long journey, and by the time I got to the bus stop where Ghastly Ralph was supposed to be meeting me, my suitcase felt like it was full of all the sugar in the world, plus all the teaspoons to measure it with.

'You're late,' said my stepfather as I struggled off the bus.

Yes, and merry Christmas to you too, I thought.

'The train got delayed at Plymouth,' I said, too tired to pretend to make conversation. I got into the old Peugeot, and as I smelt the familiar smell of stale beer and fresh methane, suddenly felt incredibly depressed.

'How's Mum?' I said. 'And how was Kevin? Has he gone?'

'Your mother's all right. Kevin wasn't any trouble. Supports the right team, anyway. And, yes, his dad's just picked him up.'

I felt a bit happier at the thought of what I'd missed. Ralph, Steve and Kevin cheering on the 'right team' in front of the TV for a solid week. Poor Mum, though.

As I came in the front door, Poor Mum came out of the kitchen wearing her 'Keep Calm And Cook Bacon' apron (a crapola present from Ralph even by his standards).

'Oh, it's lovely to have you back, Chloe,' she said as she and the bacon apron squeezed me tight. 'Did you enjoy yourself? It all looked beautiful from your pictures.'

'It was great, Mum. But how's it been going here? Has Ralph got himself another job yet?' It was all coming flooding back – the very *Ralphness* of our lives. Ugh.

'The Jobcentre's going to let him come back on probation. Such a worry, but he's promised he won't let us all down again. Would you like some sausages, love?' Wonderful how Mum could deal with important issues, and always come back to the solution to any problem: processed meat.

Not many hours later, my beloved family was sitting round the breakfast table – sausage time seems to come round amazingly quickly in our household.

Monosyllabic Steve, leads hanging out of his ears as usual, was fully focused on the large pile of bacon in front of him, Mum was at the cooker frying the fifth egg, Ralph, with only one piece of sausage to go, was grunting disapprovingly over the sports pages. Situation normal *a la casa* Bennet.

I couldn't wait to head off to Amy's to hear more about Charlie and his party. Sally and I were meeting there for Coke and brownies (approx. twenty-five teaspoons of sugar, but we were NOT counting...) in plenty of time to help Sally plan her big date with Rob.

When I got there, I found the others sitting round the kitchen table, with the Dad Who cutting up a fresh new batch of brownies. He and Amy were in their running kits, and they looked so healthy and smiley I had a brief moment of wishing they were my family – until I remembered I wouldn't swap Mum for anybody's.

'Where are you meeting Rob, then?' Amy was asking.

'At the hall, where they're practising,' said Sally. 'You know, the horrible hall of the Snog Fest.'

'It won't be horrible any more, though, will it?' I said. 'Not with you and Rob, and Amy and Charlie.'

'Yes,' came a bit of a sigh from Amy. We all looked at her. She gleamed. And she had a sort of dopey, faraway look that made her appear as though she was a few sandwiches short of a picnic, if the truth be told. But of course I wouldn't dream of saying that out loud.

'It's true Charlie's shot to the top of the league table,' I said. 'All those Suitability and Compatibility points, and now all those Sustainability points...how great that you can actually look forward to the Snog Fest. Lucky you!'

354

Sally, who hadn't consumed a single teaspoon of sugar in any form (amazing how love can cure everything – even a passion for brownies), set off soon after that for the horrible/happy hall. She promised us a full report if not later, then on Sunday. I wished her luck. I really did.

Later that night, much later, I got a long message from Sally on voicemail. There was so much background noise and so much excitement in her voice I could hardly understand a word. But the general impression was that drummer boy had been fun and fond... that she'd had a great time...that she'd even had a go on the drums with Shedz...and Rob was going to see her home to chez Liv. She said she felt like she was on cloud nine. In between being happy for her, I couldn't help wondering what is wrong with clouds one to eight.

Sally came round first thing on Sunday to deliver her full report – or as first thing as it gets after so much Saturday-night excitement. Mum, Ralph and Steve had headed off to lunch at the Bear and Chipmunk, but what with one thing and another, and despite the fact they did such good Scotch eggs, I didn't really want to go there and revisit the scene of The Great Betrayal. Even though we'd so moved on...

As Sally came up the stairs we heard a lot of familiar hysterical barking downstairs.

'So how's Albert, is he happy to be home?' said Sally when she arrived – showing admirable concern for our furry friend, even in the middle of all her excitement, I thought.

'I hope so, but I haven't seen him properly yet,' I said. Although I was glad that Albert was safely found, he was rapidly becoming A Worry. Firstly because I knew that one day I would have to go back to the terrifying Mrs Munroe mansion to return the collar and lead, and secondly because I was even more terrified of finding Hortense fat and full of puppy. What happens in cases like this? Can dogs sue other dogs for child support? I didn't see Mr Underwood cheerfully shelling out the cost of vets' fees, and anyway I'd pretty much pretended I was Albert's owner. Oh dear, oh dear.

Happily, I didn't have to dwell on all this for long, because no sooner had we sat down to our colas ('diet', of course), than Sally was off.

'...so amazing. They were just brilliant, and Rob's

so good on the drums, and then we had coffee...'

'But you hate coffee!' I couldn't help interrupting.

'Oh, no I don't. It's delicious, I love it,' said Sally, proving once again that love is blind, and so are taste-buds if they want to be. 'And then we went back and Jezza was singing, and then Rob let me have a go drumming. It was brilliant. He said I was good, and then he called me a dingbat, but in such a nice way.'

This went on for some time. I thought if I didn't interrupt soon it would be Monday and time for school.

'So did he take you home, and did he meet Harris and Jock and your mum?' I asked, hoping that there hadn't been any Terrible Twins encounter or any kind of embarrassment with Liv and Mr Pinot Grigio.

'Well, yes,' said Sally a little more slowly. 'I think it was OK. I mean he saw the twins in the distance having a bit of a fight, and Mum was a bit tired sounding. I think she'd been out running with Patrick. But I do think it was OK.'

'It all sounds great, Sally. I mean, love you, love the twins. I'm sure he's big enough and strong enough to take them on,' I said, not wanting to end the report on a negative note.

'Oh,' said Sally, 'and Gemma was at the band practice too.'

'Oh *really*?' I said. Ha. I knew it. The news of Jezza's renewed interest hadn't gone unnoticed after all.

'Yes,' said Sally, 'and she went off with them all at the end for coffee too.'

All this romance. And all this coffee drinking.

Not that I was jealous or anything, but I did wish I could see Mark properly soon. And without the Queen Beeyatch anywhere near.

Apart from my worries about Albert's potential offspring and the Snog Fest, my mission for the rest of term was to get a key part in the joint production of *A Midsummer Night's Dream*.

I was so sure that Mark would be chosen to be the Duke of Athens, I thought nothing less than his queen – Hippolyta – would do for my own role.

Miss Brewer had announced that there would be three read-throughs in the coming weeks, and those of us who were chosen could all try for different parts. After my spittly declaiming as Lady Macbeth I'd got on the list of possible actors. It was very exciting, but very tense-making.

Sally had become utterly fixated on drumming

practice, and Amy on running around the park with Charlie. Gemma didn't seem to be fixated on anything, so it was only me who appeared to care about the play.

'Girls,' Miss Brewer said at the beginning of one of the important Drama lessons. 'We have now heard from St Thomas's which of their pupils are going to be in the joint school play.'

Now *that* got everyone's attention.

'You can have a look on their Drama website after this lesson.' How frustrating was that? I expect that nobody paid any attention to Miss Brewer's analysis of the last act of *Macbeth*, we all just wanted to get to our book bags and our phones.

And yup, I was right. Sure enough, the very first line of the cast list was:

Theseus, Duke of Athens: Mark Anderson

Right, I thought. So I've GOT to be Hippolyta, his queen. I scrolled quickly to the text. He calls her 'gentle sweet', quite early on. Already I was mentally practising the way I would gaze into his eyes as he said this.

For the next two or three weeks, in between all the other occasional bits of homework, I became absolutely word perfect in the part of Hippolyta. By the time we got to the read-through, I was quietly confident.

My determination to succeed in this mission provided a welcome distraction from the goofy behaviour of my friends – or of Sally and Amy at any rate, who were almost incapable of talking about anything except their respective 'him's.

Gemma was just her normal cool self, and seemed to be mostly quite absent from school. I'd have been worried about her going to the doctor so often if I'd believed she really was going to the doctor so often...

'Chloe,' Miss Brewer was saying. 'I'd just like you to read through the part of Snout, where he comes on stage dressed as Wall.'

What? But I was meant to waft on from the wings, dressed in gossamer blue to match my eyes. I was meant to say the opening floaty lines as I gazed adoringly up at my lord Theseus. I wasn't meant to be the peasanty one who stood on a brick dressed in a sack.

'But I...' I started to say.

'Page 304,' said Miss Brewer firmly.

I looked down at the page, and furious with life the universe and everything, put on an extreme yokel accent (or what I thought was a yokel accent) and began, 'In this same interlude it doth befall...'

I hammed it up, and the more I hammed it up, the

more people were laughing – in a good way.

'That was well done, Chloe,' said Miss Brewer as I finished. 'Very well done.'

I was starting to think that perhaps my future lay in comedy (Shakespearian comedy...I've always admired Shakespeare's comedies...) rather than drama or tragedy, when I became aware of Miss Brewer's voice.

'And now,' she was saying, 'Hippolyta, Theseus's queen. Maggie, would you read through this please?'

Oh no. Oh hell and tarnation, but no, no, please no, anything but this.

Maggie began to read, ''Tis strange, my Theseus...' and I stuck my fingers in my ears. Her little girlie voice, her whining, drawly, false-flirty voice was horrible. Horrible. There was no WAY any Duke of Athens would lumber himself with a dreadful little whiney witch like that.

'Good, Maggie,' said Miss Brewer, when the Q Beeyatch finally stopped. 'That's all for today. I'll be deciding on the parts at the next read-through.'

I was completely silent as we walked out of school that day. Sally was trotting at my heels, telling me I was 'so

361

funny', 'really brilliant' and 'anyway Maggie's never going to get the part sounding like that'.

None of it did any good.

'Sally,' I interrupted her. 'It's no good. I want to forget about it all. Don't talk about it. Talk about something else.'

'OK,' she said cheerfully. 'Albert. Let's talk about Albert. Shall we go and see how he is?'

That made me remember the whole dreaded saga of the collar and the lead and the puppies...

'I've got to take that collar and lead back to Mrs Munroe's son,' I said. 'I think, since everything's so horrible anyway, I might as well do it now. Will you come with me?'

Sally's face fell. It really did fall – sort of going from all upward pointing and cheerful to downward and hopeless. 'Yes, of course,' she said. She was very brave, I'll give her that. She was probably even more frightened than I was of Mrs M, and she'd never been to the house before, so there was all that to be frightened of too. But The Great Betrayal still had her on the moral low ground even now.

'Thanks,' I said. 'Let's go back and get the lead now.'

So we got on the going-home bus and headed towards my house. We were very silent as we walked up the stairs, Albert's cheerful barking somehow made us even more so.

There was nobody at home, so I just went straight to the cupboard under the stairs where I knew Ralph had thrown the lead, and we went back to the bus stop, with the collar and lead in a plastic bag.

Sally was getting more and more nervous: 'Supposing Mrs Munroe answers the door? Supposing her dog's in labour when we arrive? What if—'

'Stop it,' I said. 'It's all bad enough without imagining it to be even worse.' Although part of me was thinking that if you imagine the worst, then surely that makes you stronger and more prepared for the reality?

We walked slowly up to the front door of Mrs M's mansion, which seemed to have grown even bigger since the last time I was there. Moments after we'd pressed the buzzer the door opened and there was Mrs Munroe herself. I realised that all the imagining hadn't made me stronger.

'Good heavens,' she said. 'What are you two doing here?'

'We've come to return Hortense's collar and lead,' I said. 'At least, I think they must be Hortense's, because when we got Albert back, he had them on him, and he hadn't had them before, I mean they weren't his, so I thought they must be yours. I mean, Hortense's.' I was blushing, I could feel it.

'Ah yes, the border terrier,' she said. At that moment I saw, walking across the hall behind her, a miniature poodle. Except it wasn't very miniature at all. It was black, and small in every respect except round its middle, where it looked distinctly bulgy. Oh lord.

'Well, those are definitely her spare collar and lead, so that's good to have them back,' said Mrs M. 'Thank you for bringing them. You'd better head back home now before it gets late.'

She started to shut the door, and as we turned round, I hissed at Sally, 'Don't run, it'll make us look guilty. Don't run.' Too late, of course, Sally had reached the gate before Mrs M had shut the door.

I went to bed that night, wondering what other horrible things could make the end of the summer term worse than it already was. Then I remembered, the Snog Fest. It was looking more and more like the others were all going to have a happy time. Of all of us, the world would see that I was the only one who was an outcast. All my friends would be happily entwined, and I would have to watch the vile, whiney QBM hanging all over Mark.

Life was properly and completely hopeless.

The Dance of the Boy Watchers

It is a truth universally acknowledged that the last two weeks of the summer term are traditionally happy weeks. There are no more exams, and we're all focused on fun end-of-term activities, like sports days, and plays...and dances. Everyone's light-hearted and looking forward to the holidays, and all the plans they're making with their friends.

Everyone's happy. Except me.

There was nothing to look forward to, especially not the St Thomas's and Queen Mary's Annual School Dance. And probably not the joint school play either.

The Thursday of that week was our last English and Drama lesson – the big one, in which Miss Brewer would tell everyone who had got what part.

Unusually it was a day when Gemma had deigned

to come to school, so we all went into the classroom together and bagged the back row. The three of them were really quite uninterested in who was going to be which fairy, which peasant, or which lord, but they knew that I was white with tension on the subject, so they were rallying round.

'Now, girls,' said Miss Brewer, 'it's been difficult to choose the cast for this exciting project, and those of you who have not been chosen must not be discouraged. All of you have reached a very high standard, and even if you aren't going to be a part of this production, there will be other opportunities for you to rehearse your acting skills.'

Managing our expectations is I think what it's called. But as I looked across at the QB of them all, I could see she had an expression of such smug self-satisfaction on her face that I wanted to smack her. Again. She looked like it was her right as the Queen Beeyatch to be Theseus's queen too.

Miss Brewer started with some of the smaller parts, and then came on to the cast for the play-within-a-play.

'The part of Snout, the Wall, to Chloe Bennet,' said Miss Brewer. So I was to be the clown after all. Well, so be it. At least I'd get to go to all the rehearsals, and who knew…

'And now to the leads. The part of Hippolyta, the queen…' Miss Brewer was saying.

I held my breath and dug my fingers hard into the palms of my hands.

'…to Julie Duxworth,' said Miss Brewer. Suddenly all was not so terrible. Julie – who'd probably been coached by her famous actor mother – was quite set on an acting career. There was a chance, a real chance, that she wouldn't necessarily want her leading man to fall in love with her.

I saw the expression on QBM's face out of the corner of my eye. Oh, that was worth it too. She looked like she really had been smacked in the face.

There was a god, after all.

'But what if it gets really hot?' Sally was saying. We were in her kitchen, the one with the secret door to the larder, and the secret hoard of designer handbags. She was trying on her new pink and black dress, and generally looking quite pleased with herself, so none of us said anything about the particular pink and how well it went – not – with the particular orange of her hair.

'I mean, it's got a jersey top and I can't exactly take it off, can I?' said Sally.

'You'll have to get Rob to take you outside to cool you down, won't you?' said Gemma.

'I think you look great in it, and that's the main thing,' said Amy, ever the one to think positive.

'You going to wear that red dress you wore to Charlie's party, then, Amy?' said Sally.

'Yes, he said he liked me in it. Besides, I'm not sure I've got time to get a different one, unless maybe I wore my green one,' said Amy.

It was at this point that I decided I would have to have a primal scream. The sort of scream that they advocate for slightly mad people who need to release a lot of pent-up anguish. As that was a rather anti-social idea, and since none of them showed any sign of stopping talking about what they were going to wear to the Snog Fest, I went off to see what Harris and Jock were up to. I really fancied shooting a few aliens, perhaps even vaporising the odd zombie.

It was the end of another last-week-of-term evening with my dear friends. Even Gemma seemed to be infected with the need to talk about the Snog Fest and nothing but the Snog Fest. Apparently she'd had lots of messages from Jezza who was trying to make sure she wasn't going with anyone else, and also trying to make her meet him before it started so he could be sure he'd got her. Gemma, of course, was playing it all very cool, but that didn't stop her going on and on with the others about what they were going to wear.

I, meanwhile, had decided ages ago on a black dress that was too tight for me, but in a good way. At least I was fairly sure it was a good way. So I had nothing to contribute to the great debate.

We were, though, only two days away from It. Knowing that my so-called BFF was quite likely to desert me and go off backstage and catch up on drumming technique, I'd made Amy promise me not to abandon me. I'd be the only person on my own, but at least Amy and Charlie were nice enough to make sure it wouldn't show too much.

Just to make me feel a bit better about it all, they'd agreed that the great Getting Ready moment should be at mine.

And so there we were. Dateline Snog Fest.

With Mum hovering kindly in the background – 'Just in case anyone wants some help with their hair' – we were crowding around in my bedroom and the bathroom.

Steve was hiding in his bedroom. I think that that many girls, even if one of them was Gemma – or perhaps *because* one of them was Gemma – were just a bit too much for a monosyllabic sixteen-year-old with limited social skills.

Ghastly Ralph was, thank goodness, safely at the Jobcentre, working uncharacteristically hard to try to prove he'd earned his second chance.

The process of preparation took just as long, if not longer, than last year. I'd taken the precaution of doing extensive tweezer work on my eyebrows the night before, so that saved me an hour or so, but otherwise all the product seemed to take even longer to apply, and certainly the eye make-up required as much discussion as it did application.

'Just think,' said Sally cheerfully as she put yet another layer of eyeliner on, 'this time last year we didn't know what was going to happen, and nothing nice actually happened. But this year, we know what's going to happen and it's all nice.' She caught my eye in the mirror. 'I mean, all sorts of nice things *could* happen…'

Eventually, we all declared ourselves ready, and set off for the bus stop.

'Just give Ralph a ring when you've had enough,' Mum had said. 'He'll be more than happy to come and get you.' I tried not to think about the humiliation of being so desperate to leave early that sitting in Ralph's putrid Peugeot would be better than being at the Snog Fest.

'Come on, Chloe,' said Amy as we climbed on the bus. 'Might not be as bad as all that.' Guess I hadn't got as good as disguising my feelings as I'd thought.

As we approached, we could hear the loud music from the hall two streets away.

Mentally I tried to imagine the worst in order to make myself stronger for the reality. Just as I thought I'd cracked it, and was prepared for anything, I saw Mrs Munroe's son standing by the entrance. He had an official organiser's badge on.

Great.

'Hello,' I said, because it was impossible to pretend I hadn't seen him as he was standing exactly by the only entrance.

'Oh, hello,' he said, clearly rather taken aback to see me. Perhaps I just looked a different – obviously much more sophisticated – person in a little black number rather than a school uniform. That was a nice thought. 'Thanks for bringing that lead back, I'd forgotten I'd left it on your dog.'

'That's all right,' I said. This was going unexpectedly well. I took a deep breath, 'How's Hortense?'

'She's doing fine. She had the puppies – seven of them – and they're all fit and healthy.'

Oh. My. God. But he seemed so *calm* about it – not accusing at all.

'Oh great,' I gulped. 'What do they, er, look like?' I wondered if they were little Alberts or little Hortenses.

'They look just like you'd expect them to look. The product of two pedigree poodles mating. She was already pregnant when your border terrier turned up, which was why I needed to keep them separate.'

I breathed out my most enormous ever sigh of relief. All that worry had been for nothing, Hortense already had her buns in the oven, or whatever the expression is, and Albert was innocent after all.

'I'm so glad everything's all right,' I said, and I really, really meant it.

I went into the hall feeling much, much better about life, but then I heard the noise (deafening) and saw my friends (paired off). Charlie and Amy were either side of me in a sort of protective way, but Sally was already disappearing in the direction of Shedz who were getting ready to play. I saw her turn round and give me a great big beaming smile. I tried very hard just to feel happy for her, and I didn't think that the pink of her dress clashed horribly with her hair *at all*.

Jezza had left the rest of the band and had come over towards us. He put his arm round Gemma in quite a…proprietorial – I think's the word – manner, but she didn't seem to be minding. In fact, as he bent down to her and said something in her ear, she stared laughing in a relaxed and happy way.

Great.

And then just behind them and slightly in the distance I saw Mark. He was in a group of people, one of whom was the QB herself. She was standing in front of him looking up at him and doing her sweet little girl impersonation – 'sweet little girl' who was heavily underwired and cleavaged, and wearing so much eyeliner you could hardly see the eyes.

More great.

By this time the noise was even noisier. Charlie came and danced with me, and then a random tall boy came towards me. He probably meant no harm, but he looked so like the Six Foot One who had caused Sally so much grief last year, that I avoided his eye and headed off to that place of safety we all know so well: the toilets.

They were full of girls needlessly reapplying their make-up, shouting and giggling with each other. I decided to head outside. At least it wouldn't be boiling hot and I could hear myself think.

I went down the back stairs, quite a slow process in the very high heels I'd chosen to wear, where there was a big courtyard that backed on to the rest of the high street. There were a lot of couples being coupley, which of course only served to make me feel even more cheerful.

I headed towards what looked like a quiet corner, where I reckoned I could sit and check out a few Twitter feeds. After all, you're never alone with a phone.

As I got nearer the quiet corner I saw a familiar figure. It was Mark, and he was standing on his own, looking down at his phone. Incredible.

On. His. Own.

I walked towards him. Just as I was about to screw up my courage and interrupt him, he looked up. He smiled, a proper smile – welcoming and warm, like he really was pleased to see me. He put his phone away.

'Hello,' he said. 'It's you!'

Just for once, I didn't want to make some smart

reply. 'Yes,' I said. 'It's me. I had to get out of there. I don't think I'm in the mood.'

He looked at me, for quite a long time. 'No,' he said. 'It's not really your thing, is it? But you're dressed the part – you look great in that black.'

I was glad of the dark, for I felt a huge blush coming on. How unbelievably wonderful. He thinks I look great...

'Thank you,' I just about managed to get out. I really wanted to say that he looked great too. In a white T-shirt and a jacket with the sleeves rolled up he looked so beautiful I almost couldn't breathe.

But I couldn't say that. I stuck to safer ground. 'The next part you'll see me dressed for is Wall. They've cast me as Snout. I'd rather fancied myself as the queen, but apparently I'm better at being a peasant standing on a brick.'

'That's much more fun than being the queen,' he said. 'You can make people laugh being Wall. Just try not to fall off your brick, though. You don't want to see the inside of an ambulance again, do you?'

'No, definitely not,' I said, 'except I can't help feeling a brick would be easier to walk on than these heels.' I knew it wasn't cool to admit this sort of thing, but what with one thing and another I was feeling very wobbly. I took a step back to prove it, and almost fell over.

I didn't fall over because Mark had put his arm round me.

'Honestly,' he was laughing. 'You need a bit of looking after, don't you?

'Do I?' I said. It was such an incredible feeling having his arm round me that I could hardly think straight. But I knew there was something I had to clear up. 'You mean like, well, like people like...' I had to get the name out, just had to – 'Maggie need looking after?'

'Maggie?' he looked down at me with such an expression of surprise that I felt a rush of warmth and excitement right through me. 'Maggie doesn't need looking after. She's good enough at looking after number one not to need any help, I'd say. But don't let's talk about her. This is about you, dear Chloe. You might think you're awfully self-sufficient, but I've got a feeling you might let someone in if they asked nicely enough. And this is me, trying to ask nicely. How am I doing?'

I looked up at him. His face was really close, so close that we could almost...

'You're doing wonderfully,' I said, thinking how even more beautiful he was close up, 'really...wonderfully.'

His lips were now very, *very* close.

'That's good,' he said quietly. 'That's great.' And very softly and gently he brushed his lips over mine. And then he did it again, a bit harder. I kissed him back. It all seemed to be over in flash, and yet it also lasted for ever.

We walked back into the hall, arms round each other.

I was officially in heaven.

Acknowledgements

My greatest debt is to my agent Caroline Sheldon, whose encouragement, wisdom and insight are second to none.

My other greatest debt is to Rosie McIntosh and the terrific team at Orchard Books for their professionalism, enthusiasm and all-round splendidness.

Special thanks to Laura and Jonathan, Aly and Ian, and Jane and Brian for helping me to write by locking me up in their garrets. And heartfelt thanks to all my lovely friends for their faith and support. Also to Mati, Izzy, Julia, Ottilie, Tallulah, Edie, Milly, Charlotte and Helena who in another world would, I'm sure, be Chloe's mates.

Chloe and I are as one on this: friends – can't do without 'em.

About the Author

Chloe Bennet is the pen name of Val Hudson, a former publisher and editor responsible for a number of famous bestsellers over the years. She used to love spending her time helping other people write. Now, with *Boywatching*, she has discovered that it's more fun to do it herself.

Coming soon:

BOYWATCHING...UP CLOSE

It's the summer holidays, and the charts of the intrepid Boywatchers are all filled up. But a true scientist never stops researching...which is just as well because in the course of the holidays The Boy turns out to be just as much of a mystery as ever.

Chloe and her friends discover that there really is no end to the evil that QB Maggie can do if she really puts her mind to it. And in *Boywatching...Up Close* she really puts her mind to it...

Can Chloe hang onto the heaven that is Mark? And who is going to do what with who at the after-play party?

Will Gemma's reunion with the unpredictable Jezza last or are the confusing handsome Cornish boys going to get in the way?

Is Amy destined for greatness in the Olympics, and is Steve's new Army friend what he seems?

There are some big surprises in store for Sally – whose secret father has a secret all his own – and there's some amazing and amusing news from the ghastliest stepdad of them all.

And who knew that Mark's sister was going to be such an influence, or that Chloe's mum was going to be such a worry?

Meanwhile, Albert has his own ideas about which boys to watch...

Boywatching...Up Close –

the page-turningly funny sequel.